ALSO BY C.K. CRIGGER

Western Novels

The Woman Who Built a Bridge

Letter Of The Law

The Winning Hand

Black Crossing

Liar's Trial

The Yeggman's Apprentice

Western Short Stories

Left Behind

Double Deal

Memory of Blood

The Whereabouts of Miss Nellie Thistlewaite

Ask Parrot

Aldy Neal's Ghost

A Deal's A Deal

Other Novels

Lost Girl Lake

Hometown Homicide

HOMETOWN BURNING

C.K. CRIGGER

CITY LIGHTS
PRESS
~ LAS VEGAS ~

Published in the United States by City Lights Press, Las Vegas

City Lights Press
An Imprint of Wolfpack Publishing
6032 Wheat Penny Avenue
Las Vegas, NV 89122

citylightspress.com

Paperback ISBN 978-1-64734-154-1
eBook ISBN 978-1-64734-153-4

Library of Congress Control Number: 2019956529

HOMETOWN BURNING

CHAPTER ONE

Chaotic noise greeted Frankie McGill as she pulled her pickup into the tiny Hawkesford, Idaho fire station parking lot. The rise and fall of a siren's high-pitched screech shot a blaze of agony through her head. The noise and ensuing pain paralyzed her for a moment, her vision blurring and fading to black.

Familiar anger seethed through her when thought became possible again. Why me?

Why not her? At least she was alive. Frankie forced the more positive thought into her mind.

The blast from an IED outside Kandahar, Afghanistan had failed to kill her, even if it did leave her as damaged goods. A plate in her head; part of a prosthetic foot. More than a year ago by now, but the repercussions were never ending. Never Ending.

But, unlike others in her squad, she'd made it home,

able to put her paramedic training to use in the town where she'd grown up.

Resolutely, she put the memories, if not the pain, aside and entered the lion's den.

Stepping from the Ranger, she spotted Karl Mager, the fire chief, waving his arms and rocking on his toes as he stood beside his fire department four-wheel drive SUV. She headed toward him. A couple trainees clad in turnout gear watched him with awe-stricken expressions. Karl's face was red as a boiled crab, sure sign of a temper gone south.

Alongside Karl's rig, the pumper's diesel engine, warmed up and ready-to-go with a driver behind the wheel, spewed exhaust fumes out the open garage doors.

Two more volunteer firefighters dashed into the station at a run. With a quick glance at Karl, they donned their gear, and climbed into the pumper truck. And there everyone sat, a puzzled expression on their faces.

"What's going on?" she yelled at the chief over the siren's pulsating blare. The noise seemed certain to send her into a blackout.

"Berthold's," Karl roared back at her. "Nobody knows where it is."

Including him, from the look of things.

"You ever heard of the place?" He didn't sound hopeful.

After a moment in which she drew a blank, her sometimes faulty memory kicked in and she had it. "I have." She jogged to the dispatcher's desk, leaned over the college girl's shoulder, and punched an override button. The siren stopped.

"You have?" Karl repeated, his voice too loud in the new quiet. He glared a little at the young dispatcher. She, not so craven as the trainees, glared back.

"You mean you know where it is?" His tone eased back a notch.

Frankie nodded. "I do." Thanks to constantly puppy-dogging her granddad, back in her formative years.

The two volunteers looked relieved; the trainees like a death sentence had morphed into life without parole.

"Good. There's a fire. Take the lead." He crawled into the truck and stuck his head out. "C'mon, woman, get in here. You're with me. Hustle."

Frankie, slowing only to grab a helmet off a wall hook, did hustle, swinging lithely onto the seat beside him. She was still carrying her purse and had her car keys in her hand, not the most helpful of items for a paramedic to take on a run.

* * *

Following Frankie's instructions, Karl led their cavalcade first south, then east out of town. The call into

3

dispatch, he told her as they tooled along the unpaved country road, was a foul-up from the git-go.

"The caller not only didn't stay on the line, he didn't even give directions on where to find the fire," he said. "And our dispatcher had no idea how to locate 'the old Berthold' place." His fist thumped the steering wheel as he mimicked the girl's voice. "'I couldn't find it on any of our maps, Chief,' is what she said."

Frankie suspected what bugged Karl most was that he didn't know how to find the place, an old homestead dating from the Coeur d'Alene Indian reservation land lottery of 1909. He must've been ready to blow a gasket as minutes ticked away while Arlene searched. No surprise there. The passage of time is always a huge problem when it comes to fire, a credo Karl preached over and over to the volunteers.

A glance in the pumper's side mirror showed Frankie that Lew, a seasoned fire department veteran and the head paramedic, followed the pumper in the ambulance, far enough behind to protect his windshield from the gravel kicked up by the heavier truck's wheels. Chris, one of the department's more talented volunteers, accompanied him. Like most the rest of the fire department, Chris was a comparative newcomer to the small town of Hawkesford. He'd taken some leave over the last month and on this, his second day back, wasn't yet up to speed.

4

Frankie's fault, or so she felt. He'd partnered with a man she'd seen put in jail where he awaited trial and for a while, Chris had been a suspect as well.

Best not let herself remember. In a method the acupressure therapist swore would help alleviate the pain from the plate in her head, she surreptitiously pressed her fingers against a certain spot. An antidote when overwhelming flashes of light and noise threatened a blackout.

Her opinion? The treatment had proved marginal, at best. Worked this time, though. More or less.

The squeal of emergency sirens rose and fell. Frankie, glancing again into the big side mirror, glimpsed the following rigs through the boiling dust.

"Are we expecting casualties?" she asked.

"Dunno," Karl replied, then, "Just taking precautions. Over there. I see smoke." He sounded relieved.

"Right turn coming up," she warned Karl after another half-mile. The truck slowed.

"Where?" Karl peered ahead. "I don't see a road."

Frankie didn't blame him for his skepticism. One couldn't call the barely discernible track running through a recently harvested chickpea field a real road. Nevertheless, she pointed. "There. Between those two tottery old fence posts. The house is over the hill."

He grunted and flipped on the turn signal to warn the

pumper truck behind them.

They smelled the smoke as it seeped in through Karl's window, which he insisted on leaving rolled down. It stunk of age—and of other things too. Frankie frowned.

As they gained the track, she spied the sheriff's deputy, Gabe Zantos, speeding to close the gap behind Lew. Her heart sped up, too. Though not "together", per se, they lived in the same house. With the differences in their schedules, she hadn't spoken to him in a week. Leaving him a message about the backyard gate's broken latch was the sum total of their communication. Did she regret the silence between them?

Maybe.

The vehicles breasted the last remaining hill separating them from the fire. Off to the left, down in a wide draw where a muddy stream had flowed in the spring, a derelict old building was fully involved. Flames leapt from burst-out windows, between shrunken lap siding, and through the roof. On one side of the place, where the fecund Berthold family had added a bedroom ell to house their many children, the fire was already dying, its fuel source burnt out.

Karl drew up in front of the house, the rest of the cavalcade following. "Looks like our job is to stop the fire from getting into the fields," he said, sighing.

"Nothing salvageable about the house, that's for sure,"

Frankie agreed. "Although I'm surprised it hadn't fallen in years ago."

"Looks like a sneeze would bring it down."

Speedy through diligent practice, Karl and his volunteers swung into action, the trainees observing and helping where they could. The volunteers unrolled the hose, the driver worked the pumper controls. Karl was everywhere at once, calling instructions and, being a hands-on kind of guy, jumping into action when needed. Frankie followed more slowly, taking up a position upwind of the smoke.

No wounded . . . call them injured . . . here. Her job had been to guide. Mission accomplished.

The ambulance, also unnecessary on this run, parked in an out-of-the-way spot. Gabe in the sheriff's department SUV pulled in right behind it. By then, Karl and the guys had a stream of water wetting the ground around the burning house. Gabe stopped for a brief chat with the fire chief before coming to stand beside Frankie.

"This place never ceases to amaze me." He shook his head. The resident deputy for this end of the county, he'd only been in Hawkesford a couple years. "Choc-a-bloc full of secrets, like it is. I've driven past here dozens of times and never guessed there was a house behind the hill."

Frankie shrugged. "No reason why you should. Nobody's lived here for donkey years. I expect most everyone has forgotten it ever existed. The house had been empty for ages when my granddad and I came scouting around, and I was only six or seven then."

Gabe grinned at her. "Ancient times."

He stood close enough for her to stick an elbow in his ribs. The August sun beat down on their heads. Sweat broke out on Frankie's scalp, dampening her short, dark hair. The fire made the already hot day feel hotter.

A metallic rattle of unrestrained tools and containers bouncing in the bed announced the arrival of a dull gray Ram pickup. It wheeled in and stopped beside them. A mid-fifties, dusty-faced man, clad in denims and a long-sleeved chambray shirt climbed out and tromped over to them.

"Hey, Frankie, Deputy." He gave a one-finger salute and a brief nod to Gabe. "Took you guys long enough to get here. Thought I was gonna have to start up the Cat and plow a firebreak."

"Hi, Mister Strohmeyer." Frankie recognized him right off, although it had been a few years since she last saw him. Harvey was his first name, if she remembered correctly. She'd heard he held the lease on this ground. "Are you the one who called in the fire?"

"Don't know if I'm the only one, but I did call."

Frankie gave a snort. "Unfortunately, nobody on shift

had ever heard of the Berthold's, and the name isn't on any of our updated maps."

"Oh, right. I expect not." He gave a one-shoulder shrug. "There's no Berthold on my lease anymore, either. The last grandson died twenty or more years ago. The owners now are all women, all with different names, and all in different states clear across the country. One of them lives in Atlantic City, New Jersey, for God's sake."

He said it like Atlantic City was in a foreign land, and Gabe's lips twitched.

Frankie cocked her head. "Karl and the dispatcher could've used more explicit directions."

"Huh. Sorry about that." Strohmeyer's narrowly set eyes opened as far as they'd go. "I guess that kind of dates me, doesn't it?" He folded his arms and surveyed the firefighters soaking the ground between the house and his field. "Gonna just let'er burn?"

"Nothin' there worth trying to save," she said.

He nodded. "Yeah. I suppose not. Too bad. There's only one or two of these old places left, ya know? The Buchanan place, for instance. You still own the original one hundred and sixty acres, don't you? And the six hundred forty your dad had?"

Frankie smiled. "Yes. Hank Kelton farms it."

"I'd take over the lease in a New York minute." Strohmeyer jerked a stained John Deere cap from his head and wiped sweat. "If Hank ever wants to throw in the towel, be sure and give me a call. He's getting a little long in the tooth."

Like he, himself, was not? But not, she conceded, as old as Hank. "I'll keep your offer in mind," she said, which made his beady blue eyes snap with what she imagined was anticipation.

Gabe, who leaned against his SUV's fender watching the firefighters, slewed his glance around to Strohmeyer. "How did you happen to spot the fire? You're done harvesting this section, aren't you?"

Certainly no machinery was in evidence, nor any standing crops.

"Been done for over a week." Strohmeyer pointed his whiskery chin toward the house. "But some funny stuff has been going on around here. Me and my boy noticed when we were cutting the chickpeas. Looked like somebody was camping out in the house. And there was an old car parked down there in the trees."

Frankie trudged around until she could see beyond the rapidly shrinking flames. Gabe and Strohmeyer followed. "No car there now."

"No," Strohmeyer said. "Nor yesterday, but there was every day before that."

Gabe nodded. "Easy to see where it sat. Bare ground shows through the dead grass and weeds. It must've been there a while."

"Told you," Strohmeyer said. "Somebody's been camping out here most of the summer."

Gabe's brows rose over his hazel eyes. "Squatters, you mean? Why didn't you report them?"

The farmer's face turned a dusky red. "Didn't think it was any of my business, except—"

"Except?" Gabe folded his arms across his chest.

"Thought they might be dealing drugs, cooking that meth stuff or whatever," Strohmeyer admitted. "Didn't want anything to do with a bunch of drug addicts. But it is the reason I checked on the place every day."

"Could've timed your rounds better," Gabe said coolly. "And let me handle a trespass call."

Strohmeyer shot him a neutral glance. "Could've. Hoped it wouldn't be necessary."

Gabe shrugged. "Or better yet, reported possible criminal activity and let me shut down an active drug operation."

"Hindsight," Strohmeyer said. "Wasn't sure what went on here."

Frankie twitched a look at Gabe. Not many would see the anger in him. She did.

The firefighters, with the ground on this side of house well-wetted, dragged the heavy hose around to the back. Karl reopened the valve, shooting the spray in a high arch. Dust and knee-high weeds resisted until enough water fell to beat them all down and make mud.

Close to what had been a small porch and back door, a shape on the ground became visible. She'd seen its kind before.

Frankie grabbed Gabe's arm. "Gabe, look there. Is that . . ." She pointed, finger wavering.

He followed the direction she indicated. Air hissed through his teeth, a sign of affront. The anger grew more obvious. "Karl," he bellowed, and started forward, dragging Frankie with him. "Shut off the water."

Karl turned. "Huh?"

"Shut off the water. We've got a body."

CHAPTER TWO

"Who is that?" Harvey Strohmeyer took a firm step forward, head turtled out front as if to get him there faster.

Gabe stuck his arm against the farmer's chest, barring his way. "That's what I intend to find out. Please step aside, Mister Strohmeyer, and let me get to work."

The farmer yanked at Gabe's arm. "Watch who you're pushing around, buster. This is my land and I'll go where I want."

Although his eyes flickered, Gabe's demeanor didn't change. He remained polite even as his arm remained locked in place. Frankie felt a thrill of pride in him. She didn't think she'd be as tolerant of a bully like Strohmeyer.

"I can't allow you to tamper with the evidence," Gabe said. "Not that there'll be much left after pouring water over the site, but in case there is, you can't be allowed to step over it."

Strohmeyer grunted like he hadn't expected opposition. "This is my land," he repeated. Squinting, and with his lower lip pooched out, he glared at Gabe. "Guess I've got a right to know what's happening. See who's laying out here in the weeds."

"Guess you don't have the right to obstruct the police in their duties, or to contaminate the evidence. Unless, of course, you're trying to get arrested."

"Thought you said there wasn't any evidence," the farmer said.

Gabe eyed him his face expressionless. "What I'm saying is keep back and stay out of the way."

Frankie shot a swift, startled glance at him. That had sounded like some kind of a challenge. Like he almost wished Strohmeyer would step out of line. And maybe Gabe did want him to. It was pretty clear the farmer ruffled his fur in the opposite direction.

The memory of her granddad wondering how Strohmeyer had gotten the lease on this land in the first place bobbed through Frankie's mind. An answer surfaced. Through bullying the Berthold heirs, more than likely. It couldn't have been his winning personality, that's for sure. Granddad's own lease holder, Hank Kelton, bid for the lease at the same time, and Granddad always said Hank was the better farmer. And better person. Apparently, Gabe felt the same instant antagonism toward Strohmeyer as her granddad always had.

But Gabe needed to keep his cool if he wanted to stay on as resident deputy at this end of the county. Although she—and most everyone else in the Hawkesford area— were firmly on his side, a certain Ms. Alexis Barwick, a muckety-muck attorney with political pull, had filed a complaint on him a while back. Turned out she was guilty of hiring someone to kill her husband's mistress and Gabe was coming too close. The deaths expanded to two, with Frankie and her partner Marc near misses, before Gabe actually caught the woman red-handed. Yet, unbelievable as it might be, Gabe had gotten a reprimand from the sheriff's office on Ms. Barwick's say-so.

"Watch your step," the sheriff had told him.

Frankie guessed logic—or fairness—in the justice system were not prerequisites. And Strohmeyer struck Frankie as just the sort to add to Gabe's woes.

"At least the body isn't burned." Frankie inserted herself between the two men. "It shouldn't be too hard to identify him."

"Hope you're right," Gabe said.

"Let me—" Strohmeyer took another step forward, until Gabe's steely gaze and shake of the head stopped him.

They found the body to be that of a young man. One arm outstretched, he lay sprawled on his belly in the weeds. Longish brown hair flopped across his face, obscuring his features. A crusty dark stain spread across the back of his shirt. A blackened hole gaped through the singed fabric.

Gunshot wound. Frankie knew one when she saw it. And now the water had been turned off, she heard the persistent buzzing of flies.

She swallowed once. Twice.

Gabe touched her arm, cutting off any memories that might arise.

"There's an evidence kit in the Tahoe, along with a roll of crime scene tape," he said. "It would help, Frankie, if you and Lew were to set up a perimeter around the body. I'll tell you where I want it." He kept his eye on Strohmeyer as he fished his cell phone from his shirt pocket, punched a number and with hardly a pause, began to talk.

"Zantos here. I've got a body in a field south of Hawkesford. Inform Sheriff Falsworth, please. I'm gonna need the medical examiner. Yep. Looks like a homicide. Yeah. Murder. Get hold of tribal, too, will you? Officer Swallowtail, if he's on duty." He turned and whatever else he told the dispatcher was lost—to Frankie, at least. Maybe not Strohmeyer because if anything, his face grew redder beneath the dust, and his mouth pouted more.

Ignoring him, Gabe made more calls. Karl and the

guys dragged their hose around to the other side of the house and the fire, thankfully, soon died down to smoking embers that cast a stinking pall over the site. Yet they were lucky today. No wind to spread sparks into the dry fields beyond the home site.

Glad for something to do, Frankie and Lew strung yellow tape in a broad area encircling the body where Gabe indicated. They tied the tape to sturdy weeds, the handle of a rusted out garden tiller, and finally, one of the house's door hinges. Still standing, the door itself hung askew and tilted at an angle.

The volunteer firemen soon shut down the water and coiled the hose around its spool on the pumper. Taking shovels, they went to work, patrolling the edge of the field. Karl, whether because Gabe had given him a high-sign, or because the chief was naturally gregarious, struck up a conversation with Strohmeyer, diverting his attention.

Frankie didn't know what they were talking about, but the rise and fall of Strohmeyer's voice indicated he was still a little hot under the collar. Typical of him, she thought, disgusted. His son Blake had always been just like him. She'd gone to school with him, a troublemaker in every classroom.

Rudy Swallowtail, the local tribal policeman, arrived just as Frankie tied the last knot in the tape. The one anchored to the soot-blackened hinge. She glanced up and waved. He waved back.

Hawkesford being on the Coeur d'Alene Indian Reservation, Rudy often liaised with Gabe on cases that involved tribal members. Since he was also fully trained as a Kootenai County deputy, they would work together until they learned whose jurisdiction they were dealing with. Could be this case would soon be handed over to the F.B.I. but in the meantime, they followed strict protocol.

"Who is it?" Rudy asked as he got out of his cruiser and joined Gabe. "Mine or yours?" His last question asked the identity of the dead man and whether he was Indian. If so, he'd be the man in charge, for the moment at least.

"Don't know yet," Gabe said. "Let's take a look. Want to snap some pictures?"

Rudy, as everyone who worked with him knew, had proved to have a good eye—an artist's eye—for capturing detailed crime scene photos, even using the cheap camera supplied by the sheriff's department.

Grimacing, Rudy took the camera. "If I were you, I'd lose this thing," he muttered, poking at the tiny buttons. "When they replace it, ask for a Nikon D5300 with some Nikkor lenses and a Speedlight kit."

"That your recommendation?" Gabe grinned.

"It is. I've done my research."

"And I suppose the tribe has supplied you with one."

Rudy laughed. "Not yet, but I'm working on them. I think I'm getting close." He clicked off a few pictures of the ground around the body before, both men donning latex gloves, they approached and hunkered down beside it.

Frankie averted her gaze as Gabe swept the dead man's hair away from his face, revealing his features at last.

"Huh," she heard Rudy say. "Yours."

Since she'd seen enough dead bodies to last her a lifetime during the war in Afghanistan, Frankie fixed her attention on securing the end of the tape so it wouldn't come off the reel. After all, she was a paramedic with the intention of saving lives. This man was beyond her help.

But a roll of crime scene tape couldn't distract her for long. With the task complete, and unable to stifle her curiosity, she glanced into the interior of the old house, what the fire hadn't consumed. Not that there was much to see. A table, a broken chair, a falling-to-pieces Hoosier, its top littered with junk, mouse turds, and dead bugs. All singed and black with smoke and soot.

More to the point, a series of three card tables were lined up, each with a camp stove, exploded glass beakers and bottles with tubes stuck in them. Ugh! A meth lab, for sure.

Frankie started to back away, then stopped. Over there, where a wall reeking of char had divided the kitchen from the living room—what was that?

Her breath caught. Squinting into the dark interior, she peered harder.

Frankie's gaze settled on what lay on the floor in front of an old wood burning range that was missing one leg. Her pulse began an erratic pounding. A flare of light flashed like lightning behind her eyes. The pain set her reeling.

She applied force to the pressure point on her temple as recommended by her therapist and blinked to clear her vision.

Didn't work. The object was still there.

"Dammit," she said, harsh and bitter. Turning, she bumped into Lew who stood behind her watching Gabe as he fished in the dead man's back pocket for a wallet. Lew gave her a sharp, questioning look.

"Gabe," she shouted, only it came out a whisper. She swallowed on a dry click. "Gabe!" she tried again, finding some volume with this try.

Gabe looked up. His nostrils flared as he got to his feet, studied her for a moment, and headed toward her with long strides. "Another?" he asked.

Frankie nodded. Mind-to-mind communication. How about that. She must be emoting so strongly he could read her from a distance. They'd evidently grown closer than she'd thought, these past couple months. Did he really know her so well? Or maybe he was just sharp enough to pick up on her body language. Probably the latter.

"Whew-ee." Lew, by this time, was leaning over her shoulder and seeing what she'd seen. "A real crispy-critter." He summed it up nicely.

"You can say that again."

Frankie was disgusted with herself. She'd seen plenty of bodies, even burned ones. She didn't know why this one affected her like it did. Maybe because the others had been the result of either war or accident. If she read things right, both these deaths pointed toward murder, the burning deliberate. And although she'd seen murder before, too, these struck her as even more hardboiled than those.

A warm hand clasped her by the shoulder. Gabe, of course. "Come away, Frankie. There's nothing you can do for either of them."

She drew in a shaky breath. No kidding. "I know." She forced a smile.

Seeing everyone else's attention had been diverted, Strohmeyer could not be restrained. Not without tackling him and putting him in cuffs, anyway. He jerked away from Karl Mager and barged ahead until he, too, had stared his fill at what had once been a person.

"I always heard people smell like roast pork," he said. "Looks like this one got overcooked."

His callousness served to drive the collywobbles from Frankie's mind. Of course, Strohmeyer had to have the last word, which didn't surprise her.

"How long before you get this mess cleaned up?" he asked. "If there's anything I don't need, it's a bunch of gawking tourists prowling around out here, driving all over my fields."

CHAPTER THREE

"I can't remember even one murder occurring around Hawkesford back when I was a kid." Frankie glanced from the countryside rushing past her window to Karl, who drove the fire department SUV like he owned it. "But look at the place now. I've been home for three months and there's been four deaths and at least two near misses. Has it really gotten so lawless around here?" She directed a vent to blow cool air over her hot face.

"Looks as if," he said. "Sad to say we've got some bad apples who've taken up residence. Frickin' meth heads."

With their part of the excitement over, she and Karl were on their way back to the station. The pumper truck followed in their dust. Lew and Chris, still at the scene with the ambulance waiting for the ME to finish, had drawn the not-so-pleasant duty of transporting what Karl had already dubbed 'the Strohmeyer bodies' to the morgue in Coeur d'Alene. The firefighting crew had left Gabe and some deputies at the farm sifting through the ashes for clues into the identity of the dead people.

And good luck to them.

A snort of laughter rose in Frankie's throat, drawing a questioning look from Karl.

"What? If there's anything funny about this, I wish you'd clue me in," he said.

Frankie instantly sobered. "I was just wondering what Harvey Strohmeyer would say if he knew you'd assigned his name to the victims."

A twinkle flashed in Karl's eyes. "I hope nobody tells him."

"Me too. He was really in a mood today, wasn't he? Even more than usual, I mean. I remember once when he came to school and chewed Principal Gower's butt very thoroughly. In front of the whole student body, no less, which didn't go over too well. Gower had expelled Harvey's son Blake for smoking in the boy's locker room. Set off the smoke alarm, so we all had to evacuate."

"I remember, back when Stevens was captain." Karl shook his head. "That incident introduced me to both Hawkesford and to Strohmeyer. Had the department in a panic when they thought the school was on fire. It surprised me they let his kid back in."

"Strohmeyer farms a lot of land around here." Frankie

had no need to say more than that.

"Yeah." Karl drew the word out thoughtfully, causing her to twist in her seat to study him.

"'Yeah' what?" she asked.

"Wonder how the antagonism is going to work out between Gabe and Strohmeyer. Had me thinking they were going to come to blows for a minute."

"I know. Gabe almost lost it. Sure shocked the dickens out of me. For all her mouthiness and sarcasm, the murderer he caught last month didn't wind him up that much. Truthfully, I'm a little disturbed by his reaction."

"Well, you oughta know," Karl said. "Living with him and all."

Heat rushed through Frankie, turning her cheeks hot. For a minute she felt like she imagined Strohmeyer must when thwarted. Only she wasn't thwarted. Her anger was justified. Right about then a good swat to Karl's stubbled cheek would've made her feel better.

"Innuendo, Karl. I don't like the implication of what you said." Her voice became a little rough. "I live in the same house. Gabe leases the place from me and allows me a room for a reduction on his rent. It's a business proposition, nothing more."

"Yeah?"

"Yeah."

A sudden rush of blood suffused Karl's face, and

Frankie guessed he was aware he'd pushed the topic to the limit. "Okay," he said. "Whatever you say. Sorry."

"Okay."

Except he didn't just leave it there. "Although I don't know what would be wrong with the first scenario."

"Ask him if you want to know so bad," she said. And if you find out, please tell me.

Frankie gritted her teeth. She didn't know what came between Gabe and her either—quite. Except for her foot, her PTSD with subsequent nightmares and, upon occasion, brain flashes complete with short blackouts. She didn't think her two dogs counted against her. Maybe with some men, but not with Gabe. As far as she could tell, he liked them.

The fact remained he didn't seem interested in getting closer to her. Edged around it a couple times, both from which either he or she backed away.

"Well," Karl said, his tone mollifying, "Seems to me you two make a good team."

They backtracked to the highway. Once off the gravel road, Karl tromped on the gas. The fields, sere and golden under the sun, spread around them as they passed the grain elevators standing tall at the edge of town.

Frankie, gazing into the distance, spied smoke rising from beyond the elevators.

"Look!" She pointed the lazy spiral out to Karl.

He nodded, not much concerned. "Just old Bill Woodruff out burning trash, same as he does once every month. And every month either Gabe or I present him with a fine. He just grins and tosses the papers into the flames."

Relieved, Frankie chuckled. "I remember now. He's still at that, is he? Bill's a silly old coot. I can't help feeling sorry for him, though. Guess it'll be your turn to pay him a visit this time. Gabe'll no doubt be tied up with this new investigation."

She figured the old man's bill must've been horrendous after all these years, seeing it had never been paid. The general consensus was that he started his fires and got fined every month just to ensure someone would come around and make sure he hadn't bought the farm. Worst case would be if the fire got away from him and he was burned beyond recognition. She shuddered. Enough of that for one day.

As though tracking her mindset, Karl nodded. "A sad end when we don't even know if the incinerated one is male or female."

"I have no doubt Doctor Huong will soon figure it out." Frankie tried for optimism. "The county is lucky to have her as medical examiner. She's very good at her job."

"Yeah, but nobody should have to 'figure it out'," Karl grumped. "Shouldn't happen to anybody, dying like that."

"It's just so freaky." Frankie's train of thought was stuck on a single track. "Two murders last month, and now two this month."

Karl glanced over at her. "Month has only just started," he said on a glum note.

"Maybe I'm a jinx." Considering the body count, Frankie couldn't help thinking she might as well be back in Afghanistan dodging IEDs. Trouble is, she wasn't any too good at dodging. Otherwise she'd still be in possession of the missing half of her left foot, and she'd have an all-bone skull instead of one with a titanium plate.

"Nah, you know better than that." Bluff and hearty, Karl sent her a reassuring grin as they pulled into the station parking lot, where he let her out. The pumper followed them in and stopped outside the garage. The trainees immediately went to work washing soot, ashes, and dust from the rig.

Frankie went inside to discover Maggie Owens in charge of the dispatch desk for the evening shift. In charge of more than that, truth be known, since she had more longevity than anyone else in either the fire or police departments and wasn't shy about letting everyone know it.

Maggie's kind heart kept her from coming across as a tyrant. Her natural tendency was to take anyone having a tough time under her wing. Someone like Frankie after the duplex she'd rented when she first returned to Hawkesford got blown to smithereens. That was the reason she now lived in the house Gabe leased from the estate after Frankie's grandmother died. But first, Maggie had tried to hold a fund-raising dance for her.

Frankie put a stop to that pretty quick, the fund raising, not the dance, but she'd be eternally grateful for the thought behind it.

"Hey," Maggie yelled and waved her over to the dispatch desk. "Heard you guys caught a bad run. You all right?"

"Sure. All in a day's work." Frankie returned the helmet she'd snatched up at the beginning of the run to its hook before collapsing into the chair beside Maggie's station. The monitor was blank at the moment; a break in the activity.

"Any word on the victims?" Maggie adjusted her phone mike away from her mouth.

"Huh? What is this? You're asking me?" Frankie summoned up a smile. "I expect you'll hear before I do. Anyway, Lew won't have delivered the bodies to the morgue yet, let alone Doctor Huong preformed the autopsies."

"Yeah, but Gabe—" Maggie broke off.

"Gabe what?"

Twisting this way and that, Maggie spied out the terrain before speaking in such a low voice Frankie had to lean closer to hear.

"Gabe called the sheriff a few minutes ago. He said he was bringing Harvey Strohmeyer in for questioning. The sheriff asked what he was gonna charge Strohmeyer with and Gabe said obstruction of justice for starters and that he'd figure out something else as he went along."

"Seriously? He arrested Strohmeyer?" Frankie gaped at the dispatcher.

"Seriously."

Maggie was obviously reporting the conversation word for word. No chance she'd heard things wrong.

Dread frizzled along Frankie's nerves. This didn't sound good. Had a new outburst blown up between the two men? Gabe was a stickler for due process. He had to have probable cause to bring Strohmeyer in. What could it be?

* * *

As the result of a duel between a tiny eighty-year-old man and a washing machine, Frankie and Zane, a willing but under-trained volunteer, were kept busy until nearly nine o'clock that evening. On their way home from a hospital run to Kootenai Health, Frankie took an out-of-the-way detour past the sheriff's office in Coeur d'Alene. Gabe's SUV was still in the parking lot. Probably, she thought, not a good sign.

"Hey, that's the cops' house. What are we doing way

out here?" Zane stared over at the office as they cruised past. It had taken him a while to notice they'd turned left instead of right on their way out of the hospital.

While Zane may not have been the brightest light in the chandelier, he was a willing worker when it came to hefting patients onto stretchers and the like. Too bad he always turned green at the sight of blood or vomit. For his sake, Frankie was thankful the old man's broken arm hadn't involved bodily fluids. Her sake, too, come to think of it.

"I'm hungry, aren't you?" she asked brightly. "Somebody told me this is a good place to eat." No way she'd tell him she was keeping track of Gabe, and Zane's soft paunch indicated he liked his food.

A garishly lit drive-in restaurant shone just ahead. Frankie didn't know—or care—which one, but on impulse, and maybe as a bit of a cover-up to her snooping, she turned the ambulance into a parking lot populated by only a couple cars.

"Here?" Zane's incredulous look went from her to the neon sign. "Belly Boy Burgers?"

"I'm buying," she said, figuring that would do the trick. "And Hudson's is closed." Hudson's was the iconic hamburger joint in the Coeur d'Alene area, in business for over one hundred years in the same location with the identical menu.

Zane, busily glomming down his food, paid no attention when she discarded half of a greasy cheeseburger. He slept most of the way to Hawkesford and Frankie, in spite of his raucous snores, considered herself thankful for it. She didn't feel like making conversation. Or answering questions.

* * *

Frankie's shift ended at midnight. There'd been no calls for emergency services to carry them into overtime, thank goodness, and she was primed to leave the second the clock's hand hit twelve. She'd slung her purse over her shoulder and begun edging toward the door when Maggie, giving her the look, started with her own round of questions.

"What's wrong?" Maggie asked as they left the station side-by-side, leaving Zane to shut off the lights and lock the door.

Frankie fished her pickup keys out of her purse's side pocket, studiously avoiding Maggie's penetrating stare. "Wrong? Nothing's wrong."

"Don't try to kid the kidder." Maggie grabbed her arm. "Something in your world is off kilter. You're always the last one out. So, what's up? Did Zane make a flub on the evening run? I noticed he isn't yapping his head off tonight."

"Huh? No. He was fine. Better than usual. He didn't get sick once." More oblivious, she meant, even if it had cost her fifteen dollars' worth of heart-plug food.

The other woman eyed her. "Hmm. Really?" She frowned. "Well then, have you got a headache? Or is your foot bothering you? I've got to say your color isn't good."

Maggie really ought to head up the Sheriff's Investigative Unit, Frankie thought wryly. Or the Nosiness Bureau.

"For heaven's sake, Maggie, I'm fine. Honest. We're standing under the weirdest streetlight in Hawkesford—probably in all of Idaho. Your color isn't good, either. You don't see me bugging you because you're green."

Dropping Frankie's arm, Maggie laughed. "Okay, okay. But if you do a have problem, you'll tell me, won't you?"

"Sure." Tell the biggest gossip in all of North Idaho? Never happen. Frankie inserted her key in the Ranger's door lock and climbed in. The interior needed a good vacuuming as an abundance of long white dog hair floated in the air.

"Liar." Maggie walked around to the driver's door of her shiny new Outback. "Is it Gabe?" she called before getting in.

Frankie just waved.

Maggie had hit the mark dead center, though. Did Gabe have a problem? Was something going on between him and Strohmeyer? That's exactly what she wanted to know.

CHAPTER FOUR

Frankie arrived home to find Gabe's SUV backed into the driveway, ready for a quick getaway in anticipation of a call out. She parked beside his rig and stepped from the Ranger. Heat still radiated from the Tahoe's hood, the metal ticking as it cooled. So. He hadn't been home long enough for the engine to get cold, but long enough the lights in the house were off.

She'd wanted a conversation with him although the poor guy was probably worn to a nub. He'd had a long day. And unless they caught whoever had killed those people out at the Berthold place PDQ, he'd probably be in for a long series of short nights and lots of overtime.

She took the uneven, brick-paved path around to the rear of the house, where leaves on a pin oak overlooking the patio whispered a welcome home. The gate into the backyard, hinges in need of a squirt of WD40, squeaked faintly as she forced the broken latch open. A couple seconds later the dog door set into the house wall flapped and two dogs dashed out. For all her smaller size and shorter legs, Shine, the Bichon Frise led the way, with Banner, the Samoyed close behind.

Frankie, as always delighted by the greeting, was met by two creatures ecstatic at her return. Ear scratches, tail-wagging and near trip-ups ensued before Frankie got the door unlocked and open. Once inside—Shine having taken the short route via the doggie door—both dogs headed for the old apple-shaped cookie jar that had stood on the counter for as long as Frankie could remember. The only cookies it contained these days belonged to the dogs.

"Yes, yes," she whispered, flipping on the light over the sink. "Patience, my dears."

A harsh voice spoke from the doorway. "What can you tell me about Harvey Strohmeyer?"

Sparks like lightning flashed behind Frankie's eyes. Her vision bounced. A little heart-shaped dog biscuit dropped from her nerveless fingers into Banner's gaping maw.

She spun around, hand over her heart. Heaven only knows what her expression was like because Gabe said, "Oh, God, Frankie. I'm sorry. I didn't mean to scare you."

"Startle me." Her voice was too loud. Her throat

scratched. "That's all. Not scare me."

Deny, deny.

"Startle you. Either way, I apologize. I know better."

Shaking, she turned and reached into the cookie jar again, selecting, according to dog size, another of the heart-shaped crunchies for Shine, and a larger, jerky type treat for Banner.

"It's not your fault I'm screwed up," she mumbled, avoiding Gabe's worried gaze and allowing the dogs to claim her attention. "I'm just extra jumpy tonight, is all."

"Got reason to be." He leaned against the door jamb and studied her. "It was a bad scene, out there at the Berthold place."

There seemed a little emphasis when he said "Berthold", as if he didn't want to give Strohmeyer any weight in the matter. As for excusing her reaction, well, to her supreme embarrassment, she'd awakened him more than once, crying out while in the throes of a bad dream. Bombs, noise, blood—and dead friends. Yeah. He knew. About those anyway. She hadn't told anyone about the occasional blackout.

Forcing a smile, she lifted her chin. "Now I've forgotten what you asked. I have a couple questions for you, too."

"You do?"

"Yes. But you first."

Gabe came on in, brushing past her to fill a glass with water at the tap. He was barefoot—the excuse Frankie used for not hearing his approach—shirtless and wearing an old pair of jeans. Stubble sprouted along his jaw. Frankie liked the way he looked. Comfortable. At home. Tired.

A little upset.

"I asked what you can tell me about Harvey Strohmeyer. For instance, has he always been a loud-mouthed hard-assed SOB or is this behavior new to him? Maybe something he learned from his son?"

Make that a lot upset.

"He's always been all that—and more. Ask anyone. They'll all tell you his son learned it from him." Frankie pushed back a smile, although it wasn't exactly a smiling matter. It's just that Gabe's serious expression and his rare outburst were so out of character. "But if you're asking me if he's capable of murdering those people we found today, I'd tell you I don't know. At one time I wouldn't have thought so. Nowadays . . ." she shrugged, " . . . who knows? Anyway, I never knew him that well. Harvey or Blake either one. I guess the first thing I'd want to know is why they would want to kill anyone. Especially on their own land, then have the chutzpah to call in a fire."

Gabe drained his water and got a refill. "Motive, you mean. Frankie, after talking to Harvey for three hours this evening, I think he'd do anything he wanted, just for the pure hell of it. I find him a man of impulse. I don't think he'd actually need a motive. As for Junior—"

"Who's a limb cut from the same tree," she interjected.

"A complete clone of his parent," he agreed, "although it might be easier to see a motive for him."

"Like what?"

"Like a drug deal gone wrong. The victims were using the old house to cook meth in. I think you saw their set-up. You think Strohmeyer—both Strohmeyers—weren't crazy mad? Then they, or someone, killed the cooks and managed to catch the place on fire and almost spread it to the stubble. Only I can't figure out if they're mad now because of the fire danger, or because a lucrative bit of side business got shut down."

"So, you're asking if I think they could be part of a messed-up drug operation?"

"Among other things."

Did she? Well, Blake had always been the bad boy at school. And very good, if some of his classmates were to be believed, at putting the blame on someone else.

"Blake, maybe," she said, brow gathered in a frown. "I wouldn't put it past him. Harvey, though, well, it just seems he'd have too much to lose if he got found out."

Gabe was silent, his face blank, before finally saying, "That's what I thought. Although maybe we're giving him too much credit. A man like Strohmeyer Senior thinks he's too smart to be caught by someone like me."

"Someone like you?"

"Small town cop. Dirt beneath his feet. Less than dirt. It's clear he puts a lot of value on good topsoil."

"Maybe." Frankie had almost forgotten the pain flashing behind her eyes. Wasn't she used to it, after all? Gabe in a mood was something else, claiming all her attention. He'd never opened up to her regarding a case before. Not even the one that had almost gotten her killed right after she moved back to Hawkesford. Perhaps this said something about their unconventional relationship.

Not that they had a relationship, exactly. She owned the house they both lived in, although he'd leased it from the estate while she was still in Afghanistan. When she'd come back home, the place she'd rented got blown up and he'd offered her a room in her own house.

And that was that.

Mostly.

Even though the pain had rapidly faded, Frankie still felt a little dizzy. She sat down at the kitchen table, a 1950s affair of chrome legs and a red Formica top her friend Jesselyn said was worth a small fortune on eBay. Shine immediately jumped onto her lap, while Banner sat on her foot, the one with all the toes.

She cleared her throat. "So, did you let Harvey go?

After talking to him, I mean. Him and Blake?"

"Yeah. Had to. He lawyered up almost before we got to the station." Gabe refilled his water glass and brought it with him as he sat opposite her.

"What did you charge him—them—with?"

To Frankie's surprise, Gabe's Mediterranean complexion flushed. Must be a story behind that, she thought. But if so, he kept it to himself.

"Obstructing a policeman in his duties," he said. "Both of them. Strohmeyer the younger is not only foul-mouthed, but malicious besides. His father is downright mean." He swirled the water in his glass. "Too bad I couldn't arrest them for having rotten personalities. All I can say is it's a good thing Rudy got to the crime with his camera real fast or half the evidence would've been destroyed."

"How?"

Gabe's upper lip curled. "After you left, they overheard the ME say identification might be difficult, and took it into their heads to do their own examination. Or so Harvey said. Tromped around the body in the weeds before we could stop them, destroying any trace evidence there might've been."

Frankie huffed a breath through pursed lips. "Wow! I suppose Harvey is back to saying it's his property and he can go where he wants."

"You nailed it. All while pointing out that everything

had already been hosed down by the fire department, so it didn't matter anyway." Gabe sipped his water. "Worst part is that he was probably right. Even so . . . So, I cuffed them, put them in the Tahoe out of the way, and let them sit while we worked the scene." His eyes narrowed, as if viewing a movie on a far-off screen. "Didn't go over real well."

If she remembered correctly, the Tahoe had been parked in the sun. Frankie couldn't help it. She giggled. "No. I expect not. I wish I'd been there."

Gabe's face darkened again. "No, you don't. These are not pleasant people, Frankie."

"No kidding. But do you seriously think they killed those two?" The idea took some getting used to. The Strohmeyers might never be described as pleasant—well, no might about it—but they were people she'd more-or-less known all her life. It was hard to wrap her head around the thought of them as killers.

She ran her fingers through Shine's soft, curly hair. The little dog, shot and left for dead a while back, was fully recovered thanks to a blood transfusion from Banner. Even so, she'd forever sport a bullet hole through her ear.

What had happened to this bucolic little town while she'd been in Afghanistan? When had it gotten so violent?

"Are they killers?" Gabe rolled the word over his tongue. "I don't know. Not yet. But I'm going to find out."

CHAPTER FIVE

Frankie believed Gabe when he said he'd discover who killed those two drug dealers. But the first item on his agenda was to find out exactly who the victims were. She went to bed, leaving him emailing various agencies.

She heard his phone ring during the night. Two sharp tones only. Then his voice, a soft murmur wafting up the stairs to her room. She loved the old place, really, she did, but regretfully, the 1911 house lacked something in the soundproofing department. Rolling over, she faced her clock. Four a.m. Not that it mattered. She'd only been dozing anyway.

A short while later, she heard him stirring around. Water in the pipes. The sound of a drawer shoved into place too hard. A muffled curse.

Banner, lying on the soft sheepskin rug beside her bed, lifted his head and whuffed a question.

"Let's go see," Frankie answered. Moving carefully to keep from awakening Shine—who slept harder than any dog she'd ever heard of—she swung her legs over the side of the bed and stood. After a brief check to ensure any part of her body that needed cover had it, she and Banner made their way down the steep staircase.

She didn't bother with her prosthesis. Gabe had seen her mutilated foot often enough she was no longer embarrassed by it.

Gabe, in the act of taking a cup of instant coffee out of the microwave, swooshed his mug at her as she hesitated in the doorway. "Sorry. Didn't mean to wake you."

"I wasn't asleep. Is there news?"

He nodded. "A missing person report just got called in. Sounds as if it could be one of our victims."

"Sad news for someone. Couldn't they wait until morning to call you?"

Gabe eyed her over his cup brim. "It is morning."

"Technically, maybe," she grumbled. "But it's not daylight."

He grinned and reached down to pat Banner who'd ambled over to sniff—then sneeze—at the odor of fresh gun oil. Gabe was a stickler for maintaining his gear in top condition. No gun of his would dare jam.

He was in uniform now, his Glock secured on his hip, his face freshly shaved. Alert, so you'd never know he'd had less than four hours sleep after a long day on the job.

"Where from?" Frankie stepped farther into the room.

He cocked a brow. "Pardon me?"

Huh. She must be incoherent from lack of sleep. "Where did the call come from?"

"Oh. Missoula."

She didn't realize her expression changed until he said, "You're pleased about that?"

"I'm not pleased with any of this. But, yes. I hope it means they're not local. I don't like having people I went to school with turn up dead."

He finished his coffee and turned to rinse the cup. "I suppose you don't," he said over the splash of water.

He left after giving Banner a last pat, saying, "Go back to bed, Frankie. You've got dark circles under your eyes."

Not very flattering. Nor informative.

* * *

Taking Gabe's advice, Frankie did go back to bed and, to her own surprise, slept a solid five hours. A record for her, these days. Refreshed and full of energy, she put in a stint of housekeeping, mowed the lawn, and made a batch of chocolate chip cookies. By then it was lunchtime. Surrounded by dogs, she had just sat down to eat when her phone played a couple bars of Beethoven's Fifth.

The image of a strawberry blonde woman grinned out at her on the phone's screen. Frankie touched the answer button.

"You'd better not be getting mixed up in this latest crime wave," Jesselyn Pettigrew announced before Frankie could even say hello.

"Crime wave? What crime wave?"

"Oh, c'mon, don't be stoopid. The one those dang drug dealers are bringing down on our town."

Frankie didn't take offense at Jesselyn calling her stupid—or even stoopid. They'd been best friends since the first grade and were used to insulting each other.

Sighing a little, Frankie picked up her fork, speared a small shrimp out of her salad, and poked it in her mouth. "Is it a real crime wave?" she asked around the bite. "Had you heard any rumors about a meth operation around here before yesterday?"

The dogs sat close to her, eyes fixed watching her chew.

"I've heard a mention," Jesselyn said cautiously, "just speculation, really. Rumors about how it might be easy to set up out here in the boondocks. But we were just talking. Nobody thought it would happen for real. And at the time, we were thinking marijuana. Not meth. That crap is ugly stuff."

Jesselyn, Frankie thought, had no idea how ugly.

"So," Jesselyn went on, "who are the dead people? The paper said their identification is being withheld until next of kin can be notified, but has Gabe said anything? He knows who they are, doesn't he? Are they from Hawkesford?"

Shaking her head at all the questions, Frankie dug a shrimp for each dog from her salad. Banner and Shine both leapt to attention and gulped down the treat.

"I can't answer any of that," she told Jesselyn. "I worked until midnight, remember, and when I got up this morning, Gabe was gone. Not that he'd tell me anything. He keeps all his sheriff business to himself. Don't forget I'm just a lowly paramedic, not a sheriff's deputy."

Mostly true, she excused herself, and if there were a few omissions, well, Jesselyn need never find out. She crossed her fingers against the little fib. Jesselyn did have a way of digging these kinds of things out.

"Hah! A paramedic who lives with the resident deputy," Jesselyn retorted. "Give. Tell me what you know."

Frankie took another bite of her salad and said, "I don't know anything. Maybe you should talk to Blake Strohmeyer. I'm sure he'd be happy to fill you in on what happened yesterday. Just don't believe everything he tells you."

"Frankie!" Jesselyn's screech nearly broke her eardrum. "Blake Strohmeyer is involved? Really? He'd lie just because he doesn't like to tell the truth. You know how he is."

"Got an idea," Frankie said. "He doesn't seem to have changed much from our high school days." She thought maybe she shouldn't have mentioned Blake's name. But she had to tell Jesselyn something, didn't she, with the object of diverting her? What better than siccing her onto Blake? Besides, the location of the bodies was no secret. Too many people were involved in the discovery, for one thing. The whole area knew by now where the fire had occurred, and that the Strohmeyers were the farmers of record.

"If he's involved, the rumors just became more believable." Jesselyn still sounded excited.

"What rumors?"

"Oh, about a big drug bust, and some dead people, except nobody is saying who they are."

Frankie sighed. "Yeah, well, on second thought, don't believe everything you hear and go accusing anyone. In fact, forget I mentioned Blake and his dad. All I know is that the dead people were found on one of the sections the Strohmeyers farm. Which," she warned her friend, "doesn't really mean a thing." A thought occurred. "Don't forget bad stuff always used to happen to people Blake took against. It's a trait he learned, or inherited, from his father. Could be he hasn't outgrown it."

"He hasn't." Subdued now, Jesselyn related how late in the winter Blake had been arrested for beating up one of the high school basketball players. "In theory because the kid had talked back when Blake told him he sucked and should go play with the Special Ed kids. Only he wasn't that polite. And then, too, the kid is Native American, which didn't help."

"So Blake got away with it?"

"Not entirely. He had to pay a fine. No jail time, regretfully, even though he's an adult who beat up a juvenile."

"Was Gabe the arresting officer?" It would explain the obvious bad blood between him and the Strohmeyers.

"I believe so, although Rudy Swallowtail was on the scene first. You can guess what happened with that."

Frankie sighed. Oh, yes. She could. Poor Rudy. The Strohmeyers were, if not complete holdovers from Aryan Nation days, the next thing to it.

As part of the background noise, she heard Jesselyn's work phone chime. A relief, really, when Jesselyn said, "Gotta go," and hung up.

Thoughtfully, Frankie speared another shrimp for each dog, hoping to finish her meal in peace. So, Blake hadn't changed from the same asshat he'd always been, and greedy, too. Stealing lunch money had always been a favorite game of his. Not because he needed it, the

Strohmeyers were wealthy, but because he got a kick out of it. And he enjoyed making his targeted victim go hungry. No wonder Gabe had him in his sights—as long as it didn't backfire.

CHAPTER SIX

Frankie arrived at work her customary fifteen minutes ahead of schedule. She found the station abuzz with people who'd discovered they had important business there. Calls for fire permits, driver manuals, vehicle licensing tabs, dog licenses, all the mundane stuff that usually saw only a scattering of requests on any given day. As often as not, there were none. Arlene, who's real job meant attending to any dispatch calls, appeared a bit on the frazzled side with all the extras.

"Thank God you're here," she greeted Frankie who, as everyone knew, could be depended on to lend a hand for whatever needed to be done. "We've been overrun with people demanding to know all about those dead people you guys found yesterday. And wouldn't you know? Today of all days, Maggie is running an hour late and . . ." Her dispatch line blinked and she broke off to answer.

"Hawkesford 911. What is your emergency?"

Frankie eyed the line of three formed up at the front desk. First in line, a farmer whose place was southeast of town. Taking a breath, she stepped over to see if she could help.

Vern Hendon, his face gray with dust from the fields, wanted a driver's manual—or so went his excuse for being there. "Aimee'll be taking driver's ed as soon as school starts. Figured I'd better get'er prepared." He took the pamphlet Frankie handed him. "Thanks." He didn't move and finally, came to the crux of the matter. "Uh, by the way, you heard who those dead folks are? They from around here?"

Sighing, Frankie spoke plenty loud enough for everyone in line to hear. "I haven't heard a thing, Vern. Hopefully, the detectives will have something to announce on the evening news. I'm sure they're working very hard to get this resolved." Proud of how professional she'd sounded, she looked around him to the next person in line. "Ma'am, can I help you?"

Ma'am was someone Frankie didn't recognize, probably one of the summer people who lived at the muckety-muck enclave down by the lake. The woman had two things on her mind. One, she wanted to make a complaint, she said, and two, to tell someone in charge—meaning Gabe, the resident deputy—what she'd seen when driving home from a theater production in Coeur d'Alene the night before last. She seemed adamant that it involved a stolen car. And that maybe it had to do with those drug dealers.

Frankie dug in the desk drawer for a pen and one of those ubiquitous pink message pads. "I can take a message, ma'am. The deputy isn't here right now, but he'll get back with you as soon as he can." Pen poised above the paper, she hesitated as though a thought had just occurred to her. "Perhaps you could call the sheriff's department in Coeur d' Alene and speak to someone there. I can write the direct number down for you."

The woman glared. "That's my complaint," she said. "I reached out and they completely ignored me. I want to speak to our deputy. Now."

Hendon cocked his head, unabashedly listening although he'd stepped to the side. The man behind Ma'am, Les Bitters, wasn't about to be left out of the conversation, either.

"Zantos oughta be posting updates," he stated. "Folks here are worried. We deserve to know what's going on in our community and if he won't tell us, maybe you'd damn well better."

Hendon nodded. "He's right, Frankie. It is Zantos' job to keep us informed."

An eye flash in the shape of a lightning bolt first lit,

then blackened Frankie's vision. A violent pain stabbed through her head, forcing her to clutch at the desk. She took a couple deep breaths.

"I can't tell you what I don't know," she said, hoping none of them had noticed her lapse. "And I wouldn't tell you if I did in case I blabbed something I shouldn't. I'm not a cop, after all. But I do know Deputy Zantos is working hard to find out who the victims are, and who killed them. And to keep us all safe."

Ending her little speech, she blinked and looked toward Bitters. "Is there anything you need that I can provide?"

Evidently not.

"Damn snippety women." He muttered a word or two more, most likely something uncomplimentary, before he stomped away empty-handed.

Ma'am was still waiting, her left foot, clad in cork-soled platforms, tapping the floor impatiently. "I, for one, don't care who these dead people are. I don't know any addicts or dealers and personally, don't care a thing about them, except that they stay out of my backyard. But I do care about murder taking place practically on my doorstep. And I want to talk to the deputy."

"Where do you live, ma'am?"

The woman spieled off an address.

Sure enough, it turned out that she did live down at the

lake, just as Frankie had surmised. At Pearson's Landing, to be precise. And when Frankie considered the location, Ma'am wasn't as full of hyperbole as she first thought. A short hike across the field and over a steep wooded hill and one would indeed be right in her back yard.

Frankie copied the address and looked up at the woman. Forties, long blonde hair, not a single wrinkle between her eyes or trace of crow's feet at the corners, thanks either to botox or extremely good genes. "Can you give me the gist of what you saw? I'll see the deputy gets the note as soon as possible."

The woman cocked a brow. "You'll hand it to him personally?"

"I will, the moment I see him."

Ma'am's name was Laura James. Mrs. Donald James she informed Frankie, as though it should mean something special to her. She repeated the part about driving home from the theater and that she'd seen a car parked under the big lone pine that, as she put it, "marks where the farmer takes his machinery into the field."

Kids used to park there to make out. The memory flashed through Frankie's mind, and probably through Hendon's, too, as he opened his mouth to speak. Ma'am— make that Mrs. Donald James—didn't give him the chance.

"I noted the car in particular because our real estate

agent has one like it. It's a red Lexus LC500 sports car. A rather ostentatious car for a man in his position and very distinctive. I probably wouldn't even have noticed it except that my headlights glanced off the windshield and caught my attention."

"Windshield?" Hendon asked.

"Yes." Mrs. Donald James gave Hendon's dirty face and dusty clothes a disparaging glance. "It was backed in, which struck me as odd. Out of place."

A fancy car parked on that little used road? It struck Frankie as odd, too. Not that she knew what a Lexus LC500 sports car looked like, but if Mrs. James said ostentatious, it had to mean expensive.

"You know anybody around here with a red Lexus?" she asked Hendon.

He shook his head without having to think about it. "Farmers don't have that kind of money—except maybe Oswalds. Or Fremont."

Frankie didn't think he was actually hurting either, but that his taste in rigs probably leaned more toward seventy-thousand-dollar pick-up trucks than sports cars.

Mrs. James brushed all this aside. "Our agent told me it's the only car like it in the whole area. Which is why I thought it might be stolen."

Over at the dispatch desk, Arlene hit the button that set the siren to screeching, the sound making Frankie jump.

"I'm sorry. That's me," Frankie said. "Got to go. I'll see the deputy gets the message." Ripping the note from the pad, she stuck it in her pocket and ran, leaving Mrs. James agape. She headed for the ambulance, aware that once again she hadn't had time to put her personal things into her locker or collect her gear. Frankie took the shotgun seat, what with Chris having climbed in on the driver's side. He gunned the motor.

Arlene, sounding remarkably professional, sent out directions. Southwest of town, for this run. Out on Highway 95 for two miles, then take the turn off toward Hawkesford Mountain. Injury and a structure fire.

Lights flashing, the fire truck led the way. Chris hung back far enough not to rear end the truck if Karl, known to barrel up on turn-offs, slowed without warning.

She looked over at Chris. He drove with his hands white-knuckled on the wheel, eyes fixed on the road.

"You all right?" she asked.

He swallowed, the up and down movement of his Adam's apple's prominent. "Sure. Why wouldn't I be? You don't have to worry, Frankie. I can do my job."

Back when she was still going to the veteran's hospital, she'd hated overly zealous questions. Still did, for that matter. Chris probably felt the same. So she'd take it easy.

"I know you can," she said. "I just figured . . . well, yesterday can't have been much fun."

"No." He snapped out the word, short and sharp. He hesitated, his head jerking. "I can still smell it. The stench of burned human flesh. It's like I can taste it."

That last part, Frankie noted, had been a whisper just for himself. He hadn't meant for her to hear. She answered anyway. "The taste stays with you. I know. Anybody who's ever experienced it will say the same." Lieutenant Jay had burned, back in Afghanistan.

Black spots danced across her vision; pain stabbed at her temple. Odd, really, for the pain to hit there. The plate in her head was farther back and up, above her right ear.

She pressed the painful spot. Damn it. The spells, while shorter than they used to be, were definitely increasing. What did they mean?

"Do you think those people were dead before they burned?" he asked. "Has Gabe told you anything? Who they were, maybe? God, I hope I didn't know them."

"You think you might? Are any of your friends . . ." She hesitated. What now? Chris was a bit of a loose cannon, easily led and not always a good judge of character. Look at the disastrous friendship he'd formed with Darryl, who'd proved to be a killer. But seriously? Would he be tight with this kind of people?

"No!" he said. "Not my friends. But still, I know most

everyone around here. I just—"

Frankie relented. "As far as I know the police are still trying to identify them." She eyed his set jaw and added, "I think they were dead, Chris. I think the fire was set to destroy the evidence."

Did Chris relax just the least little bit? Maybe. Enough for him to nod and glance over at her, anyway.

"I've been meaning to ask you," he said. "About Darryl. You know, when he shot Marc and then came after you."

A moment passed. Frankie waited for him to speak, but he didn't. Not right away. They were nearing the turn to their destination before she said, "What about him?"

His breath caught on a kind of hiccup. "I thought him and me were friends, you know? All of us, even Lew. But Darryl? He shot Marc down like he was a paper target nailed to a post. If I'd been driving that night, he would've done the same to me, right? How do people get to be like that, Frankie?"

"No clue," she said.

"I wondered, did he say anything after he got caught? Like maybe he was sorry? I mean, we all hung out to-gether. Had a few beers. Worked on saving people's lives, for God's sake. And then—" Chris, in the midst of taking a deep breath, choked as he slammed on the brakes. Karl, hardly bothering to slow, had just turned onto a narrow, recently graveled road leading to a small, weather-beaten farmhouse where a woman stood halfway between the house and a huge machine shed. At some time, a south-facing lean-to had been tacked on behind the shed. Smoke boiled out through the lean-to's wide-open doors.

"Psychopath." The word jolted out of her. She threw out a hand to stop her body's forward motion as Chris braked hard and the ambulance came to a juddering halt. "For the record, he didn't say anything. Just pointed his gun at Marc and then me and started to shoot."

She, for one, was happy to abandon the topic as they piled out of the truck. Grabbing the medical pack, she headed toward the shed, ready for the reported casualty. Ahead of them, Karl ordered the firefighters to roll out a hose and start the motor on the pumper truck, while he strode to the building and paused at the entrance.

"Roland Ginz," Frankie heard him bellow, "where are you? Call out."

He turned around and waved the rest of the crew forward. "Get that water running," he said, then, in direct contradiction to what he taught the volunteers, rushed inside by himself.

It felt like minutes, although Frankie figured only seconds passed before Karl dove back through the smoke. He had a short man slung over his shoulder. The man's screams were enough to stop everyone in their tracks.

"Crap." Frankie, seeing his left arm held stiffly out to the side as if frozen there, plunged forward. "Bring the gurney," she called to Chris.

Karl paused beside Frankie long enough to let the victim slump onto the ground before rushing back toward the shed. Flames rose in the interior of the building.

Kneeling beside him, Frankie saw the victim's face was burned a deep red, although not blistered. More like the flash burn from a welder, she thought. His bloodshot eyes streamed tears and, unblinking, he stared straight ahead.

At first glance, his hand appeared the most immediate problem. Fingers mangled, two hanging by mere flaps of skin, the thumb simply gone. A deep gash scored the palm, the tissues peeled back like the layers of an onion, and there were deep burns that traveled all the way from hand to elbow, ending somewhere in his armpit.

She lifted the arm, then, closing her eyes, let it drop.

His screams stopped dead.

By then Chris had the gurney situated beside the man. "Here, sir," he said, swallowing convulsively. "Let's get you onto the gurney so we can help you."

For one fraught moment, the man seemed to be complying—until he toppled over onto his side. Chris caught him, lifting him on to the gurney while Frankie felt for a pulse. "Get his vitals," she snapped. "Quickly. We need sterile water. Extra water is in the bus. There's not much I can do for the exit wound, but I'll get an IV started."

Chris couldn't seem to move. "Exit wound? Has he been shot? Him too?"

"Vitals," Frankie said again, ripping open an IV insertion packet and searching for a viable vein without much luck. A full minute passed before she found one good enough to support a needle. "No, he hasn't been shot. Electrocuted. The charge traveled. Hustle. The water."

"I'll get the water," a voice said from behind her. Gabe, already on the scene. She hadn't been aware until now.

"Electrocuted?" Chris fumbled for his stethoscope, the blood pressure cuff, the oxygen monitor, apparently unable to decide what to do first.

"Sir?" Frankie said to the man. "Sir? Can you tell me your name?" She snatched the blood pressure cuff out of Chris' hands and wrapped it around the man's right arm. Barely discernible. He had no visible respirations. His heartbeat faded by the second as she dug an intubation bundle from the bag. One look told her it was no use. The state of his trachea made intubation impossible.

A jug of sterile water appeared, thrust into her hands. She motioned for Chris to take it and began irrigating.

The man's eyes rolled toward her. They were suffused with blood and Frankie knew he couldn't see anything. He didn't speak. His body convulsed suddenly, jerking hard enough she had to hold him down. She heard something snap, a bone, possibly a ligament, and then he went still.

The cuff went slack. She put her stethoscope to his chest.

"He's gone," she murmured. Perhaps a relief.

"Son of a bitch," Karl said. He, a little pale as sweat ran down his face, stood behind her looking down at Ginz's body. "You're sure?"

Gabe, standing beside him, patted his shoulder.

She hadn't been aware of Karl watching her work, or that enough time had passed for the fire to be extinguished. Frankie nodded. "Yes. Was he a friend of yours?"

Karl's shoulders hunched. "A friendly acquaintance. What a way to go."

"Awful," she said.

The sounds of Chris and two of the volunteers vomiting on the ground only steps away were loud as someone turned off the pump and killed the truck engine.

Sinking back on her heels, Frankie found a black tarp and unfolded it over Ginz's mutilated body. Her pulse pounded in her temples, lightning zig zagged through all parts of her head, the pain almost overwhelming, and yet, she dared not let any of that show. She'd promised when she took this job that she could handle it. She'd only been back two months, just starting on her third.

Still probationary, and now this. Her first death on the job.

The first that wasn't death by murder, at least. Although . . .

Her brow creased.

"All right?" Gabe asked, and she nodded. A lie.

Only later, as they transported the body to the morgue in Coeur d' Alene, she belatedly remembered the woman she'd seen hovering between house and shed. A woman who not only failed to come forward or to ask any questions but disappeared before the deputy arrived.

CHAPTER SEVEN

The sheriff's department Tahoe Gabe drove sat backed into the driveway when Frankie got home around midnight. As always when she worked the night shift, he'd left the slot nearest the door for her to park the Ranger. His thoughtfulness never failed to touch her.

The lights were on inside the house, so she guessed Gabe either hadn't able to sleep or he'd just gotten off work. If so, it'd been a very long day for him, too. She moved to touch the Tahoe's hood. Cool.

The dogs rushed through the flapper of their door to meet her. Shine, small even for a Bichon, ran between Banner's legs like the operator of a Star Wars AT-AT. The sight always made her smile, and right now, she was grateful. This had been a grim shift with nothing much to smile about.

The giving of ear scratches and the receipt of doggie

kisses lifted her spirits. Frankie physically felt a stress knot in her chest unravel as they all tromped into the house.

She found Gabe, paperwork spread before him, sitting at the kitchen table, a red and chrome Formica affair left over from the 1950s. Nothing much had changed in her grandparent's old house, except the people who lived there.

He gave her an absentminded salute.

"Hi." She ran herself a glass of water and plopped down opposite him on one of the red vinyl-covered chairs.

Gabe looked up from where he'd been copying notes from his voice recorder to his ever-present notebook. She'd learned he preferred the recorder for verbatim words but liked his notebook to remark on the facial expressions and body language of his witnesses or suspects.

"Hi, yourself. Another bad day, over at last." His own face looked weary to her discerning eye.

"Not the best of days, for sure. For you, too?"

A faint smile touched his lips. "Nope, not my best, either." He made another note in his little book and touched the recorder's go button. "Listen to this."

Harvey Strohmeyer's voice boomed out. "You better watch your step, deputy dawg. Me and my boy, we aren't answering any more of your questions until our lawyer gets here. You're already over the line as far as I'm concerned. Any more and I'll have you up on charges. Where the hell do you get off hauling me and Blake in here, anyway? You got no right. Those dead people and the fire? I figure we're the injured party." A second of silence, then he said, "Parties."

"Deputy Dawg? Really?" Frankie's eyebrows went up as Gabe pressed the stop button and wrote a couple more lines. "So, he claims he's the injured party, regardless of who's dead. Is that from last night?"

"Yeah. I wanted to get this down before I forget half of it. And today's business, too." He leaned back in his chair. "As you can tell, Strohmeyer wasn't exactly cooperative. Strohmeyer Junior?" He shook his head. "Even worse, only with a more . . . action-driven . . . vocabulary."

Frankie scoffed. "Blake always did cuss like a logger, even in the fourth grade. I think that's about the time his mother departed for parts unknown. Who could blame her?"

At this, Gabe frowned. "Parts unknown? Does anybody know where she went?"

"One assumes Strohmeyer does. Otherwise, I don't believe I've ever heard." Frankie took a sip of water and patted her lap for Shine to leap up. Banner snuggled down atop her toes.

Gabe made a final entry in his notebook before closing it. He yawned. "Gotta get to bed. Another early day tomorrow."

"Before you go, is there any word on who the dead people are? You mentioned a missing person's report out of Missoula. Everybody keeps asking me."

"I suppose they do. But apparently, that lot isn't our victims. We're still looking."

"That's rough. It's hard to move forward without knowing who the victims are."

Gabe yawned again. "Yep. And then there's what happened to the old fella this afternoon. Pretty gruesome. You all right, Frankie? I'm afraid—" He stopped.

Compressing her lips, Frankie met his eyes. "Afraid of what?"

"Afraid it'll trigger bad dreams."

Damn it. Exactly what I'm afraid of. Deep inside, her innards quivered. "You and me both. I hope not. If it does and I holler, ignore me." Deliberately, she deflected that line of thought. "Did anybody figure out what happened?"

"What happened?"

"To Mister Ginz."

"Aside from getting killed, you mean? But, yeah. Karl is saying faulty equipment. Old wiring and it looked like he'd spilled a bucket of water he was using to cool the welds and somehow managed to stand in it. We haven't figured out why he was using that old welder without wearing his helmet or gloves. He had new equipment right there. Karl says Ginz had plenty of experience and it didn't seem like something he'd do."

"It really doesn't." Frankie shook her head. "I wonder if that woman has any idea."

Gabe, who'd turned toward the hall, spun back. "Woman? What woman?"

"At Ginz's place. I imagine she's the one who called in the alarm. Wasn't she?" She looked up at him in surprise. "Didn't you go up to the house and talk to her?"

"On general principles I went up to the house and knocked. Nobody answered, which came as no surprise. Karl had already told me Ginz lived alone. That his wife died years ago. We figured a passerby called in the fire when he saw smoke." His eyes narrowed. "Where did you see this woman? When did you see her?"

Had she heard a hint of distrust in those questions? What the heck? Did he think she hallucinated the woman? Conjured her up out of thin air?

"I saw her standing about halfway between the shed and the house when we first drove up." Frankie drew in a breath. "She had blonde hair and wore a very short and strapless blue sundress. We were moving too fast and were too far away for me to see anything else."

"Where did she go? Did you see a car?"

Frankie sought to recall and came up blank. "I don't know where she went, and no, I didn't see a car. Karl and the pumper truck were stirring up a dust storm ahead of the ambulance. They must have gotten a better look at her. I don't know if Chris noticed her at all." She stood, dumping Shine off her lap. "But if that's the case, why didn't Karl tell you?"

But she knew why. Karl was famous—or maybe she meant notorious—for his single-minded approach to a fire. More than likely, his attention had been concentrated on the smoke issuing from the building. As for the others, well, their view wouldn't have been as open.

"I'll ask him." Gabe began stripping himself of his gear prior to locking it away for the night. His Glock always went in a lockable walnut sewing table, a holdover from Frankie's grandmother, that sat beside a recliner in the living room. Another giant yawn stretched his mouth. "Tomorrow."

* * *

Frankie dumped her fouled clothes in the hamper before she turned on the shower. Her shirt was stained with fluids from working with Mr. Ginz, which made unbuttoning it doubly distasteful. What a relief to wash the day's activities from her body. And thank goodness for her short hair. At least she didn't need to spend an hour drying it.

The shower helped her sleep, dreamlessly, as it happened, and when she got up the next morning, Gabe had already been gone for hours, the coffee in the pot stone cold. He'd left her a note. Thanks for the tip, it said. I'll ask around about the woman.

Frankie smiled as she dumped the cold stuff and started a new pot brewing. So, Gabe believed her after all. Oddly enough, she felt vindicated.

Having barely settled at the table—crumbless of course, since Gabe never ever left any mess for her to clean up—with her first cup of coffee, the rumble of a heavy truck backing into the driveway brought her up from her chair. Shine began barking like a little white maniac, and Banner's fluffy tail waved in joyful greeting.

It wasn't until she read the name Boyd Brothers Construction on the truck doors that she remembered this was actually a much-anticipated appointment. Her faulty memory at work again. Her homeowner's insurance had finally paid up, and the old house was getting a new porch to replace the one that burned when a crazy woman set the place on fire a couple months ago. Ms. Barwick had meant to burn Frankie up with it, but thanks to the dogs, she'd gotten out in time. The old porch had been the only victim.

Frankie had decided to go all out with the rebuild and had selected Mick Boyd as the contractor to do it. She ordered fancy wrought iron rails instead of plain wooden ones, for instance, that Mick created himself. Maybe they were not quite in keeping with the old farmhouse, but she liked them. The porch would have a knotty pine ceiling, built-in flower boxes, and seating that lifted up to conceal hoses, gardening supplies and even to store pillows and blankets. If she wanted to, she could live on this porch when the construction was complete.

Consequently, she considered herself late when the clock showed only seven minutes to the hour when she pulled into the station. Karl had hung around waiting to speak to her.

"Come into my office for a minute," he called from his office doorway.

For the third day in a row, her purse still hung over her shoulder as she complied. Hoping against hope the alarm didn't go off today before she got a chance to get squared away, at his gesture, Frankie closed the office door and took a seat.

"What's up?" Something about the look on Karl's face gave her a qualm.

"That's what I want to ask you," he said. "What's this about a woman out at Ginz's place yesterday?"

She frowned. "What about her?"

"How come you're the only one who saw her? Where exactly did you see her?"

He sounded remarkably like Gabe had last night. Skeptical.

Frankie eyed him. Most of the time Karl appeared completely satisfied with the way she did her job, but for some reason, he looked puzzled and a little aggravated right now. She sat up straighter in her chair.

"I don't know why I'm the only one who saw her, except you, and Chris, who drove the ambulance yesterday, both probably had your eyes fixed on the road. Or were looking ahead at the fire. I saw her on that gravel path between the house and the shed." Crisp and succinct, just as a good report should be.

"I asked the volunteers. None of them saw her."

"Well, I didn't see her after that one glance either." Frankie could only shrug. "So what? Do you think I saw a ghost or something?" She forced a smile. "I assure you she was real."

Karl merely stared back at her, his blue eyes squinting. "Gabe says he didn't see anybody at the house when he went up to check. Who do you think this woman is, Frankie? And where is she now?"

"I have no idea," she said, her thought processes slow in kicking in, "unless . . ."

"And how did she go?" he said over her hesitation. "There weren't any cars parked at the house. Not that I saw. Did you?"

She tried to think, drawing a blank. "No, I didn't see a car, either. But, as to who I think she is, well, I imagine she's the one who called the accident in."

Karl tapped a thick forefinger on the desktop, a sure sign of impatience. Or maybe something else. Distrust? "The call came from Herb Jonas, the mailman on that route. Gabe checked."

"Yet another mystery." Frankie got to her feet. "As if enough of them aren't already making the rounds."

"Yeah, well, I hope to God you're not getting involved in another damn firestorm." Karl got up, too, and opened the door. "You watch your step. Marc is just coming back to work. I don't want anybody else in this department getting hurt."

She couldn't help flashing on Marc lying on the ground, bleeding. "Me, either," she said fervently just as Maggie, back on the job today, toggled a switch and the alarm went off. Frankie was never so glad to be called out in her life, even if she hadn't, once again, gotten her purse put in the locker.

What had gotten into to Karl, for heaven's sake? Was he actually blaming her for Marc being shot, or for Ginz's death? She ran for the ambulance, her purse bumping against her hip.

Lew Carpenter, head of the EMS team, had already claimed the driver's seat.

"Chris is late," he explained, of a not-too-unusual occurrence. "He was a little shook up yesterday, ya know, with Roland dying like that right in front of him."

Soberly, Frankie nodded. "I do know." She stopped herself from adding, "Me, too," just in time. One of those things the boss didn't need to be told.

Their call turned out to be one she often suspected was initiated because Ruby Lyons, naturally gregarious but lonely, needed someone to talk to. Also, her calls for help occurred with a rate of about twice a month. This would make Frankie's fourth call to the address.

They drove up Ruby's gravel driveway, Lew giving the siren a couple toots to let their patient know they were coming. The front door stood open, just a little, an invitation to let themselves in.

Frankie's lips twitched. Had Ruby somehow anticipated her fall and left the door unlatched just in case?

"Missus Lyons," Lew called as they entered. "Call out, please. Let us know where you are."

"Here," a woman's quavering voice answered from the depths of the house. "In my bedroom. Through the living room and down the hall to your right."

Actually, both Lew and Frankie, by this time, knew just where to find Ruby's room, but they always acted as if they didn't.

In any case, their course of action involved picking

the elderly woman off her bedroom floor, one thankfully padded with a thick carpet. Not an easy task, as she weighed in at around two hundred fifty pounds. It struck Frankie as odd to find their patient had managed to apply makeup, do her hair, and insert earrings, but then, she surmised, maybe Ruby made herself beautiful every day as a matter of rote. Frankie's job entailed providing help, whatever kind of help required.

Anyway, who was she to say loneliness didn't register on the scale of both mental and physical health? Of course, it did. But she couldn't help thinking maybe Ruby should get a dog or a cat. Or even one or two of each. Anything to save Frankie's back, and the back of her partner.

They'd already found Ruby possessed of a normal blood pressure and steady pulse. "I just don't have the strength to get myself up," Ruby said. "I've gained a little weight, you see. But I'm not hurt."

Probably not. Frankie had an idea a carpet the depth of a mattress took care of any potential broken bones.

Lew started to say something, probably to chew the old lady out, before he turned it into a cough. "Ruby," he said, scowling his concern, "you have got to start using your wheelchair, and parking it next to the bed. If you don't, one of these days you'll take a fall that really does hurt you."

The chair in question sat tidily against the wall out of the way until Frankie pulled it forward. She squeezed in on Ruby's other side and at a nod from Lew, they braced themselves and hoisted her into the chair.

Barely settled, their patient had questions about the dead people found at Strohmeyer's field.

"I saw them a few times, you know," she said, excitement putting a lilt in her voice. "The two who were murdered. Although they probably didn't know I did. You see, I often sit out on my front stoop of an evening when the sun dips behind the western hills. The house is always hot this time of year and it's cool out there. These two people would come walking over the hill out to the main road. A young man and a young woman and they always had those backpacks over their shoulders. I knew they were camped out at the Berthold homestead."

"How'd you know?" Lew demanded.

Ruby shrugged. "Only place they could be."

With a start, Frankie realized Ruby lived on the other side of the old Berthold place. Odd, really. First, that woman, Mrs. James, reporting a parked car over on the lake side, and now Ruby on this side, with the homicide scene sandwiched in the middle.

"Did you ever speak to them?" Lew asked before Frankie could open her mouth.

"Oh, no. They kind of scared me, you see. Strangers

acting sort of furtive. Especially after I saw them meet with someone a couple of times and when they walked back, their backpacks were gone. I see the news, about the drug trade and all, so I suspected something fishy was going on. Especially as they always met after dark. Once I heard them arguing with the man they met, all of them shouting their heads off from down on the road. I locked my door that night. And every night since."

"If it was dark, how could you see them?" Frankie asked, thinking the old lady better learn safer habits than leaving her door open even when she expected EMS to show up.

Ruby gave her a cool stare. "I should've said dusk. Not light enough to see their features, except the girl had light-colored hair, but not dark enough to entirely hide them, either. And of course, those backpacks always make everyone, even children, walk sort of hunched over and look like a turtle on its hind legs. Made it easy enough to see they'd passed whatever they carried on to the other one."

"Other one?" Lew said, his attention fixed now. Frankie's, too.

"The man they met. The fellow with the loud voice. He," Ruby added in a whisper, "did a lot of cursing."

Frankie's heart gave a lurch. Cursing, eh? And who'd she automatically associate with cursing? Something more to share with Gabe. Or rather, for Ruby to share with Gabe.

A full half-hour passed as the three of them chatted, mainly Ruby talking while Frankie and Lew listened. Lew told Ruby about Roland Ginz, leaving Frankie out of the report, for which she was grateful.

Ruby's eyes filled with tears. "How awful. Well, he hasn't been the same since Althea, his wife, died. But what a way to go!"

Frankie couldn't have agreed more.

"We'll have to let Gabe know what Ruby had to say," Lew said as they finally escaped and drove back to the station.

"Do you believe she saw and heard as much as she says?" Frankie asked.

"Oh, yeah. You may think she's just a fat old woman, but I figure she knows what she saw. And heard."

Frankie huffed at him. "I don't think she's just a fat old woman. Why would you say that?"

"You challenged her about seeing in the dark."

"You challenged her about how she knew where they came from."

Lew chuckled. "I guess I did. The thing for us to do is have Gabe get after her. Maybe she'll remember a little more about who said what."

"Yes. ASAP."

"Right."

An agreed upon course of action. Except the idea didn't quite develop as planned. Gabe, it turned out, had been called to Coeur d'Alene to meet with the brass and Maggie reported him as currently unavailable.

CHAPTER EIGHT

In between runs that evening, Frankie tried calling Gabe. Tried calling him several times, in fact, aiming to tell him about Ruby being a potential new witness. She dialed both his personal phone and his police line. No answer on either. Nor to a text asking him to call her, reiterating that she had important news.

When she got home after her shift, she found Gabe's Tahoe parked in the second spot in the driveway, leaving plenty of room for her Ranger closer to the house door. Quelling a flash of anger—couldn't he have at least answered a text if only to say he was busy?—she gave a sigh of relief. At least he hadn't been detained somewhere or sent off to the other end of the county.

Pausing in the driveway, she used her headlights to examine progress on the new porch. The pillars and the rafters were set, with most of the framework done.

Another day or two and the whole structure would be complete.

She stepped from her truck and hit the remote lock, reminded again of Gabe's consideration in leaving the best parking spot to her. Never mind that she was a former combat medic, and now a civilian paramedic, conversant with the most gruesome forms of torment to the human body. That he took such care so she wouldn't have to walk across a dark driveway tickled her.

Odd, though, that he'd ignored her messages. Maybe he didn't believe a new witness had been found. Maybe he'd been taken off the case. For instance, if the dead people were Native American, the FBI would be in charge.

Hushing the dogs, who in all honesty seemed to know they should be quiet, she closed and locked the door. Soft snores came from the downstairs bedroom that had been her grandmother's, and which Gabe had taken for his own. He was asleep then and getting some well-deserved rest. She wouldn't disturb him. And yet, she couldn't help wondering how he'd react if she went in there and maybe sat on his bed. Just sat. Would he welcome her?

She was tempted to try it—until Banner stepped on her foot and she looked down at the clodhopper packer boots she wore to hide the prosthesis.

Sighing, Frankie whispered to Banner and Shine, spreading largesse with a treat from their cookie jar.

Before mounting the stairs to her part of the house, she wrote Gabe a note detailing Ruby's news and saying she'd talk to him in the morning. Leaving the note on the kitchen table where he couldn't miss seeing it, she placed his favorite coffee cup on top to hold it down. Certain she'd hear him stirring around before he left in the morning, she went upstairs to bed with the intention of getting up early and talking to him in person.

A well thought out plan, except it didn't happen. Around dawn, just as birds chirping in the tree next to her window combined with the beeping sound of a far-off heavy-duty machine to rouse her, she heard the Tahoe start up and tires whisper on the driveway.

Banner lifted his head from the rug where he lay beside the bed and gave a "ruff."

Frankie sat up, still mostly asleep. "I heard. Darn it. Do you suppose he's deliberately avoiding me?" Banner scratched his ear in reply. Shine, stretched out with her head on the other pillow, didn't stir. The Bichon had the right idea, Frankie decided, and yawning, lay back down and followed suit.

Later, when she did awaken and went downstairs to make coffee, she found the note she'd written and the cup still there, still clean, just how she'd left it. Another emergency? A scary thought yet must've been for Gabe to leave without his coffee.

It didn't appear he'd even seen the note. What could've happened to get him on the road so early? Resolving to try calling him again later, she took Banner and Shine out for a short before-breakfast run in the woods out back of the house.

An hour later, Mick Boyd's construction crew, all two of them, were hard at work on the new porch, hammers pounding, saws screeching, driver whirring as Boyd screwed down some pretty knotty pine boards. Or maybe she meant screwed up since the boards were going on the ceiling.

Only vaguely aware of a rig having stopped at the road, a disturbance drew Frankie to her open bedroom window. By this time, she'd gone upstairs to change the sheets on her bed and air the room. Loud voices rose from below. She amended the disturbance designation to altercation. Shouts and virulent curses highlighted a temper tantrum so red hot she could almost feel the air burning.

She knew who to blame, too. Blake Strohmeyer had arrived, and his voice rose above any and all sounds of construction. In fact, all work ceased as he made some kind of demand. From the sound of things, he appeared to think Mick and his helper were working for him, not her.

And apparently, he intended on breaking her door

down, judging by the way he battered at it with his fist.

Well, he had no business here and she had no qualms about telling him so. In no uncertain terms. She didn't like his attitude. Her house, her rules.

Taking two steps at a time, she dashed down the stairs, totally forgetting her foot. Banner kept pace, with Shine close behind.

Frankie flung open the door, which Mick Boyd had considerately closed to keep out some of the construction mess and noise.

"What's going on?" She glared pointedly at Blake who'd just raised his fist to pound on the door again. "What in the world are you yelling about?"

"Where is he?" Blake roared, his tenor voice almost breaking Frankie's ear drums. The metal plate in her head always seemed to magnify certain sounds, and this was one of them. A nerve behind her eye twitched a warning of pain to come.

"He? He who?" As if she couldn't guess.

Face red, he shoved up against her. "Your shack job, of course. You stupid or what?"

"Hey!" Mick Boyd said.

Behind Frankie, Banner growled. His tail, always an indication of the Samoyed's well-being, drooped low. Shine froze in place, her small body trembling.

Blake failed to scare Frankie. She shoved him back,

both hands against his chest. It was like pushing an ele-phant. "Watch it," she said. "I don't know what's gotten into you, but I suggest you leave, right now." High road, she told herself. Take the high road.

He sneered. "What's the matter. Did I interrupt your nooner?"

The man working with Mick stood up from where he knelt, his eyes flashing. Mick took a step forward. "Hey," he said again.

Hanging onto her temper with an effort, Frankie laid her hand on Banner's head. She felt his body shaking, but he didn't back away. "I have no idea what your problem is, Blake Strohmeyer, but one more word, and I'm calling the cops. Go away. If you have a problem with Deputy Zantos, talk to him. Don't try to intimidate me. It won't work."

Stepping back, she closed the door on him. Except Blake managed to stick his steel-toed work boot into the opening before it could latch. His fist slammed into the door, causing it to fly wide open, bash Frankie's arm and even scrape her nose. "Ow," she gasped. "Son-of-a . . ."

Alarmed, Shine squealed. Banner, growling, lunged forward.

Which is when Frankie saw Blake reaching behind his back. When his hand appeared again, it held a small automatic. He pointed it at Banner.

"Miserable freaking mutt," he yelled. "I hate dogs. Attack me? I'm gonna kill the son of a bitch."

Frankie had time to think, Banner means to protect me, before she stepped in front of the dog.

Banner wasn't her only defender. Mick also charged in, barring Blake's way with his arm. Could be he'd forgotten he still held the driver he'd been using on the ceiling planks. Or that he had his finger on its trigger.

Or maybe he hadn't forgotten.

The driver tip burred into Blake's arm. He bellowed— surprise or pain? Frankie sort of hoped pain—before he swept around knocking the driver out of Mick's hand. It landed on the porch boards, denting the new wood as the battery jolted loose and skittered away.

"Get away from me, you interfering bastard," Blake shouted, his pistol pointed at Mick.

Frankie hadn't been afraid before, but fear struck her now.

Mr. Furnough, Frankie's elderly neighbor from next door, headed toward them, stumbling a little in the deep grass of his yard. "Want me to call Gabe?" he yelled over at her, waving his cell phone in the air.

"Yes. Call nine one one."

Has Blake gone completely insane? The question burned in her brain. Or could he be under the influence of some mind-altering substance? Like from that burned out meth lab on his and his dad's rental property?

Whatever, seeing his driver go sailing and with some of the work he'd just completed now needing replacement, Mick, his Irish temper roused, went on a tear, apparently feeling no fear of Blake's little pop gun. He batted the pistol to the side.

Infuriated, Blake came around with the pistol, landing a blow on the side of Mick's face and opening a gash that immediately spilled over with blood.

Seeming to hardly feel the wound, Mick threw a punch that rocked Blake on his heels. Blake, evidently having forgotten that a man who did construction for a living was not exactly a weakling, raised his pistol to shoot.

Meanwhile, Mick's partner danced around trying to stay out of the combatants' reach, his phone held out in front of him recording the whole altercation. Over on the lawn, Mr. Furnough yelled into his phone. Shine had disappeared into the house, no doubt to hide under the table or maybe the bed, far away from the shouting.

Banner stayed with her, ready to defend his person. And he knew who the friends were. He bounced on all four legs, ready to back up Mick, too.

"Stop it," Frankie shouted. "All of you. Stop right now."

But nobody did, which is when, as Blake's back turned to her, she stepped in and jerked his free arm up behind him. She used the super-efficient hold she'd learned in unarmed combat training to contain him. At the same time, she used her free hand to twist his little finger backward. He screamed and dropped the gun.

Unfortunately, it went off.

Fortunately, the bullet didn't hit anyone. A hole appeared in one of the new porch pillars Mick had just erected.

Blake didn't shut up until Frankie finally remembered to release his pinky.

"Cops are on their way," Mr. Furnough bellowed over to her, his whiskery old face flushed with excitement. But Frankie already knew that, because down on the highway, a siren had begun screaming.

Unwisely, Mick bent to retrieve the pistol, until Frankie said, "Don't touch it, Mick. Use your foot and nudge it over to the other side of the porch. And you . . ." she meant Mick's helper, "keep recording. We want this all on video."

In less than a minute, Rudy Swallowtail's tribal police car drew to a halt behind Blake Strohmeyer's big Ram pickup. A good thing since Frankie's grip keeping Blake's arm corralled had begun to fail. For the first time, Frankie noticed that in his rush for a confrontation, Blake hadn't even killed the engine on the pickup. He'd left the door open, alarm pinging, while diesel fumes from the badly tuned engine spewed their stink all over the neighborhood.

Rudy got out of his cruiser, reached in and shut off Blake's rig before closing the door and striding toward them.

"Keep your hands off my truck," Blake shouted. A pointless objection since Rudy was already picking his way through scattered building materials to the temporary steps. "Damn Indian," he added, but more softly, as if thinking maybe Rudy wouldn't hear.

A mistake Frankie figured as Rudy flicked him a cold glance. She jerked Blake's arm, reefing it a little higher and causing a pained grunt.

"Show some respect, butthead." The words hissed out of her.

Nodding first to Mr. Furnough, then Mick, then the helper, Rudy stopped to survey the scene. Finally, he looked at Frankie half-hidden behind Blake. "Got a problem?" he asked.

Always the funny guy.

Four male voices burst forth in explanation, all with varying success. Rudy let them vent without interrupting, his dark eyes switching back and forth between the speakers. Frankie listened, too. Let them talk. She'd have her chance when they finished ranting.

"Send your video over to my phone," Rudy said to

Mick's helper when the noise ran down to reasonable level. And to Frankie as he indicated Blake, "Your invited guest?"

"Not hardly," she said.

Rudy studied them all a moment longer before saying, "I think you can let him go, Frankie." And when she did, he added, "Do you want to press charges? Do I understand gunfire is involved? If so, he's under arrest anyway."

"You can't arrest me. I ain't no damn Indian," Blake said, twitching away from Frankie as she released him.

"What are you, stupid?" Mick said, throwing Blake's words about Frankie back at him. "Even somebody as dumb as you are oughta know that along with being tribal police Rudy is a Kootenai County deputy."

Blake lunged at Mick who sidestepped and slammed him against one of the new porch pillers. A little stunned, Blake shook out his arm. The one with a bit of blood running from the hole Mick had drilled in it. By this time, it probably felt quite useless. Pure hate glinted from his pale blue eyes. Frankie thought observant people might see a similar expression in her own dark ones as she glared back.

"What is your problem, anyway?" she said. "You come to my house waving a gun not only at me, but at my dog, my neighbor and the people working for me. Are you completely out of your mind?" She turned to Rudy. "Yes.

I'm pressing charges. His gun is under the pile of lumber. I think he came here with the intention of shooting Gabe, only Gabe isn't here, as anybody can plainly see. Apparently, he figured it'd be just as much fun to vent his rage on me, Banner, Mick, and anyone else he could reach."

"Must be high on his own meth," Mick said, voicing Frankie's concern. He dabbed at his bloody face with his shirttail.

"You could probably use a couple stitches in that," Frankie said. "I'm sorry, Mick."

"I'm good," he said. "Not your fault. The only one to blame is the meth-head, himself."

Blake, who'd always been a slow learner, made another lunge at Mick, only to have Rudy plant himself in the way.

"Enough of that. This fight's over. Doesn't appear to be working out real well for you anyway." Rudy, over Blake's loud protests, read him his rights, slipped plastic zip ties around his wrists, and prepared to walk him down to the patrol car. With his prisoner settled—or at least securely confined, Rudy returned to the watching group, silent now.

"I had word Gabe arrested Harvey Strohmeyer early this morning," he said. "I expect that's what set Blake off. A night in jail ought to cool him down some. If it doesn't make him worse." Rudy sounded a little pessimistic.

Frankie gasped. "Arrested him for what? Harvey, I mean."

"Arson," Rudy said. "They found proof he's the one who started the fire to cover up the murders."

"Do they think he killed those people?" Mick asked. Mr. Furnough nodded as though he were the one wanting to know.

Rudy shrugged. "That's what the detectives are trying to find out." He sighed. "I'll send someone around to move Blake's truck, Frankie. If anybody asks, it'll be in the station parking lot."

"Thank, Rudy," Frankie said. "For everything. Especially for getting here so quickly. Don't tell anybody, but I'm not sure how much longer I could've held him."

"We aim to please." Rudy touched his hat in a salute.

* * *

Mick sat still while Frankie cleaned blood from his face and applied a butterfly bandage to the gash on his cheekbone. He'd categorically denied stitches were in the offing.

"It'll be fine," he insisted. "Me and Jock got work to do. I've got another job lined up starting the day after tomorrow. Can't be taking time off for a little thing like this. You want your porch completed on time, don't you?"

He grinned at her, so she knew he had the timing down. But he also winced when the grin stretched at the wound.

"Your call," she said. "I'm so sorry you got railroaded into a fight with Blake."

"Don't apologize. It's not your fault Blake is an ass, first and last." He got up from the chair she'd brought onto the porch for him to sit in while she worked and picked his driver off the floor. "I just hope he didn't ruin this. I need it."

"If you guys hadn't been here," Frankie said, but Mick cut her off.

"Well, we were. Forget it, Frankie. Let the cops take care of Strohmeyer. Besides," his grin grew wider, painful or not, "I had fun taking Blake on. I've been wanting to do that since middle school."

Jock, Mick's helper, grinned and pumped his fist in a victorious kind of way. Even Mr. Furnough, who'd stuck around in case there was more excitement in the offing, bobbed his head.

Fun? Seriously? As for Frankie, she didn't think they'd heard the last from Blake. Not by a long shot.

CHAPTER NINE

The first half of Frankie's shift that evening almost... almost... made her long for a call just to get her out of the station. Not that boredom was the problem. No indeed. Trying to stay sharp and dodge the many questions aimed at her proved to be the problem. Karl, oddly enough for one who seldom joined in the group talks, began the questioning, and they kept right on going from there.

"What happened?" Karl demanded in his boss tone of voice. No, hello, how are you. Just, what happened? "Rudy was in the station shooting the breeze when the call came in. He shot out of here like he'd been stuck in the butt with a cattle prod."

"Oh." Frankie didn't want to discuss Blake's... um... visit. "Nothing happened to me, as you can see.

"I hear Blake shot at you," a volunteer said, and someone else broke in, saying, "No, he shot at Mick Boyd. You know, Mick's in business for himself with his construction company. He's building Frankie's new porch after that crazy Miz Barwick tried to burn her house down."

So nice for her to tell everyone Frankie's business. Frankie didn't have to speak at all considering so many were willing to do it for her.

"Well, I heard Blake must be on something, that he showed up there higher than a kite." Another of the volunteers leaned forward, his eyes sparkling. "And that he resisted arrest when Rudy took him in."

"I heard the same thing," a second volunteer agreed. "He might do actual jail time when he comes to trial. It's about time somebody took him on and won."

Karl reclaimed the lead. "What about it, Frankie? Any of that true?"

She hesitated. "Some of it. Sort of."

"Him and his dad are a rough pair. You should never aggravate them. If you do, you'll pay." Frankie didn't catch who said that, but the speaker sounded like he had experience.

"What really happened, Frankie?" the second volunteer asked.

With everyone talking, Frankie was almost surprised when Maggie, back on dispatch for the evening, spoke quietly to her and actually waited for an answer.

"Yes, Frankie," Maggie said, "did Blake really shoot at

Mick?" Maggie was as curious as ever, but at Frankie's uncomfortable nod, changed the subject. "I take it your insurance payment finally came through so Mick could get to work. It took them long enough."

Frankie could only be amazed anew by the small-town grapevine, which appeared to flourish in Hawkesford's fertile soil.

"I didn't know Blake took drugs," Marc, being one of those unwilling to drop the Strohmeyer controversy, said thoughtfully. "Are you sure about that?"

Frankie sighed and continued wiping crumbs from Marc's "Welcome Back to Work" cake from the table into her open hand. It had been a celebration, having him return to work after being shot. Everybody had been served and very little remained of the cake for him to take home.

"No, Marc," she said, wondering how she'd slipped into the center of attention ring and not him. "I'm not sure Blake takes drugs. I'm not the one who started that rumor. All I know is that he acted like a wild man when he showed up at my door. Unstable, to say the least."

Blake, and who he'd actually been shooting at, got a little lost in the following debate. Frankie didn't have the nerve to tell them he'd drawn his weapon with the intention of shooting Banner. That wouldn't have gone over well in the station, either, as she'd been known to bring the dog to work where he was a favorite of everyone on the staff. Yes, even Benton, an older, self-contained volunteer who always said he preferred cats.

"Banner likes cats," Frankie had told him once, and, despite Benton's skepticism, it was the truth.

Karl simply shook his head and sighed. "Seems almost like you're a catalyst, Frankie. Never thought when I hired you that all this excitement would follow."

She hadn't either. Now she hoped his next move wouldn't be to fire her. Not that any of the—as Karl described it, excitement—could be construed as her fault. How could anyone blame her, for heaven's sake? She helped provide emergency medical help to the community and nothing else. No drugs, no arson, no murder.

Around nine o'clock, Maggie's dispatch board lit up and they, meaning Marc and Frankie, the EMS personnel on duty, got the call. In a weird quirk of fate, they had to follow the same road they'd traveled the night Marc got targeted by a hired killer. Frankie drove the ambulance, her concentration broken by Marc's uneven breathing from the passenger seat. She knew he was reliving that night and didn't blame him.

"Getting back on the horse when he's bucked you off is always tough." She glanced over at him, noting his set jaw.

"What?" He gave her a look that asked if she'd lost her

mind.

She smiled. "Something my granddad used to tell me. And it's true. A saying that means if you've had something bad happen, a similar run-up will be hard to face. You just need to do it, Marc. You don't need to act as if you're good about riding down this road with me. I can tell you're not. And I sure don't blame you. It still bothers me, too."

"It isn't you," he said in quick denial. "If it hadn't been for you that night, I'd be dead."

A fact. And yet . . . "If it hadn't been for me, maybe Darryl wouldn't have shot you."

"Oh, he would've. He didn't need to shoot me at all." Marc glowered. "He pulled the trigger out of pure meanness."

Also a fact. Even so, it surprised her a little that Marc knew it.

They passed the spot where the shooting had taken place. The single pine still stood tall a piece of its bark peeled away where Darryl had run a car up against it. Marc gave an audible sigh of relief as the site fell behind. A half-mile farther on, Frankie turned onto a narrow country road so overgrown with scraggly trees and drooping bushes it looked like something from a horror movie.

"Does anybody actually live out here?" Marc peered

ahead into the Stygian darkness.

"Guess we'll find out." A quarter of a mile later, Frankie drew up in front of what their headlights showed as a tiny rundown house. A rusted-out pickup hulk squatted at its side, resting on bent rims. The pick-up seemed to have grown almost into the earth, while the house appeared abandoned. "The GPS says this is our destination," she said, more than a little puzzled.

Getting out of the truck, she stood listening. Marc came around and, head cocked to the side, listened with her. She felt him shaking and put her hand on his arm. "I'm going to call out," she said, and did. Once and again. Then again.

For a minute or so, all she heard were crickets and the shush of a breeze gently moving the leaves of several poplar trees. Nothing else. Frankie thought a man named Green lived here or had. He'd been old when she was a kid. With a start, she remembered this was another of those old homesteads. One like the Berthold place, where two people had been murdered, and like Roland Ginz's farm, where a man had died under unusual circumstances. Something about that caught at her mind, then disappeared as she heard a sound.

She hushed Marc, who'd started to speak. "Did you hear something?"

"No. What?"

"A voice." Frankie called again. "Fire department emergency services. Is anyone here?"

They both listened intently.

"There." Marc turned away from the house and peered into the dark. "Over there. A man. He said, 'help'."

"Yep. I heard it. Grab the bag." Frankie flicked on her flashlight, an LED jobbie that would carry most of the way to the moon and shined it into the brush. A quarter turn to her right, the flashlight illuminated a path leading God only knows where. They followed it until, after another fifty yards or so, they spotted the figure of a man lying on the ground. As they neared, they saw he was old, his movements feeble, and his breathing harsh. He lay almost obscured by milkweed and mullein stalks. As they hurried toward him, Frankie saw he wore a long-sleeved raggedy shirt and bib overalls that she suspected hadn't been washed since spring.

Bib overalls. She didn't know they were even sold anymore. From the apparent age of these, maybe they weren't.

To her surprise, a dog that appeared as old as the man, only in dog years, lay by the fellow's side. The mutt struggled to its feet, panting and trying to growl.

Frankie dropped to her knees beside the man and spoke softly to the dog. "You be quiet. We're here to help your person. We're not going to hurt him." Not much to her surprise, the creature subsided.

"Jeez, Frankie, what are you? A dog whisperer?" Marc gaped at her.

Shrugging, Frankie set her flashlight on end where it lit up the sky, but also the area and the man. If the dirt on his britches was any indication, he'd crawled here from farther down the path. Or more accurately, he'd pulled himself along leaving a marked trail. A trail that glistened wetly, the moisture dark. Blood, she knew the look all too well, and when she bent over him, she could smell it. One of his legs dragged behind him at an unnatural angle.

He didn't seem to be quite cognizant of who they were or what they were doing.

"Don't hurt me," he whispered. "Please, don't hurt me again."

Hurt him again?

Frankie looked at Marc and frowned. Yes. He'd heard that, too.

"No, sir. We won't hurt you. We're here to help. My partner and I, we work for the Hawkesford fire department. We're going to get you fixed up and to the hospital in Coeur d'Alene." She didn't know if he understood, as he mumbled something about a blonde lady, a demon, and Elmer, none of which made the least bit of sense.

"Sir," she said, trying to get his attention and make

him focus, "sir, can you tell me your name?"

All he could do is mutter something, and then fell silent.

Between the two of them, Marc and Frankie got him turned over without doing more damage to his leg. Marc tended to his vitals while Frankie got out her scissors and cut his pant leg up the side. The broken ends of his tibia jabbed through scaly white skin. There wasn't much she could, or even should do for his leg, except apply a blow-up splint and get him to the hospital and surgery as quickly as possible.

"Vitals?"

"I get a weak pulse. Blood pressure is barely registering. I think he's turning blue, Frankie. I don't know how he's still breathing." Marc looked pale himself.

"He's in hypovolemic shock. Get the gurney." Frankie looked up at him. "I'll start an IV here, but we've got to get him to the hospital ASAP. Hurry, Marc."

Not surprisingly, the old man's veins rolled under the needle, making a normally easy task difficult. Marc returned with the gurney about the same time she got the saline flowing. It was a simple matter to get the patient loaded onto the stretcher. Old Mr. Green, if this were indeed he, had shrunken in size as he aged, and hadn't, most probably, been a large man when young.

All of which made it easier for the two of them to

carry him out, the IV bag on its pole attached to a corner of the gurney.

Back at the ambulance, it took only seconds to load him. His breath came in intermittent short gasps now, and Frankie placed the oxygen mask on him. Almost immediately his breathing steadied, shallow but more regular.

"Float a blanket over him. We need to keep him warm," she told Marc, who settled on the bench beside him.

"What are we going to do with him?" Marc asked, eyeing the old mutt who'd followed them. The rusty brown creature looked at them out of sad eyes.

"Oh, rats!" Frankie jumped to the ground. In a moment she'd scooped the dog up and plunked him down inside the ambulance.

Marc grinned at her.

She slammed the first door shut. "You don't expect me to leave the poor old thing out here all by himself, do you?" The other door banged closed.

"No," she heard Marc say. "You'd never do that."

The moment they hit the highway, Frankie set the ambulance siren wailing, and put the pedal down. From there, delivery of their patient was routine, with ER personnel taking over as soon as they arrived at the medical center. Fortunately, they found their patient carried a battered wallet with the sum of eleven dollars, a ragged-edged Social Security card, and an expired driver's license made out to Gerald Green, so at least the man went in with an identity and not as a John Doe.

Mission completed, Marc came out of the hospital carrying items to replace the ones they'd used on their patient. Frankie held the door open so he could step up, which is when they took notice of their other passenger. The brown dog sat there, waiting patiently. After a moment, his tail wagged, just a little, as though to ask a question. Marc lent his voice to it.

"What are we going to do with him?" He laid a tentative hand on the dog's head. "He looks thirsty." As if on impulse, he found a clean puke pan and poured some water from his own bottle into it. He set the pan down by the dog, who lapped, tail waving more vigorously. "I think he's dehydrated."

"Probably." Frankie ignored his question. "I wonder how long the two of them were out there like that? What they were doing? The house didn't look lived in anymore. And how did Mister Green get there? I didn't see a rig."

"Good question." Marc poured more water into the pan. "I didn't see a vehicle either. You think someone dumped him?"

"Possible." She thought a moment. "Funny they'd bring the dog, though."

Marc nodded. "And I wonder how far Mister Green dragged himself?"

"Another good question."

Frankie stared down at the dog. "But you know what I really wonder?"

Something, maybe the tone of her voice, had Marc staring at her. "What?"

"Who knew he was there and that he needed help? Who called nine one one?"

Later, back at the station, they found the call had come from a pay phone, possibly one of the last on the planet, located inside a small bar in Spokane Valley. But Frankie, and Maggie, when Frankie involved her in the mystery, discovered nothing else.

"Does it matter?" Maggie asked, looking at Frankie in a puzzled sort of way.

Frankie shrugged, even as a wandering idea coalesced in her mind. She needed to speak to Gabe.

As for the brown dog, well, at quitting time, Marc opened his car door and the dog jumped in. So that, as they say, was that.

* * *

She dreamed of Banner, dropping to the ground, dead as dead could be. They'd been standing in the road keeping watch over the bright red sports car parked beneath a huge old pine tree—until a shot came from out of nowhere. Except to start with, the dog at her side was the old brown dog she and Marc had found. When she looked again, he became her own lovely Samoyed. His glistening white fur stained red from the blood pumping from a round hole in his head. It made her sick to see it. And the victim wasn't that poor old man with the shattered leg, but Frankie herself, with a hole in her head that matched her dog's, and a bloody leg that matched the old man's. The knowledge that she'd have to wear a bigger prothesis after this and that she'd never be whole again, ground at her. So much sadness. So much anger. Why was she still alive? Why?

Frankie awoke, weeping, with the Bichon, Shine, standing over her licking the tears from her cheeks. A regular little nursemaid.

"Damn it." Frankie stuck up a hand to guard her eyes from Shine's busy tongue. Her clock showed five a.m. Downstairs, the creak of floors more than a hundred years old indicated Gabe moving around as he got ready for work. He spoke, his voice quiet.

Had she cried out and awakened him? Frankie didn't know, and Gabe would never say.

Her dream quickly fading, Frankie gave Shine a hug and set the small dog aside. She had to talk to Gabe, now, before the meaning of the dream slipped away.

Getting out of bed took determination as a depressed sort of exhaustion dragged at her.

One thing at a time.

Blanket tossed back. Check.

One leg flung over the side. Check.

Second leg over the side and sitting almost upright.

Scoot to the mattress edge and place both feet on the floor.

Stand.

Bathroom. Cold water to cool her burning eyes. Check, check, and check.

Yesterday's clothes, grabbed from her laundry hamper, would do for now. But she had to burrow deeper into the muddle of dirty clothes to find what she was really looking for. And then race downstairs to catch Gabe just as he patted Banner—his conversation partner—and opened the door to leave.

"Gabe, wait. I need to talk to you." She knew her voice sounded husky. A problem caused by tears trapped in her throat overnight. That and the silent screams. At least, she hoped they'd been silent. From the look Gabe gave her, she wasn't so sure.

He grinned crookedly at her. "Must be important to get you out of bed at this hour."

"Yes. I think it might be. Can you sit for a few minutes?"

He glanced at his watch and nodded. "If it's about Strohmeyer showing up and pulling a gun on—"

"It's not. Although it might be connected." Not only did the scent of coffee fill the kitchen, but Frankie noticed the pot was, as usual, still half-full. And hot, for a change. She filled a cup for herself and waved the pot his way. "Do you have time for another cup?"

He removed his four-dent hat, pulled out a chair, and sat. "Yeah. I guess. What's going on?"

Frankie closed her eyes and took a long sip of her coffee. A little strong, for her taste, but maybe it would help her think.

"What's up, Frankie?" Gabe asked again. "Or should I be asking what's wrong?"

She opened her mouth, just as the thought struck that maybe she should hold off. Too late, anyway. The words were already pouring out.

"I'm pretty sure Roland Ginz was murdered," she said, "and Gerald Green, too."

CHAPTER TEN

Gabe, although Frankie had expected—and maybe wished for—an argument, didn't dispute her opinion that Roland Ginz had been murdered. Not even though his death had, at first sight, appeared to be an accident. Or, at a stretch, suicide. Why hadn't he? Did he have information that she did not? Had the medical examiner completed the autopsy and found new evidence?

She watched one of his eyebrows go up. Scant reaction to what she classified as a bombshell.

"At least," she continued, "I think he, Mister Green, was supposed to die. As of last night, he hadn't. Maybe he has by now."

With his coffee cup halted an inch from his mouth, Gabe didn't say anything for several heartbeats. Then, in a wondering sort of voice, "Who is Gerald Green?"

"Sorry. You must not have heard about this yet."

Frankie set down her cup and dug through the pocket of her Wranglers, pulling forth a crumpled slip of pink paper. She pushed it across to Gabe, who smoothed it out with his forefinger. "I should start with first things first. Or maybe this is second." She added about the second part almost to herself, studying her fingernails while he read the note.

He shifted in his chair. "What's this?"

She looked up. He was apt to be upset with her, and she'd deserve it if he yelled. Not that she'd ever heard Gabe yell. He didn't this time, either.

"I forgot to give this to you the other day. I took down this information from a lady named Missus Donald James just before we got called out to attend Roland Ginz. This is the message. I . . ." She shook her head. "I'm afraid it kind of got lost in the whirl of things."

"Kind of?" Gabe stared down at Frankie's once neat handwriting, now smeared and worn looking, and pushed it back toward her. "You think? How about you just tell me what this says. It seems to have gotten wet."

No doubt. Frankie remembered pouring sterile water over Ginz's wounds and soaking herself in the process.

Banner, back from his morning foray into the backyard, sat down between the two people. He pointed his nose at Gabe. "Ruff?"

Gusting out a breath, Gabe snorted. "Rough, all right."

His lips twitched. "So. About Missus Donald James?"

Speak up, Corporal McGill. Report.

A fortifying swallow of coffee gave Frankie back her voice. "It's something this lady—she lives at Pearson's Landing—saw the night before the Strohmeyer fire. She said she was on her way home, late, after a summer theater performance when she saw this car parked under the big tree that marks the back road into the house that burned. It's where Strohmeyer moves his machinery onto the land, not where we drove up to the house."

Gabe's hazel eyes locked on her. "What makes this important, Frankie? I think I know the place, and I agree, it's an odd place to spot a car. Hard to see, for one thing, but why is it remarkable?"

"Hard to see, all right, which is why kids have chosen to park there while they make out. They have since my mom's day, from what I've been told." She wrinkled her nose. "But the reason it may be important now is, for one thing, the time of day—or night, rather. A second reason is because the Berthold place is just over the hill from there, an easy walk. Due to what we found the next day, well, it just seems important. But that's not all."

Both of Gabe's dark eyebrows lifted, as if they were asking a question.

"The third thing is the car itself. Missus James, who struck me as a car enthusiast only as long as the vehicle is big and expensive, says this one caught her eye because she'd seen one like it before. It's not a car you see on the streets very often, let alone parked and seemingly abandoned on a country road late at night. And it's definitely not a kid's car."

"Are you going to tell me what kind of car we're talking about?"

"I am. A Lexus LC500 sports car. Red. I looked it up. It costs over a hundred thousand dollars."

At last. Something to make Gabe sit up and take notice.

"She's sure?"

"She is sure. Says her real estate agent has one like it and it's quite distinctive."

"For that kind of money, I imagine so." He frowned. "Kind of hard to figure what a sports car would be doing parked in a farmer's field late at night."

"She also said it was gone the next morning. So, it's unlikely to have been stolen, especially if it wasn't reported."

"I don't suppose she mentioned her realtor's name."

"No. Sorry. I should've asked."

"I'll check into that." Gabe dug his little notebook from his shirt pocket and jotted down a few lines. Finished, he put it away and patted Banner on his head before nodding to Frankie. "Anything else?"

"Not about the car, but I wanted to ask, have you spoken to Ruby Lyons?" She hesitated. "You did get that message, didn't you?"

"Yep. Two of them. One from you, one from Lew." Sighing, Gabe got out his notebook again. "But I haven't talked to her yet. I've been too busy with these dead kids. The detectives assigned the case, Armbuster and Rimmel, take great pleasure out of leaving most of their grunt work to me. Is there some hurry with Missus Lyons?"

"I think maybe so. I wanted to brush her off. She calls us a couple times a month, just wanting to talk, although there's always some excuse. Usually it's that she's taken a fall. And I think that's why she called this time, too, except as it turns out . . . Well, you should talk to her. The sooner the better." Frankie grinned. "She'll love you for it. And by the way, pay real close attention to where she lives."

"Okay." Frowning, he made a note and started to get up, then sat back down. "Roland Ginz and Whosit Green. What about them?"

Helpfully, Frankie supplied the old man's name. "Gerald Green. But first, there's what happened to Mister Ginz."

"Yes. Mister Ginz," Gabe said. "An accident—or not. I'll tell you plainly, since from the sound of things you've already got questions, his situation is under further investigation. Partly, Frankie, because of you."

Frankie had a sinking feeling in the pit of her stomach. She didn't want involved in whatever was going on here. Really, she didn't. Captain Karl Mager wouldn't like it, either. Even so, she doubted any of her wants figured into anyone's equation.

"Because of the woman I saw?" she asked.

"Yes."

Frankie sighed. "Then you're going to be thrilled with this next part."

Gabe's narrow-eyed look spoke volumes.

"When we found Mister Green, he spoke to us. Not that he knew who we were." She stopped, thinking back. "Just mumbled bits and pieces of speech, really."

"What did he say?"

"He said, 'Don't hurt me. Please don't hurt me again.' But he must've realized we intended to help him because he more or less cooperated with us. Marc and me, I mean, so he wasn't totally unaware. And Gabe, he muttered something about a blonde lady, and a guy with a gun. Oh, yes, and Elmer. I think Elmer might be his dog, though, because the dog's ears pricked when Green said the name."

Gabe blinked. "And?"

"You may not have gotten all the details yet." Frankie flinched inwardly just thinking about the information she had to pass on to Gabe. Nothing that would make his life easier, for sure, and most likely only add to the mystery. "Somebody shot Mister Green in the leg, you see. The knee, to be more exact. We were some time getting to him, so he was within a whisker of bleeding to death. He'll probably lose his leg, at best." She shrugged. "He may have died during the night. I don't know. But the thing is, he had no phone on him, aside from the fact there's no service out there."

He caught on quickly. "Which means someone else called you. Someone who left before you got there."

Frankie nodded. "I asked Maggie to see if she could find out who called it in. The call came from a bar in Spokane Valley. A woman made it."

"A blonde, by any chance?" Gabe's mouth twisted. "Wearing a blue sundress?"

"Kind of hard to tell over the phone, but . . . would you be surprised?"

"No." He stood up, tucking away his recorder and notebook. "Damn it, Frankie, I ask questions and take notes, but I'm not the detective on this case. And neither are you. Leave the inquiries to those in charge. Tell the detectives what you hear and let them handle it. You know you'll have to repeat all this for Detective Arm-buster anyway, don't you? He's the one in charge of the murder investigation and he isn't going to be pleased to find you've been meddling."

"Meddling? I beg your pardon." A sort of guilt struck her. "I admit to being curious but I'm not meddling. I get called to tend the victims because it's my job. I'm involved whether you or Armbuster or anybody else likes it or not. It's not like I have a choice."

"Yeah. I know," Gabe said, smiling a little.

"I wish you were the detective." The words burst from her. "You should be." In her experience, although admittedly slight, Armbuster, whom she'd met a while back, wasn't the wiliest coyote in the den.

"I wish I was, too," Gabe admitted.

And why not? Frankie continued the thought. As far as she could tell he was the only one on the job.

* * *

Frankie went back to bed after Gabe left, secure in knowing she had two whole days off. Not that she slept much, the cycle having been thoroughly disrupted. But she lay there with her eyes closed and thought. And thought some more, odd conclusions coming to her as her mind drifted, bits and pieces flowing in free-form.

A meth lab and murder on the old Berthold place.

A murder—most likely a murder, anyway—at Roland Ginz's home.

The attempted murder—no doubt about it—of Gerald Green.

All sudden occurrences popping up out of nowhere to plague their sleepy little town. Why these places? Why here? Why now? What did they all have in common?

Frankie grunted, eyes blinking open as Banner jumped onto the bed beside her. He joined Shine, already there. The dogs spent a few moments seeing who could get closest to her. Banner won, until Shine climbed onto her chest and stared at her with big round eyes until she had to laugh. "And the winner is. . .Shine!"

Another idea occurred to her, one that made her laughter die.

Giving up on trying to sleep, Frankie decided she should quit fooling around and concentrate on the core questions.

To begin with, the Berthold, Gintz, and Green farms were all quite remote, the houses hidden from the main road. The Berthold house had long been derelict and almost forgotten. The Gintz buildings were situated at the end of a long, private driveway; Green's rundown old abode was hidden behind overgrown trees and almost inaccessible. Another similarity: two were occupied by old men who didn't associate regularly with anyone, while the first location was known to be abandoned. All were homesteads passed down in families since the distribution of Indian reservation land in the 1909 lottery.

It just so happened she owned a property much along the lines she'd been thinking about. Another part of her inheritance, it involved the one hundred sixty acres of the original Buchanan homestead currently rented out to Hank Kelton which, along with the remnants of her dad's place, Harvey Strohmeyer had made no bones about saying he wanted to farm. Or, preferably, own.

Although, in either case, Blake going after her like he'd done was surely the wrong way to persuade her into kicking Hank out and signing a lease favoring the Strohmeyers.

Unless, of course, he thought he could get away with intimidating her at the least, killing her as the ultimate. After all, three people were dead already, with a fourth hanging on by a thread. Or, at least, she hoped Green was still hanging on.

Frankie resolved to drive out to the Buchanan property. She hadn't been there in years and it was the only piece of land she owned, aside from this house, that had buildings on it. Maybe. They'd still been standing the last time she'd been there, although ramshackle and un-livable. What she'd do is pack the dogs into the Ranger and take them out to visit. See what's what. She'd been back in Hawkesford for a couple months now. Time to give all of her inheritance a good once over.

Just as soon as Mick finished restoring the porch, she decided, the whir of a drill below her window making Shine bark and Banner give his signature low "ruff" before they bounded out of bed to investigate.

First, though, a trip to either Spokane or Coeur d'Alene went on Frankie's to-do list. She intended to stain and clear coat the knotty pine porch ceiling herself as soon as Mick got it done, and she'd need supplies.

* * *

Mick Boyd, bent over drilling holes in the new porch floor, straightened as Frankie opened the door. Not before she got a good look at him, though. No butt crack. She'd be willing to bet Blake Strohmeyer, judging by his oddly bloated appearance, showed a butt crack whenever he bent over.

All of which, Frankie reminded herself, meant nothing. The only concern she had was in a well-built porch. The holes Mick drilled with such intent care were for the bolts anchoring the wrought iron posts at the bottom. He'd already attached the panels to the smoothly sanded wooden top rail. All Mick and his helper had to do was measure accurately and bolt everything together.

And then the porch would be complete. Frankie looked around, her glance satisfied. More than satisfied—delighted.

"Morning, Frankie." Mick patted Banner's furry head, the dog having beaten her out the door and promptly gone to greet him. "How's she look?" She, of course, being the porch as a whole.

"Great." She grinned at him. "If you need a recommendation, send the client to me. I can vouch for on time, on budget, and talented workmanship. Not to mention serving as a personal bodyguard."

"Go, Mick," Jock, Mick's helper, grinned and pumped his arms like a boxer. "My hero. Well, Frankie's hero."

"It's true. He is." Frankie and Jock shared a fist bump.

Besides, she reflected, Banner, who'd been abused by his previous owner, distrusted most men on first sight but took to Mick just fine. The dog had taken to Gabe, right off, too. She figured dogs always knew.

Mick's face grew red and he turned on his helper. "Shut up, Jock, or I'll fire you."

"Good. I'd make more on unemployment, anyhow."

"Like hell. Get back to work." Mick's order inspired Jock, smirking all the while, into picking up a can of wood filler and proceeding to fill in the bullet hole in the new roof post. Mick'd decided the filler to be a better option than tearing out the post and starting over. Frankie agreed.

"We'll be done here in another hour or so, Frankie.

You gonna be all right on your own?"

Frankie couldn't help but be charmed by Mick's concern. It made her feel . . . well, she didn't quite know. Maybe a little thrilled that a man, an eligible man, would gaze at her with interest in his eyes. Interest, not pity, or discomfort, or any other of the undesirable things she'd been seeing whenever anyone became aware she'd been wounded in Afghanistan. And, unfortunately, the news seemed to have spread to just about everyone she knew.

"I'll be fine. I came out to pick your mind."

"Yeah?"

"Yeah. And to ask how your face is doing. Does it hurt?"

"I'll live." He waved away her concern. "About picking my mind . . . don't know if there's anything in there worth your time."

She sent him a look that said she knew better than that. Maybe the look leaned a bit towards flirtatious, although what she asked was to the point. "What do you recommend to seal the porch? What brand of paint? How soon can I put an outdoor rug on the porch surface?"

Frankie had more questions, and Mick answered them all, no extra charge, which could've been a fair trade since, inspired by the work on Frankie's house, Mr. Furnough came out and asked Mick to make an estimate on repairing his own porch.

"Came dang near to putting my foot through a rotten board," he told Mick. "Be bad news if I got stuck next time Frankie needs a hand."

He seemed, Frankie noted a little sourly, quite certain there would be a next time.

CHAPTER ELEVEN

Frankie, having completed a final inspection of the new porch, initialed Mick's work ticket, and signed her name on a check made out to Boyd's Construction. She waved goodbye, watching as the dust spewing from beneath Mick's truck wheels settled back to the ground. The summer had been dry. They needed rain.

Her phone rang.

She tapped the answer button, but even before she could lift it to her ear and say hello, the person on the other end began talking.

No surprise. Jesselyn Pettigrew always said what she had to say without going into the frills of a back-and-forth conversation. "Hey, Frankie," Jesselyn said, "have you seen Ruby Lyons since you've been home? Seen her to talk to, I mean?"

Frankie gave a start. "As a matter of fact, I have. Why?"

"Well, if you've seen her lately you probably noticed how she loves to talk, but she just told my sister Victoria something that strikes me as odd. I wonder if it's something that maybe you should report to Gabe. You know, in view of those meth lab murders. And what's this I'm hearing about old Roland Ginz? Are those two things connected somehow? From the gossip that's going around, it seems the general consensus."

Frankie sighed. Typical Jesselyn. As always, knowing everything there was to know in the Hawkesford community, and wanting to be right in the middle of it. At least she made the attempt to get the facts straight. That's why Frankie proceeded with caution before answering.

"Something odd?" Unwilling to even mention Ginz alongside the meth murders, Frankie wisely skipped over that part of the conversation. "Why don't you tell Gabe, then? Or better yet, have Ruby tell him. Or Victoria. Victoria would be good. I'm sure she'd get to the point sooner than Ruby is known to do."

Jesselyn emitted a curious sounding little huff in Frankie's ear. "Don't look at me," she said, as if Frankie had said anything different. "I'm not going to be the go-between. That's always a thankless job."

True. Even so, in Frankie's experience it would be a first if Jesse didn't sign up. After all, it was through

Jesselyn's intervention that she had gotten this job in Hawkesford.

"And the thing is," Jesselyn continued, "Ruby said you promised to pass something on to Gabe a couple days ago and she's been waiting to hear from him ever since. This might be too important to wait."

Wincing at the truth of it, Frankie said, "I know I promised. And I did tell Gabe—so did Lew—but I don't think Gabe has had a single minute to get out to Ruby's place as yet. he's working on about four hours sleep a night."

"Poor guy. Even so, you'd better tell him to drop everything and step on it. Among other things, Ruby is, well, maybe not scared exactly, but feeling kind of uncomfortable."

"Yes. She told me. Lew and me, when we went out to help her off the floor. I feel bad for her, but she really needs to sell her big old farmhouse and look into assisted living."

Jesselyn sounded sad now. "Yes. She knows. But do you blame her for being reluctant?"

"Can't say as I do."

"Except, this isn't about those meth people she saw, if that's what you mean. Or thinks she saw. Something else happened." Jesselyn fell silent, as if she were thinking. Frankie heard her breathing speed up. "Ruby called Victoria this morning and said she'd had a change of mind. Said she's ready to sell out and wanted Vic to give her an 'off the top of your head' estimate of what her place is worth. She said some other real estate person had been pestering her to make a deal. Somebody way too aggressive and insistent, and being Ruby, she doesn't want to deal with a total stranger. Ruby and my grandma were friends, way back when, so she feels a connection our family."

"I remember." She did, too. She recalled visiting Jesselyn and seeing Jess's grandma and a friend drinking coffee. She learned later the coffee most likely contained a hefty shot of Kahlua stirred in. God only knows how many cups of "coffee" the old gals consumed in an afternoon. Anyway, that friend had been Ruby. Frankie's own grandma had been left out of the visitations. Due, no doubt, to her preference for bourbon.

Victoria, Jesselyn's sister, had been almost grown up then, and she'd been the one to whisper about the booze. Now Victoria was a hot-shot real estate agent out of Coeur d'Alene and making a mint dealing with the rural properties that came up for sale. It only made sense that Ruby would want to do business with someone she'd known forever.

Frankie, her attention drawn from the admiration of her new porch to the seriousness of Jesselyn's call, wandered back into the house and dropped into a chair. Both dogs immediately sat at her feet and stared up at her.

"What do you want me to do?" she said, butting into something else Jesselyn was saying.

Jesselyn sighed, her impatience traveling through the ether loud and clear. "I want you to make sure Gabe goes out to see Ruby, that's what. Immediately, if not sooner. Hog-tie him, if you have to, and drag him out there behind one of Victoria's horses. Which, by the way, she says you can ride anytime you like. Wishes you would, actually. And if you can't get Gabe there, go by yourself. Somebody needs to listen to that old lady."

"I can't interfere in sheriff's office cases, Jess. You know that."

"Hah." Jesselyn's reply gusted like a miniature explosive. "Since when? Today, Frankie. I mean it." She broke the connection without saying goodbye.

Her 'or else' was implied, although for the life of her, Frankie didn't know what Jesselyn would do. Start calling every five minutes until she got her way?

Not going to happen.

Frankie pushed the contact button to connect with Gabe's personal number. When he answered, she could tell he was in his car and on the speakerphone. The siren screamed loud enough to nearly drown his voice.

"Kind of busy here, Frankie," he said.

"I can tell. But I just got off the phone with Jesselyn. She says Ruby Lyons is being intimidated by someone and we—you—need to find out who is doing it and stop him. Ruby is scared and about to sign papers selling her house, which she doesn't really want to do. And she, Ruby, that is, still needs to tell you what she saw regarding the meth deal."

The siren continued to wail. Gabe took his time about answering.

He seemed to be in pursuit of a suspect? she wondered. Or rushing to the scene of an accident?

"Intimidation, huh?" he said. "I promise I'll make time for her. This afternoon, just as soon as I get through here. Call and tell her so, please. Or this evening, for sure."

"You want me to call her?"

"Sure. Why not? A friendly chat."

Then he was gone. Frankie touched the 'end call' button. This seemed to be her day for abrupt departures.

But not, as it turned out, as abrupt as her own change of plans. Having dealt with the call to Ruby—whom she didn't think quite understood who she was, but clearly got the message she was being put off again—her own plans were shot.

For one thing, or maybe she should just call it the only thing, by the time she got back from Spokane Valley with cans of sealer, brushes, rollers, drop cloths, and a several other items needed to finish her porch, it was too late to start work. Fingers clenching, she crumbled the bill from Peter's Hardware in her pocket so she didn't have to look at it again.

A decision well made as another terse text from Gabe said he wasn't going to make it to Ruby's this afternoon but would make time for her this evening. "Please let her know," the text ended.

The message set Frankie to thinking. Since Jesse-lyn had reminded her of Victoria's open invitation to ride whenever she wanted, the opportunity—no, the need—had fallen right into her lap. Victoria, being a wealthy real estate mogul, had invested in a forty-acre gentleman's or in this case, gentlewoman's, farm when land prices dropped during the recession. It possessed a decent house, a better barn, and room for her stable of four horses.

Handed the perfect excuse, Frankie decided to take Victoria up on the offer. Lord only knows she needed something to clear the events of these last few days from her mind. Besides, Victoria's little ranch was only three or four miles away from Ruby's farm. As long as you ignored the roads and kept to the open fields and draws and the game paths that wound among the farms, it made for a pleasant ride as the day cooled.

At Victoria's ranch, Frankie tried calling Gabe one

last time before throwing the saddle aboard a dun mustang named Corporal. Victoria had picked him up for practically nothing at one of the wild horse auctions. She'd been heard to say breaking the animal to ride had been the expensive portion of the deal. Oddly enough, Frankie thought she may have been the only person to ever ride the little gelding, excepting only Victoria's trial run. Corporal wasn't really showy enough for Vic's taste, aside from the fact he could be a real bugger when fresh. But when he went, he went, and with a sweet gliding gait. Having ridden him twice now, Frankie loved him. Besides, the gelding tolerated Banner chuffing along at his heels, and for these excursions, she wouldn't leave her dog behind for the world.

Her feelings for Gabe were not quite so generous when he finally answered. "What time shall I tell Ruby to expect you?" she asked, aware of the annoyance creeping into her voice.

Gabe, catching her aggravation, hesitated. "Sorry, Frankie, I'm not going to make it back to Hawkesford until late. Let Missus Lyons know, will you? And my apologies. I'll see her tomorrow, I promise."

"You shouldn't make promises you can't keep." Pissed, she didn't care if he knew it.

"I'll find time to meet with her," he said, guilt coming through loud and clear. "These farm women get up early, don't they? I'll go in the morning before shift."

She didn't speak for a moment, and when she did, the words came out short and tight through clenched teeth. "She's an old lady, Gabe. I'm sure I don't know her sleeping habits. And by the way, I can give you her phone number and you can call her yourself."

"Sorry. No time," he said, and hung up. Again.

"What am I, his personal assistant?"

Banner looked up at her as she gathered the reins and mounted. "That is just rude. He's going to get an earful about it, too, first chance I get."

The dog shook himself and, grinning as only a Samoyed can, took up his favorite position at Corporal's left rear.

CHAPTER TWELVE

Frankie guided Corporal down Victoria's poplar-lined driveway, letting him lope along the grassy verge and stretch the kinks out of his legs. Banner kept pace, his pink tongue flapping with the joy of running. As for Frankie, she loved not only the feel, but the smell of the horse beneath her. She breathed in deep, enjoying the gentle breeze on her face.

At the road, she slowed, cautious of the gravel under her horse's feet. After a quarter of a mile, knowing the farmer, Alex Henderson, wouldn't mind, she cut through a field where lentils had been harvested. Unlike Strohmeyer, either Harvey or Blake, who'd pitch a fit on general principals.

They toiled up, then down a half dozen rolling hills before she loosened the reins and let Corporal run, leaving the dog behind. At the opening to the first draw, she turned the horse to follow it. A creek, dry now except for a couple low spots where water seeped to the surface, helped provide some carefully preserved habitat for upland birds and a few deer and coyotes. They slowed to a walk with Corporal's hooves muted on the soft earth. Panting and happy, Banner soon caught up.

They were almost to where the draw opened out behind Ruby's barn in a short windbreak of poplar trees, when Frankie heard a scream.

"What the . . ." She drew back on the reins, holding Corporal still. His ears pricked toward the sound.

Banner heard it, too. His nose lifted, pointing at the buildings as he responded with a low sort of gargle in his throat.

There was silence for a moment, then another scream, this one not so loud as it ended on a sob. Frankie could've sworn she heard a man laugh.

"Oh, Lord. This can't be good." Too much had happened lately for her to rush in. Caution seemed called for. Worse, today of all days, she'd left her concealed carry, a Sig Sauer P938, at home. Stupid.

Dismounting, Frankie tied Corporal to a low limb on one of the trees. She winced as the horse shook his head, the metal parts of the bridle rattling.

"You be quiet," she whispered to the horse, and held her hand, palm out, at Banner. "You too."

"Stay," she told him, then changed her mind, dropped her hand and said, "Come. Heel." There'd been times, more than she liked to remember, when he'd saved her bacon. Not bad for a dog breed more noted for amiable personality than training for war. Could be she'd have need to call on him to repeat his heroism.

Hidden from the driveway and the house by the bulk of an old, three-section barn, Frankie crept, soft-footed, around the corner of the building. She ducked back as the screen door at the rear of the house swung open, her heart almost failing when a man looked out.

So simple an act shouldn't be frightening, but his furtive air alarmed her. What had he done to Ruby? The question clamored in her head, needing an answer.

Something, she knew, even though no more screams pierced the warm summer afternoon.

Not only was the door in deep shade, but far enough away the man's features remained hidden. All she knew for sure was that he appeared to be of medium build, wore a white, short-sleeved shirt, and what looked like slacks. Not farmer duds, for certain. And no hat. What farmer didn't wear a hat, usually of the billed baseball cap variety? His hair shone under a ray of sun, denoting either fair-haired or gone gray.

After the one look around, he went back inside and closed the door. Both the screen and the outer door, which, to her consternation, had a window.

"Blast," Frankie muttered, not daring to move for fear he might be looking out. "We're stuck here."

Or at least, she was stuck. But maybe not Banner.

"Banner?" she said.

The dog looked up. His tail wagged. Slowly, she made an encircling movement with her arm as he watched.

He knew what the gesture meant, but would he understand the full scope of what she needed him to do?

"Go," she said, regretting for an instant that he wasn't a border collie. She needn't have worried. Her snow dog worked just fine as he dashed off and made a wide circuit around the yard, pausing only once to stop and sniff at an interesting scent in the grass. Even so, her heart almost failed her as he disappeared around the front of the house.

A second later, her hands curled into fists as he began barking. She recognized it for his worried bark, not the one he sometimes used to greet friends.

Frankie heard a man say, "Shut up, you stupid mutt. Get away from me. Where'd you come from, anyhow?"

The same man? If so, he'd gone out the front of the house. Leaving? She heard no other voices. No Ruby, seeing a visitor off. No one commenting on a strange dog's sudden appearance, or any of the thousand things people might say to one another as they departed. Just a curse indicating Banner may have drawn too near.

Then a car door slammed, and Frankie heard the purr of a powerful engine starting up.

He must be leaving.

Where was Banner?

Concern raising her heartbeat, Frankie broke for the house, rounding the side just in time to spot the flash of a red car as it fishtailed down the gravel driveway to the road. Hurrying? Why?

Banner stood in the yard staring after the car, his tail tucked between his legs instead of curled over his back.

Frankie trusted his perceptions, just as she trusted her own sixth sense as it told her now to move it. To get inside the house and find Ruby, because it sure hadn't been that man uttering those screams she'd heard.

Banner close on her heels, she ran for the door, trying it only to find it locked. No real surprise. Even so, she spared a moment to pound on the front panel and punch the doorbell. Punch, punch, punch. She heard the bell chiming inside, over and over.

"Ruby," she called. "Are you there, Ruby? It's Frankie McGill from the fire department."

No answer.

The door, a heavy one, had been made back in the days before hollow-core became the standard. The lock, an old-fashioned one, required a big key. Would Ruby have a spare hidden somewhere here on the stoop? Under the welcome mat or the pot of wilted hot pink petunias on the wrought-iron stand.

Frankie flipped the mat over and scooted the plant aside.

"Nothing. Damn it."

The back door had appeared more modern, less sturdy.

"C'mon, Banner."

Frankie sped around the house again, arriving at the back in time to see a puff of dark gray smoke escape through a kitchen window via an inch-wide gap at the bottom.

"Oh, no. No."

Certain it would be a waste of time to knock or even call out, Frankie yanked on the screen door's handle. The door opened an inch and stopped with a jolt. Peering in, she saw it was latched by one of those safety thingies used to secure hotel rooms. No way she'd get that open without tearing down the whole door, hinges first. The window looked to be the only feasible entry point, and fortunately, it had some size. Big enough for a slim woman to fit through.

But the window, notwithstanding the inch at the bottom, turned out to be locked too.

Desperate measures. Frankie cast about for something with which to smash her way in.

There. A brick from an edging around an old over-grown herb garden caught her eye. She snatched it up and without hesitating, threw it through the window. Glass shattered, sprinkling the ground liberally but leaving some in the frame. Picking up another brick, she used it to clear leftover lethal appearing shards.

More smoke found its way out, escaping in a dark cloud around the window. Peering down a hall hazy with gathering smoke, Frankie could see the red glow of a fire coming from another room.

"Ruby!"

No reply. She hadn't really expected one.

First things first. She dialed 911. Talked to Maggie. "Fire, ambulance, police," she demanded.

"On it," Maggie said. "Stay on the line."

Frankie ignored the standard caution. Had to. "Gotta make this fast," she told Banner, and without pausing to think, leapt for the opening.

Pain immediately radiated through her hands as they caught on the sill. It occurred to her maybe she should've taken more time to clear the glass. Too late to worry about it now. Ignoring the cuts, which she realized weren't deep even if they did hurt like hell, she pulled herself up and dived through the frame, leaving smears of blood on the casing. First her head, then her shoulders as she wormed hips and the rest of her inside. She ended up in a big old enameled iron sink full of dirty pots and pans.

Fighting a way through Ruby's neglected housekeeping, Frankie pulled herself over the counter and got her feet on the floor.

A choking cloud of smoke immediately surrounded her, life-threatening fumes already filling the house. Being an old house, it would burn fast. She didn't have much time. An alarm had activated somewhere in the interior and a robotic female voice screamed out repeatedly, "Fire, fire, fire. Wake up. Fire, fire, fire."

Although unaccustomed to entering Ruby's house from this direction, Frankie was no stranger to the layout, common to many of the old farmhouses. The main source of the blaze, rapidly growing as it licked at anything combustible, burned in Ruby's bedroom. Taking a last deep breath of relatively-clear air, she dashed down the hallway leading there.

Frankie knew the second she entered Ruby's room the scene facing her had been staged. No doubt meant to look like an unfortunate accident, Ruby lay face down on her bed. But only partially so. Her wheelchair was tipped forward, as if the woman had started to lie down and hadn't been able to get that far. Her knees were on the floor, with only her torso flopped half on, half off the bed. Her oxygen tank was tipped over on the floor beside the chair, the port out of Ruby's nose and no longer serving any need except to feed the fire.

A fire which, to all appearances, had begun at the wall outlet on the other side of the bed. It had already burned along the baseboards and up the wall and was moving fast toward some lacy curtains. Too fast. Even as she watched they burst into flame with a curious popping sound.

"Ruby!" Frankie called out, coughing as acrid smoke scratched her throat. "Ruby, can you hear me?"

Ruby didn't move.

Is she dead? Don't let her be dead. Please, please.

Frankie snatched her phone from her back pocket. Activating the camera, she hurriedly clicked a couple photos of the scene before shoving the phone back into her pocket and kicking the chair aside. No way she could get the victim into it.

She had a notion Ruby was in this position because the man she'd seen hadn't been able to move her into a more likely setup.

"Ruby?" There may have been panic in her cry. The finish on the corner post of the bed crinkled and began to smolder. Frankie coughed harder and more often now, in the futile attempt to clear her lungs.

Ruby didn't respond.

Lord help us both. I can't carry her by myself. She's too heavy.

The only way she even had a snowball's chance at moving the elderly woman on her own, Frankie concluded, was to drag her. And if that meant Ruby suffered a few bumps and bruises along the way, that was just the breaks.

Better than burning to a crisp.

A folded quilt lay across the foot of the bed, probably one Ruby had pieced herself. Staying low to avoid as much of the smoke as possible, Frankie yanked the quilt to the floor and spread it open. Setting herself, she gave Ruby's legs a sharp jerk, dislodging the heavier woman from the bed and onto the quilt.

Ruby landed with a heavy thump, her head bouncing as it connected with the carpeted floor. Frankie winced. Even so, she gathered new strength as Ruby made a sound. At least she wasn't dead. Not yet.

"Ruby, wake up." Frankie arranged the old woman's arms at her side, pushed a thick leg until it fit within the confines of the quilt and, squatting, pulled hard on the quilt's corners. To her dismay, she couldn't get the burdened quilt to move, the carpet's depth preventing its slide. Meanwhile, her own strength seemed to wane with every breath, shallow as they were, she took. The fire's heat seared the side of her face, her arms. Every hair on her head seemed likely to burst into flame.

Coughing harder, Frankie felt a muscle in her back

tweak as she yanked. Pain flooded through her.

"Oh, God. Oh, God." How was she supposed to do this? She couldn't. But she must. Fear joined the pain. Her back jolted again and the strain suddenly dropped her, butt hitting the floor hard. At the same time, she heard Banner outside barking. Loud and long. Frantic.

Come on, McGill. You can do this. You've done it before.

And she had, when she'd dragged her platoon leader out of their Light Tactical Vehicle after they ran over an IED in Afghanistan. She'd been wounded then. Blood from the head wound in her eyes; her foot in shreds. Now she was whole, her pain just a muscle spasm. But Lieutenant Jay hadn't been as heavy as Ruby Lyons, either.

The 100-pound discrepancy between the two rescues felt like a ton. C'mon!

Shuddering, Frankie took a firmer grip on the quilt's corners and hauled on it as if she were raising a loaded net from the sea.

It moved, and the momentum kept them going. A couple feet at a time, she dragged Ruby out of the bedroom, then ran back to slam the bedroom door shut on the growing conflagration, hoping to slow it down. Seconds counted. She worked her burden down the hall to the front door, a closer way out than through the kitchen, the quilt sliding more smoothly on hardwood floors. The door opened easily when approached from this side, and she fell into the fresh air even as sparkles lit behind her eyes. The precursor of a black-out, as she knew from experience.

A final yank shot Ruby through to the outside, and careless now of damage, Frankie let the woman tumble down the steps to the ground.

She lay there on the stoop, coughing and fighting for breath as the world around her faded. For a while all she could hear was the sputter of flames, then the scream of a distant siren penetrated her near black-out. That, helped by what she recognized as a dog energetically licking her face. How long had she been this way? Not long, she thought. A glance over at Ruby showed the old woman hadn't moved. Still alive?

"C'mon, Frankie," she muttered. "Get to work." Then, "Enough," not quite sure whether she was talking about the dog's wet tongue or the siren's harsh wail. Both, she decided.

Grunting, she pushed Banner away, aware of the pain in her back burning hotter than ever as she got up. Kneeling beside Ruby, she started CPR. After a couple minutes, Ruby emitted a little sound, more a release of air than an actual utterance.

Startled, Frankie laid her finger on Ruby's carotid and

found a pulse. Yes, alive. So far.

"They're coming to help, Ruby," Frankie said, hoping the woman heard her. "The fire department. You'll be okay. We'll be okay."

Fighting the pain, she leaned against Banner. "Good boy," she breathed. "What a good boy."

The fire leapt and crackled behind her. She imagined it burning through Ruby's bedroom door, spreading quickly toward the main part of the house. Frankie was never so glad in her life to see a fire truck as when, Captain Karl Mager at the wheel, the pumper truck roared up the driveway. He jumped out and headed toward her as the ambulance stopped behind the pumper. Lew hit the ground running, grabbing up their equipment, as did Chris.

Relief struck, making her go weak. Thank God it was Lew. He'd know what to do for Ruby better than anyone, except maybe herself. But right now, she could barely think, let alone practice good medicine.

Karl jammed his helmet onto his head and shrugged into his coat as he surveyed the scene. Orders issued from his mouth in a steady stream. "Larry, get the pump engine going, fast as you can. Alex, the hose, man. Connect the hose. Might be an outdoor spigot out back we can use, too. See about it. We've got to get some water on this fire before the whole thing goes up. Hartwell, call Avista. Get the power turned off. I don't want any-body electrocuted. The Ginz fiasco was enough for a lifetime. Got that? First thing. Meanwhile, watch your ass. Frankie, what's happened here?" He waved for Lew. "Got casualties, men. Hustle."

She almost missed the part directed at her. "Ar-son." Frankie choked in the word. "Attempted murder. Somebody tried to kill Ruby." She took a couple shallow breaths, coughing again as the smoke reached outside and surrounded them. "I didn't think I could get her out . . . but I did."

Karl patted her shoulder as Lew, toting his medical bag, knelt beside her. "You done good, kid," he said. "Lew, they're all yours." His attention on the fire, he went to direct the crew, shouting more orders as he went.

"Get some oxygen on Frankie," Lew told Chris. He ripped open an intubation packet for Ruby and bent over to insert the tube down her throat. "And let's get them away from the house. It could explode at any minute. Ruby had oxygen tanks in there."

Chris shied like a startled horse.

An exploding house was a road Frankie had been down before. She had no desire to travel that way again. Glad to leave Ruby's bulk to the men, she managed to move herself and her dog to the rear of the parked am-bulance.

Lew got back to work. "Any burns?"

Frankie said, "no," but Chris contradicted her.

"She's got a bad scorch on her back."

Do I? Oh, yes. She felt it now, competing with the spasming muscle.

"Red, second degree burns, a few blisters," Chris said. "I'll put on some salve and a dressing. Don't want to chance infection. Is there anywhere else?"

"Tweaked my lower back trying to move Ruby," she admitted, sucking in a big gulp of oxygen.

"Don't doubt it. We'll do x-rays at the hospital. Tell me what happened to Ruby," Lew said, drowning out Frankie's quick denial about the hospital and x-rays. He attached his monitors to Ruby's arm. "Pulse is 51, blood pressure 84/46 and dropping, oxygen levels are dangerously low. Where did you find her?"

Frankie lifted her oxygen mask to talk. "In her bedroom. I think she's been drugged. I heard a scream when I rode up—oh, my gosh, I forgot Corporal!" She shook that line of thought off as irrelevant at the moment. "There was a man here when we arrived. He acted suspicious, kind of poking around, and then, although I didn't see Ruby or hear any more screams, a few minutes later he took off in a car, going fast. I approached the house and knocked and called out to Ruby but didn't get an answer. So, I tried the doors, which were both locked tight. But in back, I saw smoke escaping through a window, so I broke the glass and crawled inside. I found Ruby in her room. It appeared as though her wheelchair had dumped her, but I'm not buying it. I'm pretty sure that man intended to kill her, and he set the scene to make it look accidental." She snapped the oxygen mask back up and took a couple deep breaths before, ignoring Chris' move to stop her, took it off again. "I took a couple photos."

"Good girl," Lew said.

Lew, Chris now helping, worked steadily over Ruby's heavy form. She moaned a couple times, whispered a few words none of the EMTs could decipher, but clearly said, "Don't hurt me."

Just like Gerald Green.

"Looks like you're right, Frankie. She has been inject-ed with something." Lew eyes were narrow and grimly angry. "And not gently, either. Look at the bruise on her arm."

Chris and Frankie looked. "Straight into a vein," Frankie said.

"Wish I knew what it was. I'll administer Naloxone, just in case."

Over at the house, firemen ran in and out and around. A cascade of water combined with the firemen's heavy boots trampled Ruby's flower borders into the mud. An acrid stench settled over everything, held close to the ground by the cooling air as dusk settled in. Within a few minutes they had the fire knocked down and most of the house saved, a credit to Mager's ability as the leader of Hawkesford's volunteer fire department.

Two minutes later, Gabe made it out to Ruby's house at last.

CHAPTER THIRTEEN

Gabe's face set in grim lines as he stepped from his Tahoe and surveyed the scene. He slammed the truck door shut with unnecessary force. Frankie saw him look toward her and shake his head, but he went to greet Karl first, obviously asking him the details of the fire.

Inwardly, Frankie snorted. He should be talking to her. She was the one on the scene. But he and Karl nodded at each other in some sort of agreement before he headed her way.

"How is she?" Gabe directed his question to Lew, who was inserting an IV into the vein of Ruby's unbruised arm with infinite care.

Lew shook his head. "Need to get her to the Medical Center ASAP. She's been drugged with something. Don't know what. I suspect heroin and have administered Narcan."

Gabe's eyes narrowed. "I assume the drugs were not taken voluntarily?"

"You assume right. Observe." Lew lifted one of Ruby's arms. It hung flaccidly, as though without bones within the old woman's thick, sagging flesh. "You can see ligature marks on her wrists, too. Somebody had her tied up while they injected her. Looks like she tried to fight them."

"Did you remove the ligatures?" Gabe's voice sharpened. He took out his phone and began taking photos of the raw damage to Ruby's fragile skin.

The arch of Lew's eyebrow passed the question to Frankie.

"No," she said. "He must've taken them off after she passed out."

"He?"

"The man who did this." A gesture indicated not only Ruby, but the burning house.

Gabe stared at her. "A man? You saw someone?"

The thought crossed Frankie's mind to say something about the way he'd blown off not only Mrs. Laura James and her report of seeing a red sports car, but Ruby, too, after she'd asked for help. About how this might not have happened if he'd made it out here to talk to the old woman. Anger roiled through her.

She couldn't bring herself to do it, though, he looked

so tired and, dare she say, guilty. He knew this could be partly his fault. If he'd gotten here sooner—

Some acerbity still made its way into her reply. "Yes, I saw a man. Just for fun, I borrowed one of Victoria Pettigrew's horses from her place and rode him here across country. As I came up through the draw behind her barn, I heard a scream. Two screams, to be precise."

She saw his frown and anger flared. "Hey," she said. "It's my day off, and I don't happen to be a cop. I wanted a ride and figured I'd deliver your message at the same time."

Frankie drew in a breath as his lips tightened. "Anyway," she continued, "when I heard the second scream, I tied Corporal to a tree behind the barn, and sneaked closer trying to see what was going on. Just before I walked into plain sight, a man stepped out of the house and looked around." She thought a moment. "His actions struck me as furtive. Something about him that raised my hackles, anyway. Banner's too."

The dog, hearing his name, wagged his tail.

Gabe nodded encouragement. Or maybe he meant, 'Hurry the hell up.'

Frankie fondled the dog's ears and went on with her story. "I sent Banner around front and heard the man cuss him out. Banner was okay, though. A minute later, a car started up and tore off down the drive, spinning his tires in the gravel. When he'd gone, I circled the house and knocked and rang the bell but got no answer."

Lew and Chris listened almost as tensely as Gabe.

She straightened. "So I tried the door, and found it locked. But, Gabe, I was worried. Those screams . . . I couldn't let it pass. So I went around back again, looking for an easier way in, and then I saw smoke coming out through the kitchen window." She shrugged, raising a storm of pain in her back. "I broke the window, climbed in and found Ruby, and managed to get her outside. That's it."

She held up her hands, suddenly aware of the blood seeping from the cuts.

Gabe got out his notebook and activated his phone's recorder. "What kind of car was the man driving?"

Frankie felt her face go blank. "I don't know. I only saw it for an instant, from behind, and he was already halfway down the drive. But a sporty car. Red." A connection sparked in her mind. Check with Laura James.

"Red isn't very helpful, Frankie."

She shrugged again. "I'm not much up on cars. Sorry. That's why I drive the 1993 Ranger pickup my granddad left me."

Lew huffed out a chuckle. "Bet a dollar that old as it is, your grandad's rig doesn't have fifty thousand miles on it." He cycled the blood pressure cuff again and counted Ruby's pulse. "She's stable. Chris, check Frankie's hands and get them bandaged, then let's get this lady loaded up and to the hospital. I'm afraid she's going to relapse, and we don't want that." His glance took in Gabe. "You don't, either. She needs to wake up and start talking. Frankie, you'd best ride along with us. You need to get yourself checked out."

Five minutes later they were ready to go. Ruby, stirring under her own power as they loaded her into the ambulance, mumbled a few words. Not many, but enough to lighten Frankie's heart. Lew gave a thumbs up. Score one for the good guys.

Frankie stood up, too, thankful to no longer be in need of oxygen although coughs still wracked her now and then. "I can't go, Lew. I've got a horse tied up over in the draw. I need to get him home."

Which she did, regardless of both Lew's and Gabe's protests. By then the fire was the same as out, with Karl beaming because he and the crew had saved the house. Damaged but still standing, as it had for more than one hundred years.

"Another job for Mick Boyd," he said. "He can fix this old place good as new."

Frankie, pessimism hitting her hard, wondered if that would ever happen. Would Ruby be able to return home, even if she wanted to? Did she have the money to pay for repairs or would insurance cover it? Questions,

questions. But the one that hit the hardest was the one Gabe posed.

"Who would do a thing like this to an old lady?" He snapped his notebook closed. "And why?"

She had no answers. Only suspicions, although she wondered if they were the same ones he had.

* * *

The detectives, Armbuster and the other one, a guy she'd met before but whose name she could never remember, showed up fifteen minutes after Frankie arrived home.

Corporal had been safely returned to his stall for the night, a scoop of grain in front of him to make up for leaving him tied to a tree for more than two hours. The ride back to Victoria's stable had been pure misery. Even once she got in the pickup to drive home pain-filled exhaustion dogged her. She wanted nothing more than to shower, take some ibuprofen and apply ice to her back. Preferably with one dog on her lap and another cuddled beside her on the couch.

Consequently, Frankie was not exactly welcoming when, the only accomplished item on her list being to swallow some pain reliever, she answered the door. She found Armbuster's head swiveling as he inspected her new porch. The fragrance of fresh-sawn lumber pleased her senses, and she thought it did the detective's, too. At least it helped overcome the odor of smoke surrounding her and Banner.

"This is a nice piece of work," Armbuster said. "Who'd you have build your porch?"

Frankie told him, wondering all the while if he remembered the old one burning.

"You got his number? I could use a cover over my deck. And how about that iron railing? Pretty spendy, was it?"

She didn't quite know how to answer that. It wasn't really, after all, any of his business.

She muttered something about the railing being part of the overall estimate, which seemed to satisfy the detective's curiosity. His partner just looked bored.

Detective Armbuster solemnly copied Mick Boyd's number into his phone contacts as Frankie reeled it off. But then the detectives got down to business so quickly she had to wonder if the porch inquiry had simply been a way to put her off guard. If so, he was trying to tree the wrong cat.

By this time, full dark had long since fallen. Next door, Mr. Furnough's porch light came on. A moment later, he stepped out the door and called over to her, "Everything all right, Frankie? Got my phone right here. Need me to call the cops?"

"All is well, Mister Furnough," she called back to her

neighbor. "Thank you for checking."

"Stupid old . . ."

Armbuster's sharp shake of the head put a stop to his partner's remark. "Maybe we'd better step inside," he said.

Frankie agreed.

"Deputy Zantos called in the results of his preliminary evaluation of the crime scene," the second detective said when they had all seated themselves. "We're gonna talk with you and see if you've remembered anything more."

Frankie had claimed a straight-backed chair to sit in hoping to ease her back. Turns out she didn't have anything new to add to what the detectives already had, his questions and her answers a simple rehash of what she and Gabe had already discussed. For the most part. It seemed to her he came close to crossing a line once or twice, nearing what sounded to her like an accusation. As for the man she'd seen at Ruby's house, he waved her story aside.

"Without corroborating evidence of another person on the scene, it's hard to know where to start looking." His marble-hard eyes narrowed into a squint.

"Corroborating evidence? Really?" Much annoyed, Frankie glared right back. "Does that mean you think I invented the red car and its driver? Or that they're a figment of my imagination?" Her voice went up. "Or do you believe I hurt Ruby, started the fire, and lied about a suspect in a bid to place blame elsewhere?"

That's it, she soon concluded. He thought she was lying. Or acted like he did, anyway. But why?

"I don't understand how you happened past at just the right time," he said. He had pale, squinty eyes, and a square chin sporting stubble too long to be the style, and too short to be a real beard. "Sounds a little too pat to me. Did you have business there? Pressing business?"

His mouth, half-hidden by the whiskers, formed into an obnoxious smirk. "I understand she's been under pressure to sell her farm, but nobody seems to know who is applying the pressure. You're a pretty big landowner in these parts, aren't you, Miz McGill? Are you looking to add to your acreage by any chance?"

Frankie's temper flared. She tensed, trying to keep the anger from showing on her face.

Didn't they know? Hadn't Gabe told them? Frankie forego to mention her presence had been at Gabe's request. If he hadn't said anything, then she wouldn't either. Not yet, anyway.

Ignoring him, she spoke to Armbuster. "My EMS partner and I were called out to Missus Lyons' house a couple nights ago. She'd fallen and needed help getting back into her wheelchair. My ride took me close to her home this evening, so I dropped by to check on her."

Squint, as she'd decided to call him, seemed not to understand. "Well, that was convenient, wasn't it? Being so close, and all."

And all what? Frankie shot him a look.

"What kind of partner are you talking about?" Squint demanded.

The question fanned flames of resentment. Frankie snorted. "Oh, please. You know very well I'm a paramedic here in Hawkesford and we answer calls for this kind of help all the time. Lew Carpenter, the head paramedic, and I were together on the call. Missus Lyons is a heavy woman. It took the two of us to lift her."

Armbuster's curiosity seemed genuine when he said, "So how did you manage to get her out of the house tonight? By yourself, I mean?"

"I don't know," Frankie answered honestly. "A rush of adrenaline, I suppose. Fear. I can tell you. I'm paying for it now. My back is killing me. But I didn't lift her. I dragged her. On a quilt."

Armbuster smiled. "Must've been difficult."

"Very difficult."

"Sure you didn't have help?"

Squint's question, to Frankie's mind, didn't even make sense. She ignored it and remained silent, which evidently didn't please the detective.

His volume rose "I'm asking you again and expect

C.K. CRIGGER

an answer, one I can believe. What were you doing out there, so close to her house? If I'm not mistaken there's nothing but empty fields out that way. The house sits in the middle of nowhere. Seems odd, a woman driving around by herself."

"It's not the middle of nowhere. What are you trying to say, anyhow? If you're accusing me of almost killing Ruby and setting her house on fire, why don't you come right out and say so?" She glared at him. "Anyway, I wasn't driving. I was riding."

"Riding? Riding what?"

"A horse." She half-shouted it, not caring if he heard the words "you idiot," tacked on under her breath. If he'd truly spoken with Gabe, she wasn't telling him anything new.

He snorted and his lip curled. "Really? Why?"

"Why? Because I fricking well wanted to." Her anger grew. She knew her face must be glowing red. It certainly felt as hot as the blood beating through her veins. "And what's with that crack about being a big landowner? I inherited some land. Pretty small spuds actually, compared to others around here. What does that have to do with Ruby Lyons? Or with anything?"

Regretting she'd let them into the house, Frankie rose from her chair, gasping with the pain in her back. "We're done here. Get out." She headed for the door, hoping they'd follow, surprised when they did.

Gabe, finally off duty, had just turned into the driveway. The Tahoe came to a stop. He got out and paused, his gaze taking in the tense tableau. Even through the full dark beyond the porch light, Frankie saw his chest lift as he took a deep breath. He appeared to sense Frankie's fury and unease as he studied them, his gaze lingering longest on Squint.

His question went to Frankie as they all met under the porch light. "Everything okay, Frankie? You okay?"

"I don't know. You'll have to ask them." A jerk of her head indicated the detectives.

"I will?" Ignoring Squint, he looked at Armbuster. "Well?"

"All okay. For now." Armbuster smiled a little. "Just rounding all our bases. You know the drill. We need to talk to every possible witness ourselves."

"Witness? You're treating me like your best suspect." Her voice shook.

"We don't rely on secondhand accounts," Squint said. sanctimonious as a reformed adulterer.

Frankie thought he might rethink that as Gabe eyed him coldly.

"Is that right?" Gabe said. "Never stopped you from relying on mine before. I've covered your ass more than once. Covered for both of you."

"Yeah, well, you never been shacked up with the . . .

witness before." A frozen silence met Squint's comment.

Along with the crudity, what was it he'd meant to call her?

Gabe's left hand clenched, the only sign he gave that he even heard.

"We got all we need at the moment." Armbuster shot his partner a quelling look and spoke quietly. "Get in the car, Rimmel. We'd better be on our way."

"Yes. You had," Gabe said.

"Whatever you say." Squint took a step toward their sedan, a stodgy beige Ford.

Taking in a deep breath, the scent of the porch's new wood reminded Frankie of something, and although she could hardly bring herself to speak with either detective, she looked at Armbuster. "I guess this means Blake Strohmeyer is in the clear. Being stuck in jail must be a pretty good alibi."

"Yeah, about that." Armbuster stopped and seemed to think about what he planned to say. "Normally, I'd say yes, but I guess maybe not in this case. He made bail this afternoon and is out. He and his old man both. He had plenty of time to get here and terrorize Missus Lyons."

"Except he didn't," she said.

Both men gaped at her, but it was the one thing she knew for sure.

"The man I saw at Ruby's was not Blake or Harvey Strohmeyer."

CHAPTER FOURTEEN

Gabe stood on the porch long enough to watch the detective's taillights disappear into the night. He came inside then, where Frankie, hardly aware of her actions, had gone into the kitchen and gotten a glass from the cupboard. Gabe followed, leaning on the counter while she, without being asked, got a cold beer out of the fridge for him, and poured ice water for herself.

Just great, she thought, dwelling on Armbuster's news. Something else for her to worry about in case Blake decided to blame her for his latest peccadillo.

She wished she dared have a shot of tequila. A nice, big shot, or maybe a double, or even a triple. This would be the perfect time for a drink. Wash away the taste of the detectives' pointed innuendo about her and Gabe, along with their barely concealed suspicion of her.

Hard telling what the booze would do to her, though,

mixed with her meds for pain and anxiety. Another month, she promised herself. She'd be off them both by then, come hell or high water. Sometimes she thought the VA doctor's prescriptions were what made the PTSD recur. She'd cut down to just the two, now, and the blackouts came less frequently than when she'd been taking so many. Cause and effect, only which way did it go?

Meanwhile, she felt the weight of Gabe's sympathetic gaze. "Where are you hurt, Frankie?"

His question took her by surprise. Another surprise was the anger she felt. Anger not just toward the detectives, but at Gabe and the whole sheriff's department.

"What makes you think I'm hurt?" She forced herself to stand up straight.

He took a couple swallows of beer and shook his head. "For one thing, I can see the pain on your face. For another, Lew and Karl both made a point of telling me you were injured getting the old lady out of the house." He grinned. "You'll probably end up with another medal. It may not compare with the Bronze Star and Purple Heart you've already got, but it's the best we can do."

The air went out of her like a balloon with a slow leak. "People don't need medals just for doing their jobs. I don't want another damn medal." Gabe was the only person in town who'd seen the medals she'd been awarded in Afghanistan. One of the few who even knew she had them.

As for her attitude? Well, the rest of her platoon died in action and she got the medal. The concept disgusted her. She couldn't bear to touch even the Purple Heart. The plate in her head and part of a prosthetic foot were everyday reminders.

"I know you don't." Gabe set his bottle on the counter before placing both hands on her shoulders, holding on when she winced away. "But Frankie, you must know you did everything you possibly could. You got your team leader out of the truck and you killed the men responsible for the ambush." He'd heard that much, and no more. "Just like you saved Missus Lyons life tonight."

"But Lieutenant Jay died anyway. In the end, I didn't save a single one, and I was the medic."

Bright flashing lights overwhelmed her then, an explosion of her own inside her brain, and Gabe's face faded into black.

The next thing she knew, she lay on her bed with Gabe pressing a cold washcloth to her forehead. Her eyes flicked open to meet his hazel ones. He glared down at her.

"Damn it, woman, quit scaring me."

"Sorry." Frankie couldn't think of anything else to say, although he might've been waiting for an explanation she couldn't bring herself to give.

After a moment, he said, "What happened? And don't bat those big brown eyes at me. Tell me the truth."

The minute she confessed that these black outs came at unpredictable moments, although high stress seemed to be a prime factor, she'd be out of a job. She couldn't tell anybody the truth.

"I guess I fainted." Avoiding his gaze, she closed her eyes again. "A drop in blood pressure, I suppose, due to a combination of dehydration and pain. Too hot and dry for me in Ruby's house tonight." An understatement. "No big deal. I'll be fine."

The bedstead squeaked as he sat on the edge of the mattress and pressed two fingers to the pulse in her wrist. He counted; his eyes narrowed. "I've seen people faint before, Frankie. None of them looked like this."

"Oh, you're the doctor now?"

Why'd he have to be so danged smart, anyway? Her electrical seizure, although in some ways mimicking a faint, showed up differently. It wasn't epilepsy, either. Just a weird thing most likely caused by the plate in her head and aggravated by stress—or so one doctor said. Even so, the blackouts, while still too frequent, were usually less severe. She knew that. The doctor also said that one day they'd stop altogether. She could only trust he wasn't feeding her false hope.

She swung her legs over the side of the bed and prepared to stand. Gabe put a hand under her elbow to steady her.

"I'll be all right in a few minutes," she said. "Don't worry. I told you. It's nothing." Forcing a laugh, she made a quasi-confession. "I think my temper got the best of me. Detective—not Armbuster, the other one—may be the most insulting and obnoxious man I've ever met. Or in a tie with Blake Strohmeyer, anyway. I wanted to clout him alongside the head, preferably with a baseball bat. To tell you the truth, since you asked for it, I didn't think I was going to get Ruby out of the house. I almost can't believe I did. And then to have him demeaning me, you, and the whole situation put me right over the top. Massive temper tantrum. That's it. The truth."

Or as much of it as she was going to tell him.

* * *

Frankie's phone rang much too early the next morning. She lay in bed with her arms folded behind her head, eyes open, but dreading the thought of getting up. She'd finally found a comfortable position for her back and didn't want to move from it. The thought of climbing a ladder and brushing sealer onto the ceiling of her new porch seemed like an overwhelming proposition, not that her sore hands could hold onto a brush anyway. The phone call goaded her into throwing the covers aside and propping herself on her elbow to read the caller ID.

"Victoria Pettigrew? What do you suppose she wants?" she said to Banner who eyed the phone as if afraid it might jump on him. It had moved an inch across the nightstand with the force of its vibration, after all. A fear struck her, followed immediately by a second. "As long as it isn't anything about Jesselyn. Or Corporal."

She picked up.

"Are you all right?" Victoria said. "I just heard about Ruby, and how you rode Corporal over in the nick of time to save her."

Frankie almost had an 'Aw shucks' moment until Victoria rushed on before she could answer. It was easy to tell Victoria and Jesselyn were sisters. She noted a definite similarity in the Pettigrew girls' phone technique.

"Browntree says Corporal is fine, that you even swabbed the smoke smell off him before you left. Thanks for that. In fact, thanks for getting him some exercise. Brown mentioned the poor creature is bored and needs some work. Take him out whenever you get the chance."

Browntree, a tribal member, worked for Victoria, caretaking the place and all that involved, putting up the hay, tending to the animals. The two of them might've had a little something going on between them, too, whenever convenient and the notion struck.

None of my business, Frankie reminded herself.

"Thanks. I—" she started.

Victoria had already moved on. "The thing is, I'd just talked to Ruby yesterday. She said she's been thinking of either selling the farm, or renting it out, and she wanted my advice. Me being a local girl, ya know, with connections. She also said a guy who told her he's with a Spokane realty outfit has been coming around to see her. Pestering her, she said, and he has her freaked. Really freaked."

"Freaked?" Frankie repeated. A teenage sentiment coming from a hip old lady. But according to what Jesselyn told her yesterday, the old lady was more than freaked. More like downright scared. And that she felt forced to sign some papers, which she didn't want to do. "What did you tell her?"

"I told her not to do anything, and most particularly, not sign anything, until I'd looked at the offer. The thing is, I've never heard of this guy or the company he supposedly works for. And I know just about everybody in real estate around this area. Spokane, Coeur d'Alene, Saint Maries, Sandpoint. I get around. I told her that if she really wanted to sell, I'd put the farm on the market for her and discount my fee. I'll do the same for you when you're ready to sell."

That last part, tossed in oh, so casually, almost sailed over Frankie's head. Almost. She ignored it with the hope she never had to sell. As to the rest of it, Victoria's advice sounded fine. "What did Ruby say?" she asked.

"She said she would do as I said, but that he wouldn't be happy. He'd told her she should sign right away to get the best deal, and that she'd be sorry if she didn't. She said it sounded like a threat."

"Really! How threatened? Tone of voice? Gunpoint?"

"She didn't say."

"Well, did she call the sheriff's department and report it?"

"She said she'd tried but nobody got back to her. She meant Gabe, you know."

Victoria rushed ahead, then, and Frankie almost sighed aloud with relief. She didn't want to be the one to accuse Gabe of neglect. Not that he was neglecting his duty, but in this case, his decisions might not have been the best. Or not for Ruby, anyway. What should come first when he received a call? The murder of two unidentified people, plus Roland Ginz's strange death and old Gerald Green being shot? Or an old lady's fearful accusations? Up until the time somebody set her house on fire with her in it, at least. That had made it all a different kettle of soup, for sure.

"She wanted to talk to him, I know," Frankie said, "but she went about getting his attention in a roundabout way. She never mentioned being threatened."

Victoria was nothing if not blunt. "How do you

know?"

"Because she called us, EMS, the other night, to help her off the floor where she'd fallen. She told Lew Carpenter and me that she wanted to talk to Gabe about some people she'd seen coming from the Berthold property. She thought they might be connected with the murder. As far as I know, that's all she meant to talk about. She said nothing about anyone threatening her."

"And did you pass what she said on to Gabe?"

Frankie heard an accusation in those words. "Yes. Of course. Both Lew and I did. But as you probably know, Gabe's been a tad busy. Worse, those murders aren't the only problems to hit our town lately."

Victoria sighed heavily into the phone. "What else?"

"Did you know Roland Ginz died?"

"Yes." Victoria's answer came slowly.

"Mysterious circumstances. Most likely murder. And then there's Gerald Green."

"Gerald Green? That old man? What about him? I thought he died years ago."

"Well, he didn't—but I'm sure whoever shot him meant him to be dead now."

"What do you mean?"

"We, EMS, got a call. We found him at his family's old homestead. He'd been shot and is in bad shape." Frankie paused. "Gabe's being run ragged trying to help the detectives and keep order in the county. And now, with Ruby, it's apt to get worse."

"I see. Yes. Bound to. Damn." Victoria hung up.

Frankie rolled out of bed then, her sore back making her flinch more than once. A warm shower helped ease the stiffness. Even as she soaped and rinsed, she wondered if she'd been too open with Victoria, if she'd given away any secrets into the investigation. Still thinking of their conversation as she donned jeans and a T-shirt, it occurred to her Victoria had never been specific about what the threats to Ruby actually were. Had that man warned of fire and then followed through? If so, poor Ruby must have been doubly terrified.

When she went downstairs, Banner and Shine ambling at her feet and doing their best to trip her, she went outside to find The Spokesman-Review tossed onto the front porch.

With the paper on the kitchen counter in front of her, Frankie stood to drink her morning coffee. There, on the front page, although below the fold, she found a news story headed, Crime Wave Hits Hawkesford.

At the time the paper went to press, the two meth house victims were still unidentified. The Strohmeyers, father and son, were not named, although the report said two men had been questioned and released. Frankie wondered if Blake was pissed by not having his name in the paper or just the opposite.

Roland Ginz's death, she read, had officially been declared murder, and Gerald Green still clung to life in critical condition. Ruby Lyons' close call had not been included in the article. Not until Frankie turned to the local news page and read a short, two-paragraph story on a house fire. No mention of arson. No mention of Frankie McGill to the rescue either, which didn't bother her sensibilities one whit.

To her relief, she hadn't passed anything on to Victoria that the paper didn't report. No big secrets. Victoria could've as easily read the paper for herself and discovered most of what Frankie told her. Except, perhaps, for the part about the man she'd seen and Gabe working the crimes alongside the detectives.

* * *

Gabe had said he'd hook up the doorbell on his next day off, it having been disconnected due to the construction. Frankie suspected it would be a while longer before that happened if these murders weren't cleared soon. Anyway, it came as no surprise when early afternoon brought a knock on the door. So, not surprised, but a little annoyed since she had to leave for work in a few minutes.

She trod down the stairs, dogs at her heels.

The face, viewed through the peephole in the door, which, in a show of caution Frankie actually peeked through before opening, belonged to a stranger. A woman. Blonde. Slim. Dressed in a tailored, dark-colored suit even as the early afternoon temperature approached ninety degrees.

Frankie stood back. "Who do you suppose that is?" she asked Banner in a whisper. The dog's tail waved.

After a suitable pause, she opened the door. "May I help you?"

The blonde's teeth, bleached to within an nth, gleamed in a smile. Friendly or phony? Hard to tell.

"Hi," the woman said. "How are you this fine day? I wonder if I could speak with Mister Frank McGill, please?"

Salesman, Frankie thought, or rather, saleswoman, and started to close the door before relenting enough to say, "There is no Frank McGill."

The blonde, while not quite sticking her toe in the opening, had a protest ready. "Please," she said, "let's not play games. The County Assessor's records show this, and several other properties are held in Mister McGill's name. I know I have the correct address. Are you his caretaker, by any chance? Please, I'd really like to speak with him. It would be to his advantage." The glistening teeth showed again.

Frank, eh? Frankie wondered if she needed to contact the probate attorney again to ask her to straighten out the name thing. If, she conceded, Lady Teeth had told the truth. Curiosity got the better of her.

"What kind of advantage?"

The woman chuckled, the sound warm and friendly. "Oh, that's information just for Mister McGill. I'm authorized to present an offer to him, and only to him."

"An offer for what?"

"Let me talk to McGill. Now." The timbre of the woman's voice changed, became stronger. "Believe me, you don't want to get in the way of our business."

At that moment, Banner, never far from Frankie's side, stuck his snout between the door and the jamb and nosed it wider. Shine, as always sticking close to Banner, upon spying a stranger began barking a loud warning.

Lady Teeth's eyes narrowed as she surveyed the pair, her gaze lingering for several seconds on Banner. "What a beautiful dog," she said. "You don't see many Samoyan's around here. Rare, aren't they?"

Banner's attitude riveted Frankie's attention more than the woman's words, even through the mispronunciation of the breed name—a common enough error. Usually, except when confronted by someone like Blake Strohmeyer, even strangers would find his fluffy tail furled over his back, his lips lifted in the welcoming Samoyed smile. Not now. His tail drooped and he stood stiff-legged, almost as though he needed to protect Frankie and Shine.

"Somewhat rare," Frankie said after a second's pause. "Does he bite?"

"Only if he senses a threat. Either to me, or the little dog, or himself." A lie. She'd never known him to bite at any provocation. "Are you threatening us? Because it did sound like it."

The woman quickly retreated a step, and then another.

"Certainly not." Her plucked and painted brows drew together in hard-to-miss dismay. "How could you possibly think such a thing? Well, if Mister McGill isn't here, I'd better be going." Spinning on the heel of her black leather pumps, she hurried down the steps and, awkward on those heels, trotted toward her car. A plain, older Honda Civic with dull blue paint and a dented fender showing some rust.

Sort of a dinky car for a woman wearing such expensive clothing and a pea-sized diamond on her finger.

CHAPTER FIFTEEN

Caretaker. The word echoed in Frankie's mind long after the woman had gone. Why would that woman think caretaker? Why not wife? Sister? Daughter? Why caretaker?

And why had Banner frightened her? Because he had, even though he hadn't growled or lunged, his most aggressive move being to stand between his human and a stranger.

Although tempted to call Gabe, Frankie kept her fingers off her phone's keypad. Yes, she planned to talk with him about the woman, but not now. He'd just say, "sort of busy, Frankie," and after all, it wasn't as if she couldn't take care of herself against some female wearing high heels and a pencil skirt.

The dogs, following her to the kitchen, provided further reassurance. They were good at keeping the bogeymen away. All kinds of bogeymen—1whether those in her mind, or those in the flesh.

Anyway, what could she tell Gabe if she did report her rather disturbing visitor to him? It struck her, as she closed and locked the back door and made sure the place was secure before leaving for work, that she had nothing to tell. The woman roused her suspicions, but really, what had Lady Teeth actually done to alarm her? When Frankie got down to it, she couldn't remember exactly what the woman had said. And she hadn't done anything. More like what she hadn't done or said, that Frankie found puzzling. Left no card and offered no information except a vague promise of some unknown something being to Frank McGill's advantage.

Oh, and commented on Banner as if she didn't even see Shine.

Anyway, what did she expect Gabe to do when a random, unidentified salesperson came to her—their—front door? He'd laugh at her worries. Or think her some kind of nut job.

She felt like banging her head against the wall. Maybe it'd work to jog her memory.

Like an idiot, she'd neglected to ask the woman's identity. Or where she was from. Or what firm she represented.

Still, she did have one positive item to go on; the

make and model of the car, and most of the number on a license plate hanging by a loose screw at the rear. Random things like that often stuck in her mind, where other, more pertinent matters did not. She'd ask Maggie tonight, when they had a private moment, if she could discover who owned an old blue Honda Civic. Maggie excelled at stuff like that, her natural nosiness kicking in. Frankie didn't ask how she did it. Probably best if she didn't know.

* * *

Turned out, to Frankie's disappointment, that Maggie had the day off, and the dispatcher taking her place belonged to the straight arrow club. Everything done by the book. Benton would never stoop to snooping merely to satisfy his curiosity. Absolutely not. Frankie would have to wait to ask about the license plate.

It pleased her no end when Marc arrived for their shift, appearing far more relaxed than on his first day back.

"I'm back in the saddle again," he sang at her question. "It's just like your grandpa told you, Frankie. You've gotta climb back up on the horse. No, really. We made it through that creepy first call, our patient is still alive—I called to check—and his dog is making himself comfortable on my bed. He's a good old boy."

Pretty sure he meant the dog, she nodded.

"We did good work, Frankie."

She had to smile. Marc had found just what he needed. A dog and new purpose. She, like no other, could attest to the therapeutic value of both.

They went on two short runs, to two different fields, both regarding bee stings. Or more specifically, yellow jacket stings. T'was the season, Frankie thought, resolving to pick up a couple extra doses of adrenaline. In both cases, they'd been required to administer epinephrine injections, and advise their patients to get a prescription for an epinephrine injector and carry it with them at all times. One of the people, a woman delivering a mid-afternoon snack to her husband and son in the field, required a trip to Kootenai Health as Frankie had to help her out with a breathing tube.

Back at the station, a trickle of folks wandered in. The evening rush, the volunteers called it, as people dropped by on their way home from work. Two wanted updates on the latest fire and inquire as to Ruby Lyons' well-being; one reported seeing smoke where none should be. A camper? A squatter? Just askin'. But it was the couple who inquired about purchasing a home fire extinguisher who interested Frankie.

A couple months ago, Karl had discovered a treasure

trove in a discontinued line of extinguishers for sale on eBay. He'd bought a full two dozen for practically nothing and put them up for resale at a nice profit dedicated to the fire department. They'd all sold but one.

"Yeah, hey, them fire distinguishers you got for sale any good?" the guy asked.

Marc, it being his turn on the help desk, choked. Stifling a laugh, he turned to Frankie for help. "Do we still have any fire distinguishers, Frankie?"

She knew he hadn't been able to help himself from repeating the joke, but the guy, unshaven and in need of a shower and clean clothes didn't seem to notice.

"One left." Frankie, stifling her own grin, directed her attention the guy. "Hi. How's it going?"

He wouldn't meet her eyes. No surprise. Garrity Weddell had always been that way. Autism spectrum, she suspected, or maybe Asperger's syndrome. They'd started school together, but he'd soon got left behind by two or maybe three years.

He shrugged her question off. "Are they? Are those things any good? I heard they got a desperation date."

Malapropisms had been known to get him into trouble, too, she remembered.

"Yes, they do, but they don't expire for almost four years. Comparable ones sell for forty bucks on Amazon, but we're asking only twenty-five dollars. Plus, it's rechargeable, when the time comes. It's good for most kinds of home fires."

Garrity turned to the girl who accompanied him. "You got twenty-five bucks, Juanita? Sounds like a deal to me. Cassidy E. forgot to pay me before she skipped out."

The girl, whom Frankie didn't recognize, was blonde and taller than Garrity by a full two inches. She wore tight Daisy Dukes and a skimpy camisole top that would've looked better if her shoulder blades hadn't been so pronounced. Scratching absently at her arm, she'd been staring around the station as if searching for gold, her gaze always returning to Frankie as though in discovery of a new species.

"Jeez, Gar, what am I? Your cash register?" Her voice was harsh, making Frankie wonder if she had a sore throat. Regardless, the girl, Juanita—although in Frankie's opinion the Hispanic sounding name didn't fit—fished in her short's pocket and brought forth some money.

"Be sure to read the instructions on how to use the extinguisher."

"I will," the girl said. "Gar, here, don't read so good." Sweat trickled along her cheekbone, catching in her dry blonde hair. The thin cami showed dark with moisture in a vertical line between childlike breasts.

Frankie nodded. She remembered Garrity's trouble

reading as one of the things that held him back in school. She'd always wondered if he suffered from dyslexia.

Marc, like a good friend, headed off to the storage locker to bring Garrity's purchase out to him. Meanwhile, Frankie stood with the fingers she'd used to take Juanita's cash outspread, vowing to wash as soon as they'd gone. She knew a user when she saw one. Or two. And money was notorious for holding on to the residue.

A silence fell, until Juanita poked Garrity in the ribs. She jerked her head in a go-ahead kind of motion, an indication they had something besides buying a fire extinguisher on their agenda.

Garrity jumped, his eyes, darker even than Rudy Swallowtail's, darting from side to side. "Uh, yeah. Hey, can you tell me who discovered the fire over at that old lady's house the other night? Did she . . .uh . . .is she . . ."

"Did the old woman die?" The blonde finally finished the question for him.

"Not that I've heard." A spark lit in Frankie's brain. "Do you know her?"

"Nah. But we live not far from there. Drove by on our way here." Garrity managed two complete sentences, stuttered, and started on a third. "Looks like you guys saved the house. Mostly."

"We did. Hawkesford can be proud of its fire department."

Juanita gave Garrity the eye, again, but he seemed at a loss. She shook her head and said, in her harsh voice, "So who discovered the fire? Somebody must've been Johnny-on-the-spot."

Marc, returning with a box, jumped in on this. "Frankie did. She—"

Frankie, who'd already made up her mind not to noise her involvement around, felt like bopping him one. Her interruption may have been less than tactful. "No big deal. I happened to be driving by, is all, saw the smoke and called it in. I may not have even been the first."

Mouth open, Marc gaped at her. She nodded sharply, as if to say, "That's it." If he started to make one mention of her rescue of Ruby, she'd stomp down on his toes with her prosthetic foot. That should shut him up.

"Frankie?" Garrity's vacant gaze fixed on her, now. "Do I know you? Are you, uh, yeah, uh, Frankie Mac Something?"

Trapped! "McGill," she said.

To her surprise, as precise as though doing a dance routine, the pair swung around and marched out. Frankie heard Garrity trying to tell the girl something, but she refused to listen. "Shh," she whispered, probably louder than she intended. "Talk later."

Marc waited until the door closed behind them before turning to Frankie. "What the heck was that?"

Even Benton, at his desk with his Bluetooth gadget on, appeared surprised. "Yes, Frankie. What was that?"

"I'm not sure, but—" she stopped, shrugging her own puzzlement. Best not to talk about the Weddells, she decided. Or the woman who'd stopped at the house earlier. Not with Marc or Benton, at least. Not until she'd spoken with Gabe.

The night dragged by after the volunteers left, seeming to her as if it would never end. At last it did, of course. At midnight after answering only one more call throughout the entire evening. A false alarm actually, no doubt caused by a wild critter seeking a drink out of a child's swimming pool.

And why the woman had called the fire department, nobody knew. Including the caller, after the fact.

Marc drove back to the station. Their windows rolled down, cool air rushed in, cleansing away odors of sickness and the antiseptic used to sanitize the ambulance's interior. After agreeing they were glad not to make a run to the hospital with a real emergency, the cab was quiet until Marc broke the silence.

"That guy about the fire distinguisher," he said at last as they turned off a narrow country road onto Highway 95. "Who is he? Why didn't you want him to know you'd pulled Missus Lyons out of the fire?"

The question gave Frankie pause. Why didn't she? On

the face of it, there seemed no problem, but— No. Not until she'd talked with Gabe. Maybe he could make sense of the connections she saw everywhere. Connections she had to wonder if she imagined.

She managed a nonchalant shrug, one that Marc, concentrating on his driving, probably didn't see. "I just don't want to make a big deal out of it, especially with people I barely know."

"You seemed to know him."

"We started school together. He had learning problems and fell behind, so no, it's not like he's a long-lost friend."

"Did you know the girl? What would you say, an eating disorder?"

Frankie looked over at him. "Oh, yes. Probably caused by drug use. I suppose you noticed she'd been picking at her skin, sweating like a horse, some blood around her nose that she didn't get wiped away. Did you notice her hoarse voice? It may be a symptom, too."

"Meth, you think?"

"Wouldn't surprise me."

"No, me either. Too bad."

"Yes."

Marc made a good job of backing the ambulance through the station doors into its slot. By then Benton had transferred dispatch to the Coeur d'Alene system and shut down his computer. With little talk, they scattered to their rides; Benton to a quiet Ford Escape, Marc to his rebuilt Harley, and Frankie to her old Ranger pickup.

* * *

Shortly after midnight, Gabe followed Frankie into the driveway. Not that she knew it was him, at first. His headlights shining into her rearview mirror blinded her to all except their glare and had her wishing she had her P938 handy. Until he drove under the yard light, at least, and she saw the vehicle with its sheriff's department insignia.

She hadn't known her amplified state of tension until then. Drawing a deep breath, she stepped out of the Ranger and locked her rig.

"You've had a long day," she said as he tossed his four-dent hat into the SUV and came to meet her. She spoke softly, aware of Mr. Furnough's bedroom window standing open to the summer night. A nosy old fellow, one never knew if he might be listening. A trait that had turned out well for her on more than one occasion, but still—

"Yep. There's a lot going on."

Having heard the familiar car engines, the dogs bolted through the dog door, eager to say howdy to their people.

Midway, Banner stopped and lifted his nose to scent the air.

"Skunk?" Gabe said, watching him.

"I don't smell anything."

"Human failing. You ever wish dogs could talk?" Gabe stepped in front of her, unlocked the door and opened it.

"All the time."

He grinned, the porch light shining down on him. Suddenly, Shine, from out at the end of the yard where it backed up on Janet Stevens' alpaca pasture, caterwauled a sharp cry. Banner's deeper voice joined hers.

Gabe spun.

At the same time, an object thudded into the door jamb between her and Gabe. Frankie knew the sound. A bullet.

Evidently, Gabe knew, too. "Get inside." He gave her a push that sent her to her knees on the mudroom floor. He didn't follow her. He'd already slipped away into the darkness. His Glock out, he ran toward the pasture.

Frankie turned off the light before sticking her head back out and calling for the dogs. In seconds, Shine, a little white blur, tore towards her, running straight into the house. The Bichon trembled violently as she rammed head first into Frankie's legs.

Unless, Frankie admitted, that was her doing the shaking. She picked Shine up. Having almost died of a bullet wound, the Bichon hated even the smell of guns. And she certainly knew the sound of gunfire.

"Banner," Frankie called, but he was having no part of obedience at the moment. She heard him out there, rooting through a big lilac bush and racing up and down the fence's perimeter. Thank God he couldn't get through the sturdy chain link fence. Couldn't go over the top, either. And neither, evidently, could the shooter, or she or Gabe might be dead by now.

There were no more shots.

Gabe's flashlight came on about the time Frankie heard a motor start up down at the end of the block. It revved, a door slammed, then a car raced away.

Carrying Shine, Frankie went to meet Gabe and Banner, who accompanied him. The dog pranced, as if he thought he alone had chased the intruder away. And maybe, Frankie conceded, he had, having been first on the scene.

Frankie started to say something, but Gabe shook his head with a meaningful glance toward Furnough's house. The neighbor's room remained dark. Better if he weren't roused, although it was unlike him to sleep through any commotion.

Once inside, Gabe pulled the shades down over the windows before, kitchen lights aglow, he spoke. "Who do you suppose that bullet was meant for?" he asked.

"You or me?"

Still feeling shaky, Frankie set Shine down and transferred her attention to Banner who basked under her praise. "I'd guess it's a warning of some sort, but I don't know. I can tell you one thing though."

"What's that?"

"I'm getting damned tired of people shooting holes in my house. Two inside two days? Looks like a woodpecker has been at it."

Gabe snorted. "Be glad it's not blood spatter."

Frankie had the last word. "So far."

CHAPTER SIXTEEN

"Why would anybody want to shoot me?" Hearing herself, Frankie thought her plea sounded whiney and pathetic.

"Aside from Blake Strohmeyer, you mean?" Gabe's mouth twisted in wry humor. "Or maybe the man who tried to murder Ruby Lyons? Or the one who probably thought he killed Gerald Green. Take your pick. That would be my educated guess."

"Well . . . well—" He just had to put her own suspicion into words, didn't he? For a second, she couldn't think of anything else to say. Then she did. "I expect it's the same guy who's doing all of this. But why?"

"If I had to guess, I'd say it's the man who tried to kill Ruby. He probably thinks you can identify him."

"If I could, you'd have him in jail by now."

"I would." The corners of his mouth quirked into a

grin. "But I guess he doesn't know that. Anyway, I can't see three or four different people going on a murder spree all at once. Not in Hawkesford. What I want to know is how he—and I'm saying he because it's easiest—knew where to come looking. For you or for me."

Frankie plopped down on one of the red vinyl covered kitchen chairs and, elbows on the table, propped her chin in her hands. "Hawkesford is a small town. The fire department gets called out and pretty soon everyone knows who went on the run and exactly what he—or she—did and heard and saw. Who screwed up and who didn't. Who called for help and most of all, did anybody get burned to death or mangled in a car wreck?"

"I suppose. In other words, it's gotten around that you were the one who saved Ruby's life. And Green's." He leaned against the kitchen counter, a pensive look on his face.

Frankie's stomach lurched. "Except," she said, stopped, and had to start over. "Except it wasn't just me. There's Lew and Chris who took over on Ruby. And Marc and I together took care of Mister Green, yet I haven't heard they've become targets." The whiney note came through loud and strong this time.

Gabe sort of froze. "Which means there's some other reason to put you in the spotlight. It would also imply our shooter is a local."

She started to agree, then stopped. "Maybe. Or maybe there's more than one person involved. Somebody local, for sure, but somebody else, too."

"You mean part of a gang?"

"Yes. Well, see, it makes sense. Those two bodies at Strohmeyers, for instance. Have you learned who they were?"

"No. We're waiting on DNA results. At this rate, we'd be better off to send it to Ancestry.com."

He had a valid complaint, one common to police departments everywhere who were stymied by the back log in lab work, their investigations held in abeyance, suspects even set free pending untimely processing of evidence. Even so, she figured he didn't really mean it about Ancestry.com.

Or did he, she wondered, eyeing his set face?

"To me," she said, "that implies they were not local. If they had been, wouldn't someone know they were missing?"

"Somebody does, somewhere, you can be sure of that. They're just not saying." He studied her. "What's up, Frankie? You've got a mighty weight on your mind and you're trying to decide whether to spring it on me. I can tell."

Banner, who'd been sitting on her good foot, emitted one of his signature "ruffs."

Gabe smiled a little. "See? Even Banner knows it."

Taking a deep breath, Frankie scratched the dog behind his ears. "That's because it concerns him."

"Yeah? How?"

"He was with me at Ruby's the other evening. And . . . you know I've been teaching him hand signals?"

A tilt of his head said yes. He'd watched her work with the dog several times, applauding when Banner got it right.

"He's getting pretty good at it. I sent him around the house when I saw that guy poking around. I didn't know the house was on fire at that point. Anyway, I figured Banner would cause a rumpus when, or if, he saw the guy and maybe run him off. Which he did. I think he's what caused the arsonist to leave sooner, perhaps, than he'd planned. That gave me time to get into the house before the fire grew beyond her bedroom. At least he didn't stick around to watch the house go up—and Ruby die. He may've been afraid the dog had someone with him. Hah! He got that right. But the thing is, Banner is quite distinctive. As far as I know, he's the only Samoyed in or around Hawkesford."

Slowly, Gabe nodded. "And pretty well known after word got around about him chasing down Miz Barwick after she set your porch on fire."

"There's more."

"More? What more?"

Frankie got up and walked over to stand beside him at the counter. She didn't quite know why. It just felt like she wanted to be close.

"We had a visitor today."

Straightening, Gabe's hazel eyes bored into hers. "We?"

"Banner and I."

His gaze went to the dog. "Banner? And?"

"The thing is . . ." she hesitated, wondering if she'd sound paranoid recounting the incident.

"The thing?" Gabe stirred, seeming a little impatient.

"The thing is, I made a big mistake. I didn't ask the visitor for ID."

"Did you recognize him?" He took out his notebook and activated the voice recorder on his phone.

Maybe, she thought, the bullet out of the dark had been a blessing. At least he seemed to be taking her report seriously.

"That's another thing," she said. "No man involved. Our visitor was a woman, wanting to speak—insisting on, actually—speaking with Frank McGill."

Gabe blinked. "Frank?"

"Yes. She said she'd seen the assessor's information online about a property he owns and was adamant that he lived here." Frankie thought back. "She said she had an offer for him, and implied that I'd be sorry if I didn't let her present said offer directly to him. In person. But then she saw Banner. Her eyes bugged out and she said, 'Oh, what a pretty dog.' Or, no. She said, 'What a beautiful dog.' And, 'Are there many like him around here?' Oh, and, 'Does he bite?' But she barely gave me time to answer before she said she had to go and took off almost running."

Gabe's left eyebrow arched. "Just like that?"

"Just like that. Zoom." Frankie took a breath. "A blonde."

"Wearing a blue sundress, by any chance?"

Frankie didn't quite know how to take that. Was he treating her testimony as a joke, or just trying to lighten the moment?

Lighten the moment, she decided.

"Well, no," Frankie admitted. "No sundress. Nor was she driving a red car. The car was blue, an old beater Honda Civic. But, Gabe, it just didn't seem right. She had on an expensive looking suit, nice shoes, high heels and hose, no less, and wore a huge diamond on her left hand. It looked like it could cut through windshield safety glass."

"Do you suppose she's a real estate agent? Ruby said one had been in touch, as I remember."

"Yes, although I'm sure I heard the agent is a man.

Anyway, real estate agents don't drive old buckets of bolts. Victoria Pettigrew always says it's necessary in their line of work to maintain an image and to look prosperous. Until I saw the car, I figured this woman for a realtor, too, since she talked about looking property up on the assessor's website. But thinking about it, she didn't say so, and anybody can check properties on the assessor's site. She just talked about an offer. Like the mafia."

Gabe couldn't suppress his grin. "The Godmother making an offer you can't refuse?"

Frankie, shamefaced, grinned too. "Something like that."

"So, we're looking for someone who's a stranger around here, who knocked on your door and said she wanted to make an offer for some unspecified something." Gabe reached around her and opened the refrigerator door. He looked inside for a full minute before he closed it again without taking anything. "A woman who might be afraid of dogs."

Eyes narrowing, Frankie tossed her head, sorry in that moment that she didn't have a flying mane to whip in his face instead of short hair that barely covered the scars on her head.

"Not necessarily afraid of dogs in general." she said. "Afraid of Banner. Or what he meant by being here. All of which doesn't sound like much, I guess. But, Gabe, you didn't see her, didn't hear her. I think this may be how Ruby's trouble started. And Roland Ginz's. And very likely, Gerald Green's."

Gabe clicked the button to turn off his recorder. "Intuition? I expect the detectives would prefer something more to go. A name. A place. Anything."

On the spot, Frankie decided it best to bypass Maggie's help. Providing, of course, the detectives didn't ignore her information. She wouldn't put it past them, after all. Especially Rimmel, as if Armbuster weren't difficult enough.

She motioned for him to turn on the recorder again.

"How about most of a license plate number?" She may've sounded a little smug. "All but the last digit, and after all, there are only ten of those to choose from. How hard can it be?"

* * *

After a fitful night, Frankie arose early, although later than Gabe. He, in possession of the partial license plate number she'd handed him, had been gone for an hour or more, the coffee he'd made cold.

He'd been warm last night, though, with a kiss that'd started out as a thank you peck and ended being something more. She just wasn't sure what, yet. But thinking about him made her nerves tingle.

She packed the dogs into the pickup for a trip out to the Buchanan place. The old homestead, she meant, not the acreage of itself. Banner delighted in riding shotgun his head tilted toward the air rushing past a window rolled halfway down. Shine cuddled next to Frankie, shaking a little. Undoglike behavior in that she disliked riding in a vehicle. Frankie always wondered if the dog had always been this way, or if her fear had developed after the murder of her previous owner. She'd been trying to condition the Bichon into acceptance with short treks and a treat at the end. A run in the country seemed just the thing. Maybe.

She found the roads empty at this time of day except for one motorcyclist, his dark face- shield down. Otherwise, there was only her Ranger to kick up dust on the unpaved road out to the homestead.

It had been several years since Frankie had visited the Buchanan property. Long enough to have almost forgotten where to turn. She drove slowly as she searched for the cattle guard that marked the way across the ditch. The hundred and sixty acres had been handed down from her grandmother's side of the family and retained the original name, as most of the old homesteader properties were known to do.

Like the Berthold place, she thought, smiling a little.

Some nearby fields remained lush with heavy-headed winter wheat still waiting for harvest, although combining wouldn't start until the sun had dried the overnight dew.

She found the cattle crossing, even though there'd been no cattle on the place since the 1970s and turned onto it. Hank had planted bluegrass here and harvested the seed last month. The residue barely covered the earth, although a recent rain had brought a hint of green back to the field.

The old Buchanan house, lonely in its disintegration, sat a couple hills from the main road, then a quarter of a mile down a narrow, beaten path. Any nearby neighbors had long been gone, their homes destroyed by time and neglect. A strip of dead weeds down the middle of the path showed where over a hundred years of wheels had turned the ground rock hard.

But, Frankie observed, while the weeds were dead and dry, showing Hank Kelton had applied herbicide to them weeks ago, during growing season, the tire tracks in the dust revealed more recent traffic than Hank's spray rig mounted on his four-wheeler.

Normally, she carried her pistol in an ankle holster, and kept it hidden beneath her pant leg. Today, with the August temperature hitting the low nineties, she wore shorts and carried the pistol in the small of her back. A bit uncomfortable, but experience told her this would be the norm for as long as the recent weirdness continued. The episode at Ruby's had taught her caution. The sight of vehicle tracks made her glad she'd taken the warning to heart.

"It's a heck of a note," she said to Banner, and when he looked at her, added, "That I need to carry a firearm. Reminds me of my time in Afghanistan. Always gotta be looking over my shoulder and checking a building before I enter."

"Ruff," he said, which started Shine barking also.

They made Frankie laugh.

Merriment that lasted until they drew up in front of the Buchanan house.

"Well," Frankie said, eyeing the place with her hands on the wheel and her foot on the brake. "Shite fire and save matches, as Grandma used to say."

She sat for a good two minutes, motor running, before she stepped out of the truck.

CHAPTER SEVENTEEN

Shiny new hinges supported the door into the house. The door itself was weathered its paint worn completely away. Only one corner of the building held together enough to sport a floor and walls, as Frankie could plainly see even from this distance.

But despite windows without glass and holes in the roof, a closed door barred the way inside.

And padlocked. She didn't fail to notice that.

Banner started to jump down with her, but she stopped him with a hand gesture. "Wait."

Drawing her pistol, she listened with every fiber of her being, every sense on hyper-alert. She heard Banner and Shine panting, and the Ranger's motor ticking as it cooled. The hills around them were empty, showing only the residue left from the grass harvest. Closer, leaves rustled on a small grouping of cottonwood trees and a lilac bush planted long ago at the side of house. The south and westside walls of the structure had fallen in, victims of the sun and prevailing winds, but the lilac had bloomed in the spring. She could see the dried flower heads from here. The acrid, throat-catching smell of dry vegetation and dust rose over all.

The house was the only building still standing, and it only partially. A helter-skelter pile of cracked gray boards showed where a shed had stood. The rough edges of a barn's foundation peeked through the soil. She thought Hank sometimes parked some machinery within the barrier.

There was no good place for anyone to hide except in the house, and every sense told Frankie it was empty. She released Banner and lifted Shine down.

"Let's check this out, shall we?"

Frankie meant more than just the house. A close-up view of the ground showed a vehicle, she surmised a 4-by-4 judging by the size of tires and their aggressive tread marks, had parked on this spot not long ago. Also, a truck with an oil leak. And there, mixed in, a single narrow tread indicating there'd been a motorcycle, too. The one she'd met on the way here flashed in her memory. Too bad she hadn't been paying attention, not that she knew anything about bikes. It could've been any on the market and she couldn't even say which manufacturer, let alone model. Dark purple--almost black--and lots of chrome. Big deal.

Shine kept close to Frankie as she walked toward the house. Banner made his own circuit of the yard, nose to the ground like a hound. Every once in a while he huffed and sneezed, as though something he smelled didn't agree with him.

Frankie didn't blame him. The closer she came to the house, the more the smell grew, a strong odor of chemicals with a vinegary overtone, and she didn't know whether to cuss or to cry.

With her hand on the doorknob, she stopped. Not, perhaps, the best idea to simply burst into the house. While apparently empty, she didn't know for sure. A booby trap didn't seem out of the question. Stepping back, she and the dogs made a circuit around the place.

Several places on the backside of the structure were missing boards, leaving this part of the house open to the elements. What had been a couple bedrooms contained ragged walls held between broken two-by-fours. Warped floorboards rose to trip the unwary, the nails having given way to time and season. Frankie could see through the building to the corner still standing. Someone had reinforced these walls and boarded up the windows, a barrier to prying eyes should any chance to be about.

When satisfied the house was indeed empty, she had no compunction about getting a tire iron from her pickup and prying open the front door lock.

Working together, Banner and Frankie pushed the door open, although it soon snagged on a high spot in the floor. Frankie became aware of an odd bubbling sound from within and frowned, nose wrinkling at the stench of the place.

Shine peered inside, promptly backed away and sat down, adamantly refusing to enter.

"I don't blame you," Frankie whispered, then wondered why she felt a need for quiet. Laying her hand on Banner's head, she spoke aloud. "What about it? You with me?"

He moved forward when she did. Both slipped through the narrow opening. The door opened on to a short hall whose ceiling was open here and there to the elements. Makeshift walls had been formed out of sheets of plywood that appeared to have been rescued from the dump. Old blankets hung from horizontal poles to divide the one remaining room into two parts. On one side, the first she stepped into, she found a table and two chairs. A big battery-powered camp lantern stood on the table along with a ledger, a calculator, and a scale. A box of small zipper bags was open beside it.

Not much mystery about what this set up meant.

The floorboards creaked as she crossed to look behind the curtain.

This had been the kitchen, or part of it, anyway. A pipe through the ceiling marked where the chimney for the kitchen range had been. Two metal tables were arranged under the vent now, in an L-shape. One, from the litter on it, for mixing ingredients. The other was meant for cooking as a propane stove sat in important splendor. The model looked expensive. A pot set on one of the stove burners made the bubbling sound she'd heard. That it'd been left on the stove to cook made her nervous. It indicated the cook wouldn't be gone long.

Frankie remembered the huge cast iron wood stove that had stood here at one time, and briefly wondered what had happened to it. Stolen, she suspected. Or maybe Gran and Grandpa had sold it to a collector. Or maybe whoever had moved in here had.

She found a half-dozen Styrofoam coolers stacked in a corner, metal footlockers beside them. A cot with tumbled blankets, a camp chair, a stool serving as a bedside table were the only other objects of interest. Except, Frankie noted, a magazine featuring a Harley-Davidson motorcycle had been left on the chair. The magazine, pages open, looked as if awaiting its reader to soon return.

"How long do you suppose he'll be gone?"

Banner had no answer, but Frankie thought she knew. Not long enough for Gabe to get here. She'd best hurry.

Activating her phone camera, she clicked away, close-ups and wide-view, immediately messaging the photos to Gabe. He needed to see this. Duplicates went to Rudy.

"At least we haven't found a body," she said, adding, "yet," and Banner said, "Ruff."

From outside, Shine's sudden high-pitched whine signaled trouble. Banner bounded forward, Frankie not far behind.

The guy on the motorcycle was back.

Frankie heard the shift of gears as the bike powered down for the turn across the cattle guard.

"Oh, hell," she said. A vision of dead people floated before her eyes. Two burned corpses, an electrocuted man, another man with his leg destroyed, Ruby Lyons drugged and left to die. Was she about to meet a killer face to face?

She ran for her truck, scooping Shine into her arms on her way out of the house and calling to Banner.

But Banner, for reasons known only to himself, was slow to obey and by the time he scrambled into the truck with Shine beside him, Frankie had lost her chance to climb in and make a getaway. Which, she thought, didn't do her self-confidence a bit of good. Some sheet metal, even sheet metal as thin as a car door, would've made her feel a little better.

She slammed the door shut on the dogs and turned to face the man riding what she recognized now as a purplish-black Harley.

Her hands were damp with sweat. Ditto her back where the 9mm Sig Sauer resided in a behind-the-back holster, too far out of reach for her comfort in this moment.

The Harley, roaring up beside her, spun a brodie and stopped. Dust boiled up around them and she fought the urge to cough. The rider kept the bike running, every once in a while revving the rumbling engine as he faced her. His full-face visor remained down, obscuring his features so Frankie had no notion of what he looked like.

Deliberate intimidation. She knew the ploy.

Even so, she preferred meeting a faceless man rather than some hairy-faced dude in a Nazi skull helmet. Later she might laugh at herself for thinking so, but right now she felt a little dizzy with stress.

"Who the hell are you?" the rider said. "You lookin' to buy?"

She shook her head.

"What are you doin' here, then?" He wore a black leather jacket with steel studs decorating the seams and gold braid epaulets protruding a couple inches beyond the shoulders. Quasi-military. What a laugh. More sobering, a bulge on one side indicated he carried a weapon. No surprise, and not comforting.

Gathering herself, she made her voice firm. "I might ask you the same thing."

"Don't get cute, bitch." He cut the engine, raised the bike onto its stand and dismounted, unzipping his jacket. The butt of an automatic showed under his arm.

It seemed to Frankie as though he made a point of making sure she saw it. Contrary to what she felt were his expectations, his action steadied her nerves. Guns didn't intimidate her. Especially ones ensconced in a secured and snapped holster tucked inside a jacket.

"Cute?" she repeated. "Bitch?"

"Move along, lady. Stick around and you're apt to get hurt." The helmet he wore muffled his voice, but he sounded quite positive of his message.

Frankie wished he'd push the face shield back. She'd like to see the face of the guy threatening her.

"And you're apt to be arrested," she replied, and went on to goad him into rashness. "So, the real bitch is apt to be you doing time in prison."

His arm swung around, but not fast enough. Frankie no longer stood where she'd been a half second earlier. The guy's fist hit slammed into the Ranger's door, which set the two dogs raising such a ruckus the rig shook.

The guy yelped and jumped back as if fearful of the

dogs. Banner did have nice white, and large teeth, Frankie thought with satisfaction, and they showed clearly through the side window. Even Shine's were capable of damage if she got the chance and Banner backed her up.

Apparently, the guy didn't notice Frankie's 9 mm until he shook out his hand and started for her again. Then he went still. "What the . . ."

"What's your name?" Frankie's question rose above his surprised exclamation and the din the dogs made. She didn't expect an answer, and she didn't get one.

"You don't know who you're messing with," he said, and added deliberately, "bitch. But I can tell ya that you're gonna be sorry."

Frankie believed him. No 'gonna be sorry' to it, and in a bit of a quandary, as well. It wasn't as if she could arrest him, after all. Now she had him, she didn't know what to do with him. She'd sent those photos of the meth lab to both Gabe and Rudy and so far, had gotten no reply. God only knows when either man would have a chance to look at the photos or respond to her text when they did. Hard telling where to find either one, Kootenai being a large county. She only knew she couldn't stand here with her gun trained on a man while waiting on one or the other of them. It could take hours. She seemed to be up the creek, for sure.

Only one idea occurred to her. She didn't like it much,

but it was all she had.

"Raise your visor," she said.

He didn't move. "Nope. None of your business, bitch."

Apparently, he'd fallen in love with the sobriquet.

Frankie pasted a smile on her face that felt more like baring her teeth in a snarl. Her point of aim changed only slightly before she squeezed the Sig's trigger. The bullet neatly took the left side epaulet off the expensive black leather jacket he wore.

The way he screamed ,"Holy shit!" pleased her more than the shot.

"I'm not asking," she said. "I'm telling. Raise your visor."

"Crazy damn bitch!"

There he went again, but the shield snapped upward, revealing a visage with a strong resemblance to one she'd seen only yesterday. Weasel-faced, wheat-straw blond hair, and almost colorless gray eyes. If this wasn't Garrity Weddell's brother—of which he had several, provided her imperfect memory served—she'd be surprised.

"You're gonna be sorry as hell," he shouted, "soon as—"

He clamped down on the rest of that so fast he almost bit his tongue off.

What had he meant to say? Had he almost identified a "who"? A murderer?

She didn't dignify his threat with a reply. Instead, she

got her phone from her pocket and, left-handed, an awkward though doable function of the gadget, she snapped his picture. Twice, just to make sure she had it. Then she photographed his bike, making certain to get the license plate in the picture. Made a production of sending them off the Gabe and Rudy, too, making sure the Garrity kid knew where they were going.

Not that he thought to allow this, having turned a little green around the gills. He lunged toward her again, but when he lost the second epaulet off his fancy jacket, he quieted down in a hurry.

"You can go now." Frankie tucked the phone away and made a slight gesture with her automatic as though to ward him off. "I suggest you don't try coming back here. This operation has been shut down—permanently."

He had a measure of bluster left in him. "We'll see about that. I know somebody who ain't going to like it. Ain't gonna take it layin' down, either." Nevertheless, he flung his leg over the bike's saddle and started the bike with an unnecessary roar. He took off, the heavy machine rising slightly on its rear wheel and leaving a rooster tail of dust in its wake.

Frankie, tempted to throw another shot at him before he disappeared over the hill, decided not. She didn't, after all, actually want to hit him. He could be useful if Gabe or the detectives got to him in time.

She kept the Sig in the door pocket on the drive back to town, just in case he lay in wait somewhere along the road. Handy, but out of the way so one of the dogs didn't tromp on it. She hadn't forgotten the way he'd showed off his own gun. Concentrating on looking out for an ambush, she almost forgot to watch the road. A truck driver, barreling along at a fierce rate—time is money, after all—had to lay on his horn before she saw him and steered the Ranger to safety.

The truck driver flipped her a bird just as her phone blipped a signal for an incoming text, one she ignored until she pulled into her driveway. Even then she sat, observing the house and yard, what she could see of it. All seemed well. Better yet, she spotted Mr. Furnough puttering around deadheading flowers and spritzing the blue hydrangeas growing beneath his living room window.

Reassured, Frankie got out, lifted Shine down but let Banner fend for himself.

She waved at her neighbor. "Have you seen anyone at my house?" she called across to him.

He waved the hose in return, water slopping onto the driveway. "Not a soul. Were you expecting someone?"

"Nope. Just checking." Best not to alarm him, she decided. She'd hate for the old boy to confront some ne'er do well and get hurt. Whoever was running the meth lab seemed to have a penchant for harming the elderly. He grinned and continued his watering, and she and the dogs went into the house.

The text was from Gabe. Call me, it said.

Frankie snorted. So, she'd finally claimed his attention, had she? What a surprise.

CHAPTER EIGHTEEN

Blinking as Gabe's voice emerged from the speaker, Frankie held the phone to her ear. He'd put her off for so long that having him answer came as something of a surprise.

"Where did you get these?" he said. No greeting, no small talk, no concern for her well-being. All business.

Well, that suited Frankie just fine. "I suppose you mean the pictures?"

"Yes. Seven of them. I guess you know this is a meth lab. Who sent the photos?"

"Nobody sent them to me, if that's what you're asking. I took them."

"You did?"

"Yes. For you."

"Where?" he snapped.

Was that concern she heard after all?

"Where were they taken, do you mean?"

"Yes." A snap of a reply.

On the other hand, maybe not concern. Maybe anger. "You'll be interested to learn someone has. . . had, I should say . . . taken over what's left of the house on the old Buchanan homestead and transformed it into a meth cooking operation. You may not be aware of this, but I happen to own the property. My grandma was the last of the Buchanans, and Hank Kelton farms the place now. I very much doubt he's involved with the meth lab, by the way. He probably doesn't know much about the drug world."

"Holy—" Gabe cut his words short. "I'm sure he'll appreciate your confidence in him when he finds out you vouched for him." He paused and gave a little cough. "How did you find the lab? Or should I say, what made you go looking? Because that's what you did, isn't it? Went looking? Frankie, you could've been killed. Murdered, like those two out at the Berthold place. Why didn't you call me to go with you? What the hell were you thinking?"

Frankie's temper rose. "What was I thinking? Maybe that I'd satisfy my own curiosity before I said anything to anybody. I had no idea anything was going on out there aside from Hank rightfully farming the land. But I put together what I knew of the Berthold, Ginz, Green, and

Lyons homesteads, and figured they all had something in common. What's more, I knew there was at least one more name I should add to that list. Buchanan. Which means my own. I have a perfect right to go there any time I want. So, I did."

She decided not to mention waiting for him to go with her was apt to take more patience than she had at her disposal.

Gabe didn't say a word for several seconds, although she heard him breathing. Slow seconds, that ticked past in a sort of countdown and made Frankie nervous. Then he said, "Commonality is they're all old homesteads. Some with abandoned buildings, the others with elderly single occupants easily intimidated."

One thing about the county's resident deputy, he caught on fast. "Yes," Frankie said. "And what I discovered calls for action, wouldn't you say?"

"Are you at home now?"

"Yes. Why?"

"I'll be there in about ten minutes." His tone, crisp as a new fall apple and containing a bite, gave nothing away. "You can show me the way out to the farm, and we'll talk then."

Of course he hung up before she could say either yea or nay. But her answer would've been yea.

She spent the next eleven minutes waiting for him

and thinking that although her hands had almost healed, yet another day had passed where she hadn't removed her new paintbrush from the wrapper. Ah, well.

Frankie, sitting on the porch steps with her arm around Banner's neck, rose to greet Gabe. He didn't get out of the Tahoe. Just pushed the passenger door open and gestured with his thumb. "Get in."

Frankie, observing his grim expression, figured dis-obeying a direct order from him might not be wise at this particular moment. She climbed into the SUV, with Banner edging his way in with them.

"I don't suppose you've heard," he said as he backed out onto the road, "but Gerald Green lost his leg early this morning. It's going to be hard on him, an old man. He'll have to go into a nursing home."

Frankie, in the middle of clicking the latch of her seatbelt home, froze. "That's sad. Permanently?"

"Yes. So they say. If he survives at all. He's not in good shape. Another deputy was talking to a nurse who said he's been fretting, too. Seems he's worried about some-body named Elmer. Any idea who that might be?"

Voice soft, Frankie said, "Elmer is his dog. Can you, or someone, let him know Marc has the old fellow and is taking good care of him?"

A smile twitched Gabe's mouth. "I will." To prove it, he connected his phone and asked to speak with the nurse taking care of Green. She seemed happy to have the news to pass on. Or maybe, since she sounded young, she was just happy to hear from Gabe. He'd actually told her hello. And goodbye.

"Since Mister Green is able to talk, has he identified who shot him?" Frankie asked.

"No. He has no idea. He's still pretty out of it. Keeps talking about demons and angels."

"He said something like that to Marc and me, too. I just thought he was looking death in the eye." Frankie shook her head, although he may not have seen the motion as he watched an old pickup tootling slowly along ahead of them raising a blinding curl of dust whenever he strayed off the pavement. Her next thought left her gasping. "In fact, I imagine whoever shot him thinks they killed him. So, what about Ruby? What if her attacker comes looking for her with the intention of finishing the job? Should she have a guard?"

"Already taken care of. You're not the only one to think Ruby might still be in danger. The sheriff will put a deputy at her door as soon as she gets out of ICU and into a room of her own."

Properly squelched, Frankie directed Gabe to the Buchanan property. Even from a distance she could see things had changed in the ninety minutes she'd been gone. The door hung open, for one thing, the padlock missing. For another, a pile of straw and small sticks had been set beneath the door and set on fire. God only knows why the house hadn't gone up in a flash. An errant breeze, perhaps, had blown the tinder apart and out before it could catch. When they entered the room, they found the makeshift walls had been taken down, the 4-by-8 sheets of plywood hauled off. Ditto the boards across the windows, although in both cases fresh nail holes showed light-colored against the old dark wood.

All the drug lab equipment had been carried away, as well. The tables, the camp stoves, the coolers—all gone. Also, the cot and camping stuff. All that remained was the stench of meth and, dropped in a dark corner, the magazine featuring the tricked-out Harley Davidson.

Gabe surveyed the room. "I'll see if I can get a lab tech down here. Try to get some fingerprints or DNA off the magazine, for starters. Evidence of some kind, anyway. Hopefully, before these guys succeed in burning the place down. Funny they didn't wait to make sure the fire caught."

Standing in the doorway where Gabe had told her to stay, Frankie had an answer for that. "I think I know why. One of the photos I took was of tire tracks."

"I remember," Gabe said.

"Yeah, well, they're gone now. I think whoever carted everything off, used a leaf blower to destroy the tracks.

Must've accidentally blown the fire out, too. It's still hot, you know. I expect they knew we'd soon be on our way and had to clear out fast."

Gabe swore. "Fire seems to be their favorite disposal method. I'll be checking into the local resident's crime records, see if there's an arsonist in the bunch."

"Including the Strohmeyers?"

"Damn straight," he said.

"There's another name you might be interested in," Frankie said.

Arms folded across his chest, he stared at her. "There is? What?"

"Weddell."

"Weddell? No first name?"

She shrugged. "If I ever knew this one, I've forgotten." Thank the shrapnel that'd bounced off her head for that, she thought bitterly. "There's a bunch of them. As a family, their reputation is somewhat lacking."

"Yeah. I've made the acquaintance of a few of them. You sure?"

"You have his photo. I'm going by family resemblance. Can't mistake it."

"That's who the guy is? I thought maybe you and him are dating."

She laughed. "Um, I don't think he likes me that much."

He grinned, his tired face lighting up. "Oh, I believe that. You've given me—and the detectives—a place to start looking. Thanks, Frankie . . . only . . . "

Finally, some of the concern Frankie thought had been lacking showed itself.

"Only don't do anything as reckless again, hear me?" His grin faded, only to be replaced by a scowl. "These people are dangerous. You know that maybe better than anyone. Also, you've been first on the scene with every incident. Stop taking chances. Like today. What were you thinking, facing this guy down by yourself?"

"I—" she started, but he cut her off before she could offer the excuse that, at the time, she'd been so angry about a drug gang taking over her property that she hadn't given her own safety that much thought. Or, maybe she had, at first, but cornered by the Weddell kid, she hadn't really had a choice.

"Uh-uh. Don't want to hear it." Gabe waved his arms at her, shooing her toward the Tahoe.

Feeling a little disgruntled, she got in. Gabe called Armbuster before he started the truck, updating him on the latest developments. His face flushed once, although his voice held steady. Frankie would've paid a dollar or five to have heard what the detective said. Obviously, it had ruffled Gabe's feathers.

Finally, they got underway.

"It'd be best if you keep a low profile until we get this cleared up," he said, his gaze sweeping the countryside. His caution made Frankie a little nervous.

"I can't just hide in my room, you know. I have a job to do." She eyed him coolly.

Glancing over at her as they hit the main road, he grimaced. "I know you do. But you don't need to go looking for trouble, either. It seems to find you well enough by itself."

Frankie didn't think she'd bother denying what sounded like an accusation. Trouble had been following her since she'd gotten back to Hawkesford.

"I'm not some senior citizen living by myself in the boondocks," she reminded him. "I don't think I need to worry too much."

"I hope you're right. But watch your back, Frankie." In what seemed like an afterthought, he added, "And your partner's, too."

Remembering what had happened to Marc a couple months ago on one of their runs, she agreed wholeheartedly with at least part of his advice.

At home, Gabe drove right up to the doorstep before letting her off. Shine exploded from the doggie door to greet her, her happy welcome an indication nobody had invaded the house while they were gone. Frankie didn't know she'd been worried until then.

* * *

An idea occurred to Frankie, one she set in motion the moment she stepped into the house. Her imperfect memory might not be able to dredge the motorcycle rider's name out of her sometimes-cloudy mind, but she knew of something that might provide a clue. As long as her Grandma hadn't tossed out all the mementoes of Frankie's high school days, at least, and since Grandma kept most everything, she doubted it. She knew just where to look, too.

Grateful she had the day off, she went upstairs and got a chair from her bedroom, positioning it under a hatch in the hallway ceiling. Standing on the chair, she reached up to pull down a folded stairway. The stairs took her to the attic. Shuddering a little at the old-smelling, dark, dusty, and spiderweb-strewn room, she lifted herself through the opening.

Not only dark, the attic was hotter than Hades. A ceiling vent fan flapped away, but it didn't do much to dissipate the heat. Lips twitching wryly, Frankie couldn't help thinking of all the novels she'd read where children just loved to play in old attics, where they never failed to find treasure.

She'd never been one of those children. She hated the closed-in space and always thought of it as a prison. But she did hope to find treasure.

Waving her hands over her head, it took a moment to find the string that, when pulled, activated the very old light fixture set in the center of the ceiling. Fortunately, after Gramps had insulated the roof ceiling with thick, and reflective, fiberglass batting, the single bulb made it just possible to see.

Right away, she found the objects of her search. A stickler for order, her grandmother had filed Frankie's high school yearbooks in a rickety bookcase. They might even have been one of the last things to be stored there, as Grandma McGill had gotten very frail soon after Frankie left Hawkesford for the army.

A few minutes later, thumbing through the first book, she struck pay dirt.

When she had graduated from eighth grade and gone on to high school, Garrity Weddell had already been two years behind her. She found him easily in the grade school section of her freshman yearbook, there being only seven boys in his class. She found the girl she'd seen with him, too. At least she thought so, as another blonde girl who might've been a twin of the first was in the same class. Glancing through the upperclassmen, she found a senior who drew her eye. Another of the family, but one she blanked on, not knowing him at all.

"Huh," she said. In the hall below, Banner, who waited

patiently for her return, made a little huff.

Frankie went on to the yearbook from her senior year.

Poor Garrity, he remained in the freshman class. The girl appeared in the sophomore section. The senior must've graduated. Or quit. New to that year's senior class Frankie spotted a face she'd never seen before. Not until yesterday when it had showed up at Frankie's door.

Gathering the four yearbooks of her high school days, Frankie clambered down the ladder to the second floor. She missed a rung with her toe, which almost tumbled her to the bottom. Dropping the books—which sent Banner yelping to the end of the hall where he sat and stared reproachfully at her—she hung on to the ladder with one hand. A splinter stabbing her hand, she managed to swing herself back onto the rung.

"Damn foot," she yelled.

Banner huffed.

"Yeah? You try it when you've got no toes. I dare you."

He barked and trotted over to sniff the spilled yearbooks. Sturdy publications, they seemed unharmed by the drop.

Once safely downstairs and seated at the kitchen table with the yearbooks piled in front of her, Frankie cracked open a bottle of hard apple cider and prepared to study. But first she pressed the contact button on her phone to summon Jesselyn. Jesse knew everybody and kept track of their whereabouts. She was, Frankie thought, grinning to herself, a genuine Maggie in the making.

She considered Jesselyn slightly more likely to keep Frankie's questions to herself, however. Ask Maggie, and inside an hour the dispatcher would have it spread all over town.

"Hey." Jesselyn answered on the third ring. "What's up?"

"Can you stop by after work? I need to pick your brain, if you don't mind."

Jesselyn laughed. "Hah! Frankie McGill is asking for help? Shock of the century. Whatcha need?"

"Tell you when you get here. I have hard cider."

"Nice bribe. I'll be there."

"See ya." Smiling, Frankie disconnected and went back to studying the yearbooks, pausing now and then to read messages scrawled across friends' photos. No messages, she noted, written by any of the people she studied, though. Not surprising, really. They'd been—and from the looks of things, still were—a clan, not just a family.

A new avenue to investigate had no more than crossed her mind than her phone chimed. Gabe again.

"I thought you'd want to know," he said, as usual omitting any salutation. "The bodies from the Berthold place have been identified."

CHAPTER NINETEEN

The memory of those charred bodies at the Berthold place hovered non-stop in Frankie's brain. The one lying in the grass hadn't been so bad. The one in the old house, twisted into a contorted mass, kept her from sleeping at night.

"Who were they?" she asked, hoping she wouldn't know them.

"Both from California," she heard Gabe saying. Apparently, she'd zoned out for a few seconds.

Aware of a headache building, she said, "Repeat their names for me, please?"

"The man outside the house is Vern Biggers. The one in the house is Cassidy Ellsworth. Ever heard of them?"

She, not surprisingly, drew a blank. "No," she said slowly. "I don't think so." And yet, didn't something waver like a faded shadow in the background of her cluttered mind? She'd have to think harder.

"A missing person report came in this afternoon and we matched them up." Gabe was still speaking. "We're still trying to discover what they were doing in Hawkesford. Neither has a prison record, although Santa Barbara police arrested Biggers once for selling a little pot. But no felonies or connections to a larger drug trade that we've discovered."

"Except they must somehow have crossed somebody," Frankie said.

"You think? And I intend to find out who, if Armbuster and Rimmel don't beat me to it." Gabe hung up.

Frankie, who distrusted the detectives' investigative skills, knew who she'd bet her money on.

* * *

"Do you know somebody named Vern Biggers? Or Cassidy Ellsworth?" Frankie posed the question to Jesselyn as they sat at her kitchen table. Like any good hostess, she'd poured Jesselyn's cider into a frosted mug and had it waiting for her upon arrival. The yearbooks were spread on the table, open to the appropriate pages. Banner and Shine, having been allotted their due attention, happily munched doggie biscuits on the hand-braided rug in front of the kitchen sink.

Jesselyn took a first swallow of cider before she answered Frankie's question. "Nope. I don't think so. Why?"

"Well, have you ever heard of them?"

"No again. Not that I recall, anyway. Who are they? And why do you ask?"

That information wasn't common knowledge as yet. Frankie doubted Gabe would approve, but she said, "They're the two dead people found at the Berthold place."

"Oh, good. Or not 'good', I guess. I mean . . . " Jesselyn fidgeted. ". . . I'm glad the cops were able to finally identify them and give them back their names."

"Me too. And I guess I'm glad they were strangers. I'd hate for neighbors to end up like that."

"I hate for anybody."

"Here's something easier." Bent over the first yearbook, Frankie tapped her finger on one of the photos.

After a quick look, Jesselyn shrugged. "Yeah. Garrity Weddell. What about him?"

"Tell you in a minute." Frankie turned the page and indicated another photo. "How about her?"

Wrinkling her nose, Jesselyn flicked her fingers on the yearbook page. "Juanita Ennis. She doesn't look like this now, though. I can't remember if she and Garrity are cousins or just next-door neighbors—next-door meaning a half mile down the road. She was real cute until she got bulimia or anorexia or something. Anyway, as you can see, she used to be . . . plump." Jesselyn sighed. "Now she's rail-thin."

Frankie had an idea how Juanita might have gone from plump to skinny aside from either anorexia or strictly dieting. Having no desire to start rumors when she had no proof, she refrained from mentioning her suspicions to Jesselyn.

She turned the yearbook pages forward. "Did you know this one? I don't remember her at all."

Frowning, Jesselyn studied the photo. "Another Weddell relative, I think. Or connected somehow." She brightened. "Oh, wait. I remember now. You don't know her because you were taking that three-month course in Boise during our senior year."

Frankie knew it was a bit of a sore point with Jesselyn that Frankie had gotten a chance to take preliminary medical training before graduating high school and going into the service.

"As I recall, her mother either married or lived with old man Weddell for a while," Jesselyn continued. "This girl didn't graduate from Hawkesford. She usually lived with her dad and only attended school here for about six weeks. Just enough time to get her picture in the yearbook, I guess. Then she went back to her dad. Umm, I heard somewhere—from Victoria, probably—she became a real estate broker."

Frankie tensed. "Around here?" It occurred to her that everywhere she turned lately, she heard about real estate.

"Don't know. I imagine, or I doubt Vic would know about her."

While Jesselyn finished her cider, Frankie hunted up one more page in the last yearbook. "How about this one? Any clue?" she asked, pointing to a youngster with guileless eyes and too-long hair. She'd covered the name before showing it to Jesselyn.

"Oh, c'mon, Frankie. Is this a test? Why do you even want to know?"

"It is a test. I'm not going to tell you why. I want you to verify without prejudice."

Jesselyn's eyes rounded. "Verify without prejudice? Are you kidding me?" But at Frankie's shake of the head, she said, "Okay then. It has to be one of Garrity's little brothers. I can't tell you exactly which one because he has several, but I see this one riding around on his motorcycle pretty often. He's obnoxious, by the way. Much worse than Garrity ever thought of being."

The information gave Frankie something to ponder. Connection upon connection, but did any of it make sense? What would Gabe say when she told him?

A lot, actually, even though she knew he appreciated having at least one mystery cleared.

* * *

Two days later, about an hour before she was due on shift, Frankie had a visitor. The peal of the repaired doorbell—and what genie had done that?—brought her plunging down the stairs careless of her wonky foot. Pressing her eye to the peephole in the door brought Mick Boyd into focus. He stood square outside holding one of her own rose blossoms and grinning.

Frankie opened up. "Did you come to pick my flowers?"

Taking a big sniff of the huge pink bloom, Mick sneezed and handed it over, his eyes twinkling. "For you."

"Gee, thanks." The rose was a Tiffany, highly scented and one of Frankie's favorites. She couldn't help smiling. "To what do I owe the honor?"

Standing straighter, Mick blotted a dab of blood onto his jeans from a thorn prick on his thumb. "Yeah, well, something kind of happened this morning. I thought maybe Gabe ought to know and that maybe you could tell him."

"Me? Why don't you?"

Mick mumbled something about Gabe being a hard man to catch up with, whereupon Frankie pantomimed holding a phone to her ear. Oddly enough, as if to foil them both, Gabe chose that moment to pull into the driveway.

After a moment, he got out and started toward them, eyeing the rose in Frankie's hand as he came. A large wet stain covered the front of his shirt and a powerful odor accompanied him as he neared.

"Gross," Frankie said, wincing in sympathy and sticking her nose into the bloom. "Somebody puked on you."

"Twice." Gabe sounded grim. "Thereby fouling both the shirt I started shift in, and the spare I carry in the truck. I am not," he said, as if she'd accused him of slacking, "about to go around smelling like this. I'd rather not offend the public to that degree."

"Brother, I don't blame you," Mick said. "You stink."

"If you'll excuse me, I need a shower." Gabe, glaring, made to push past them.

Mick held up his hand like a school crossing guard. "Yeah, well, if you can wait just a minute more, I got something I think you should know."

Impatience seeped into Gabe's voice. "What?"

But before Mick started his spiel, Frankie, noticing that not only Mr. Furnough, but the neighbor on the other side of her were interested bystanders. Waving to the old man, she urged them into the house.

"What is it?" Gabe repeated once they were inside. Plucking at the wet shirt, he made a wry face.

"You probably know I'm the main insurance adjuster roundabouts for Lee Daniels' First Harvest Insurance

Company." Mick waited for Gabe's nod. "I was out at Ruby Lyon's place this morning, not . . ." He looked at Frankie to include her in his report, ". . . that there's any doubt what happened, but to verify the report for the insurance pay out. I's dotted and T's crossed, ya know?" Shrugging, he added, "And to make an estimate about how much the repairs might cost, or if it's even possible to make repairs."

"Isn't that a conflict of interest?" Gabe's left eyebrow cocked.

Jaw jutting pugnaciously, Mick's voice rose a decibel or two, "I don't know. Is it? You're the lawman, you tell me. Might be if I wasn't honest, which I am. Haven't had any complaints yet."

"Are repairs possible?" Frankie hurried to ask.

"Hell, yeah. Although I've gotta say it won't be cheap tying into hundred-year-old construction. Lumber dimensions are different nowadays."

Gabe cleared his throat. A hint urging Mick to get to the point.

Glad of the rose, Frankie held it up to take a sustaining whiff.

"Yeah, yeah, I'm there," Mick said. "To the part about finding a girl . . . a woman . . . who'd taken up residence in the unburned part of the place."

"What?" Frankie and Gabe's voices formed a chorus.

Mick chuffed a half-laugh and sat on the arm of the couch. "Yeah. Thought that would interest you."

"What, precisely, do you mean by 'taken up residence'?" Cursing as he realized he'd left his phone in the Tahoe, Gabe fumbled out his little notebook and pencil stub, fortunately stowed in the pocket opposite the vomit.

Frankie, more practical, set the recorder on her phone going in time to catch Mick's explanation. She could always transfer the info to Gabe later.

"I mean somebody—I doubt it was her—had set up a generator. She had the refrigerator running and hot water. And the stove." Absently, he rubbed his thorn-wounded thumb on the seam of his pants, pausing as though to think before he said, "The outside of the place looked as if it hadn't been touched since the fire. From the front, anyway. Plants dead and trampled. The porch dirty, the corner by the bedroom charred, the roof on the back half gone. Looking in from the road, you'd believe the place empty. But I smelled food cooking as I walked up to the front door, still locked up tight, just as it should be. Even so, close up I could see where people had been going in and out. So, I went around back."

"And?" Gabe waited through Mick's pause.

Mick snorted, smiling in a snarky kind of way. "I got around back just as this bean pole bleached blonde was closing the door. Think she intended on hiding out and pretending the place was locked up and deserted, but I got there in time to stick my boot in the crack. She didn't like it. Tried screaming at me. Said she had permission to live there, which of course, I knew for a lie. She waved her phone around and told me she was calling 911, so I told her to go ahead. If she didn't, I would." A full grin spread. "Turns out neither of us did. I told her she'd better clear out, but short of manhandling her, I didn't want to force the issue. She refused to tell me her name. Refused loud and clear. The thought struck me it might be better if you saw her yourself."

Frankie could see his point. It was entirely too easy in the #MeToo climate to make accusations that damaged reputations. Unjustified accusations, she meant, not the real ones and God knows there were plenty of them floating around.

"Even if she's a relative, she's got no business going in or camping out in a house declared unsafe. Isn't the police caution tape still up?" Bent over his little notebook, Gabe made notations as fast as he could write.

"Yes, not that it matters," Mick said. "Doesn't take a genius to know she was lying about being a relative. My family has lived around Hawkesford as long as Ruby's. I know the old gal doesn't have any relatives. Not anywhere. Last time I did some work for her she told me the line ended when she did."

"She told Lew and me that too, the other night," Frankie said.

"All right." Already starting to strip his shirt, Gabe stayed long enough to thank Mick and to put in a call to Rudy Swallowtail for back up. After the world's quickest shower, so short Frankie and Mick were still chatting over the rose blossom when he emerged wearing a clean shirt, he headed toward Ruby's farm, wheels spinning a little as he dug out when the tires met the gravel.

That he would be too late to catch the woman seemed a foregone conclusion.

A tall, skinny bleached blonde, Frankie thought. The description had begun to sound too darn familiar.

"You'd better watch your back," she told Mick. "Seems to me every time I hear about a strange blonde woman, somebody gets hurt."

Or dead.

* * *

Frankie peered cautiously through the peephole before opening the front door. She found the porch clear. Citing caution as her new favorite word, she also listened, senses on alert, before actually stepping outside. And then laughed—or maybe scoffed—at herself when she discovered the odd and remarkably suspicious sound she'd heard came from next door. She spotted Mr. Furnough hard at work using a sprayer rig attached to the end of his hose to wash his house. Not a power-washer, she noted. One of those would probably take all the paint off the old siding, as his house was almost as old as her grandparents' and even less recently painted.

"Lord help me," she muttered, thoroughly disgusted with herself. "I've turned into a Nervous Nellie."

Frankie figured it safe to go outside since the old man seemed unbothered. With Banner and Shine gamboling alongside her, she knew the little walk to the corner mailbox would do them all good. She couldn't allow the Weddell kid's implied threat to buffalo her. Couldn't? Make that wouldn't. Just as well since nothing happened along the way. Divided between her and Gabe, she found a bundle of mail had piled up, some of which needed attention. Susie Ray, the carrier, must've worked overtime to stuff it all in the mailbox.

On the way back, they all stopped to provide some sidewalk supervision to Mr. Furnough, the dogs tramping through the puddles he'd made. The old man actually seemed glad of the break.

"I talked to that boy, Mick, about fixing up my porch," he announced. "He's going to give me an estimate."

"Mick does good work. You won't be sorry," she said, smiling. That boy?

Idly wondering what Mick would think of being called a boy, once back inside the house Frankie glanced through the mail. Aside from Gabe's, which she placed in a separate pile, she'd received a full dozen adverts, two offers for new credit cards plus a hefty statement on the card she used, and a notification saying her pickup license needed renewal. Two personal-looking envelopes drew her focused attention.

Both gave her a chill.

Envelope one looked to have been one included in an advertisement of some sort and reused to send her a message. Not a pleasant message. A threatening one. Stay out of the way and mind your own business if you know what's good for you. Straight out of a book—or more likely, the movies. At least, that's what she thought it said. The childish scrawl was almost unintelligible, the word business misspelled. Although the envelope lacked a return address or a signature, she had a pretty good guess who'd mailed it.

The bigger chill came from envelope number two. At first glance, the return address, embossed in rich black and gold foil on high quality paper, should've been reassuring. Only the good guys guard their reputation with ritzy mailings. Right? And this seemed very official.

Even the heading on the letter itself, the form, the stylized signature, struck her as business-like and professional. The letter was from a real estate broker, a certain Eric Benedict. Unwelcome and unasked for in the first place, the offer to purchase the Buchanan place had a sort of "or else" tone to it. Even the request to meet with her seemed more of a demand. He said he'd drop by one day soon to discuss the deal.

But what really struck a chord was the memory of Ruby's complaint about an overbearing, over-persistent real estate broker who kept pestering her to sell. And a man in a red sports car driving away and leaving the old lady to die.

CHAPTER TWENTY

For Frankie and Marc, back at work after their days off, night shift took a peculiar turn. The first half, until around eight, kept them busy at an automobile accident out on HWY-95. Both the driver and his passenger, a man and wife, suffered serious injuries requiring transport to the medical center in Coeur d'Alene. The man, barely conscious kept calling a name. Or two names. Hattie and Belle. Marc thought the words ran together. Frankie seemed to detect a slight pause between the two. Not that either meant anything. She supposed they might belong to someone he wanted to notify. If so, they were out of luck until better information showed up.

The state policeman on the scene called Cunningham's wrecker to deal with the car. Rob Cunningham, Johnny-on-the-spot, had already hoisted the crumpled twenty-year-old two-door coupe out of a gully near

Setters when she heard a faint sound coming from the wreck.

Frankie, about to close the ambulance door in preparation to transport the couple, cocked her head, the side without the titanium plate, in the car's direction. "Do you hear that?" she asked Marc as he started to climb into the driver's seat. "It sounds like an animal." She gasped. "Or a baby!"

The state police officer had released the scene by then, allowing removal of the car and clearance of the debris. A little previous, as it happened.

Marc, sort of like a hunting dog taking scent, listened, then turned toward the car where Cunningham, his winch hooked to the car's back bumper, prepared to yank it onto his flatbed.

"Straight to the junkyard," Cunningham had said. "This heap of scrap metal will never see the road again."

Marc's eyes opened wide and he ran toward the tow truck. "Stop," he yelled at Cunningham, who had his thumb on the button to start the winch running again.

Cunningham put his hand alongside his ear, the better to hear. "What?"

"Stop that damn winch." Without waiting for the car to quit moving, Marc stuck his head through the driver's side door opening. They'd had to remove the actual door before extricating both victims as the passenger door had been thoroughly crushed to the floorboards.

Marc bent nearly double as he groped around where the back seat had flipped forward. After a moment, he resurfaced. "There's a baby in here," he yelled.

Frankie figured they could all hear that for themselves although the mewling sounds were growing weaker. Three patients were too many for one crew. She called Lew and Chris for a second ambulance a delay that soon turned critical.

But the Hawkesford crew knew their stuff. In the end, everyone made it to the medical center alive. A job well done, although, for curiosity's sake, she would've liked to know if the baby was Hattie or Belle.

After the pulse-pounding start to the night, she and Marc hoped for a quiet second half of their shift. Dealing with an entire family, two of them in serious condition, sapped even a war-hardened veteran paramedic, let alone someone like Marc, barely back from his own sick leave. Regardless, their longed for relaxation period didn't happen.

Marc had no more than backed the ambulance into its spot at the station and the pair of them made it as far as the break room than the dispatch board lit up.

Benton, their dispatcher of the night, lifted a finger in an arresting motion as first he listened, then he spoke.

Wearily, Frankie halted, thinking that a call at this

time of the evening never just needed a simple question answered. Soon proved right, only moments later, directions for their next run came through. A fourteen-year-old girl, suspected drug overdose, out on one of the most rural roads.

"Crap," she said as Benton recited the details.

And Marc, generally the most laidback person in the department, cussed a blue streak. "Could give a guy a chance to take a pee."

Frankie, agreeing, smothered a laugh.

The last laugh of the night, as it happened, as the call landed them in a situation with potential to turn dicey. Dangerous even, for Frankie, at least, the way she'd been making enemies left and right lately.

At first, she didn't recognize the place. The GPS directed them concisely sans names. But when they followed a rutted dirt driveway that led to a sprawling, ill-kempt house, there was no mistaking who lived there. Revealed by a mercury light on a tall post overhead, rusted cars and trucks, abandoned machinery, trees still standing though many years dead, all were enough for any local to make a guess as to the occupants. The house sported a couple broken windows mended with silver duct tape, peeling paint, and a crumbling, unsafe chimney. It didn't really take the black-cherry colored Harley parked on its stand next to the porch to tell her.

"Well, this sucks." Frankie made the observation without thinking.

Marc pulled to a stop only a couple feet from the bike. "What does?"

"I had a little run-in with the guy who rides that Harley the other day." Even after unbuckling her seat belt, Frankie made no move toward the door handle as she looked across the cab at Marc. "If this is a trap, if somebody in there takes a shot at me, you run like hell."

Eyes rolling like those of a panicked horse, Marc gaped at her. "Shot at? Are you serious?"

"I am."

"What about the patient?"

"Forget her. If there is even a patient."

But their job demanded they treat the situation as a genuine emergency, no matter what so, revving up her courage, Frankie alighted from the truck, got their equipment out of the bin, and started for the open front door.

Turns out they had a patient, all right.

People talking inside the house covered the sound of their approach as someone, a woman, cried loudly. A man shouted for her to shut up, that help had arrived. Someone inside had been on the lookout and spotted them. His statement had no noticeable effect on the crier, although the other people quieted.

Frankie, first through the door, glanced around. She immediately spotted Garrity Weddell and, glaring malevolently at her, his younger brother. Her eyes slid away from his. She caught a glimpse of a woman with bleached blonde hair, too, the one who'd accompanied Garrity at the station the day he'd bought the last fire extinguisher. Another blonde stood in the doorway to the kitchen. One who quickly turned away as they entered. Frankie's eye caught on an old man, shriveled and dry looking, hunched in a torn and stained La-Z-Boy recliner. Franklin Weddell, the head of the clan, himself, withered in the years she'd been gone.

"She's up here," a woman, not the crier, called from overhead. "And move your ass."

Marc, meeting Frankie's eyes, thumped the gurney over the warped threshold and followed her in. She could tell he was nervous, walking into a scene like a something out of a horror movie. His uneven breathing told her as much. But give him his due, he never faltered.

They went up a steep and narrow open stairway with most of the handrail missing. Frankie figured that in the past the stairs had been enclosed as in most of these old farmhouses, but one of the Weddells must, at some time or another, been stricken by a home improvement bug. Too bad his—or her—endeavors hadn't paid off. Or, she decided, as she reached the top where the woman awaited them, maybe someone had just got knocked through the wall and this was their fix-it solution.

"She's in here." The woman's voice shook. "I found her like this. I don't know what's wrong with her."

Frankie pushed past her and knelt beside the dark-haired girl who lay on her back on the floor. "How long ago?"

"How long ago what?"

"How long ago did she take the drugs? How long ago did you find her?" Frankie got the girl turned onto her side in the rescue position, but only briefly as the fragile looking girl flung herself onto her back again. Her skin, hot to the touch, felt ready to scorch.

The woman shrugged. "An hour maybe, I thought she'd snap out of it, but I think she's worse."

No kidding! Anger leapt although Frankie tried to keep it off her face. "Are you her mother?"

"Stepmother," the woman said. "I'm not old enough to be her mother."

Could've fooled me, Frankie thought but refrained from saying aloud. "Well, stepmom, can you get me a cold wet towel? A big one. Or two. Two would be better."

"Wet towels?"

"Yes, please, cold ones. She's running a high temperature. We need to cool her down."

The stepmother trod off downstairs. Frankie supposed this old house had never been updated with up-stairs plumbing.

Marc, also kneeling at the girl's side, opened the bag and got out the blood pressure cuff, wrapping it around the girl's thin arm. Not an easy task as the girl was flopping in circles like a fish on a riverbank. Sweat poured from her and she'd wet herself. Vomit dribbled from her mouth. She struck out at Marc as he tried to get a reading.

Frankie grabbed onto the girl, striving to hold her still long enough for Marc to take vitals. "Look at me," she told her. "What's your name?"

The girl mumbled something, brown eyes glinting through slitted lids.

"Amanda?" Frankie repeated. "What did you take, Amanda? Meth? Oxy? Heroin? How much?"

The girl had lost too much coherence to reply as her body wracked into a sudden shivering fit. Frankie figured she knew anyway. She had no doubt the fourteen-year-old had been sampling the family wares and the symptoms bore the diagnosis out.

"Pulse is irregular," Marc said. "Temp is one oh five point six." Procuring the rest of the vitals proved to be an ordeal. The girl gasped for air with every shallow breath.

The woman, returning with a couple threadbare towels she'd soaked in cold water, was just in time to catch her daughter—stepdaughter—that is, as the girl broke into a seizure and lost consciousness.

"Can't you give her some Narcol or whatever that stuff is?" Stepmom stood over them with her arms folded across her chest.

"I think you mean Narcan. Unfortunately, it's the counter drug for heroin derivatives, not meth." Frankie wrapped the girl in the towels as Amanda's breathing slowed further and turned her on her side yet again.

"Frankie," Marc said, touching her arm. A warning.

"I see it. I'm going to intubate her," she told him. "Looks she aspirated vomit. Prepare an IV, Marc. Let's get some anti-seizure meds in her while she's unconscious."

Not that she thought anything they did would do any good. She had a horrible fear the family had waited too long to call for help. From the look on Marc's face, he thought so too.

Turns out they were both right. Amanda simply quit breathing, dying as they turned into the hospital emergency entrance, although Frankie kept chest compressions going until medical center personnel took over and told her to stop.

Stepmom, who'd been selected to accompany them, shed nary a tear and Frankie never did hear who'd been weeping when they drove up. Only the cycle-riding brother, who swooped into the lot behind the ambulance seemed concerned enough to follow the ambulance.

And perhaps, Frankie thought when she caught him looking at her, his concern wasn't for Amanda, whether sister, cousin, or whatever, but for the opportunity to make the universal gesture of pointing two fingers at his eyes, then at her. From his expression, there was no mistaking the signs as anything but a threat.

"Gonna have to watch out for him, Frankie," Marc, as observant as ever, had seen Weddell's show. He checked the meds bin lock after replenishing their supply. "I don't like the way he's looking at you. What's his beef, anyway? You did everything you could for that girl. We both did."

Frankie's breath huffed out. "It's not about the girl. He and I, well, we had a major confrontation the other day." Even though she tried to shrug it off, she couldn't help being disturbed. The pocket revolver in her ankle holster made a reassuring weight. She didn't tell Marc she was going armed again since he was already jumpy as a grasshopper. But then, who could blame him after getting shot while on duty with her? It'd been her fault, or so her conscience told her. Marc himself had never mentioned blame.

Back at the station, her partner, his attitude subdued because of the girl's death, dropped into a chair as though exhausted. While Amanda may not have been his first teenaged overdose victim, she was his first fatal incident.

Patting him on the shoulder, Frankie sank onto a chair, too. Her foot hurt. Or no, her prosthesis hurt her foot.

Benton spun his chair to face them, a question on his lips when, once again, the board lit up. Once, then, immediately, again. Victims here in town, next-door neighbors, frantic parents and in the background, moaning, combative voices. "Help!"

Rising, Frankie nudged her partner, "We're on. You ready for this?"

Marc groaned. "It's a damn epidemic."

"I hope not." She headed for the ambulance. "Saddle up, partner."

They ran silent through the dark, empty streets. No need to disturb the neighbors. No need to clue the neighbors in to the Parker's and the Hamilton's business, either. Halfway there, Frankie, who'd been thinking, keyed the mic to talk to Benton.

He answered immediately. "Are you there already? What do you need?"

"Call Gabe, please" she said. "Ask him to meet us at the scene. Tell him we've had three victims so far tonight. Tell him he needs to find whoever supplied these kids and maybe he can get one of these boys to talk. One girl already died. From the way things are going, there's apt to be more."

"Gotcha," Benton came back. Seconds later, she heard

his call to Gabe.

A couple blocks later, they pulled up outside the first house. Convenient, she guessed, to be next-door to the second victim. She and Marc, they were getting to be a well-oiled team. They could handle this.

"What do you mean about the supplier, Frankie?" Marc, frowning, looked across at her as he prepared to take the Parker boy in charge by himself. "We know the Weddells are making their own stuff don't we? Don't you think the crap that killed the girl came from her own family?"

"Maybe. Maybe not. I heard the old man say something while we were passing through the living room. Pretty sure he said, 'It ain't our fault. Amanda ain't allowed. Not at her age.' And I'm already pretty sure there's a second player here. Maybe even three. Or more."

His eyes opened wide. "Three? Gawd, Frankie, say it isn't so!"

"Possible, I'm afraid." The Weddells, the man who'd tried to kill Ruby, and as the third possibility, the Strohmeyers. She counted them off to herself.

And Frankie, knowing herself a distinct target, couldn't help thinking of the difficulties of protecting yourself when you didn't know who you were up against. All three of them?

She needed help.

CHAPTER TWENTY-ONE

Gabe, wearing a serious frown on his face, stopped first at the Hamilton's house just as Frankie and Marc were loading the boys into the ambulance. Both kids, in Frankie's opinion, were lucky to have people wise enough to call for help. Neither, while still having bad reactions, had deteriorated to anywhere near the condition they'd found Amanda Weddell in.

"You may not have heard yet." Frankie caught Gabe's arm and pulled him aside before he spoke to the parents. "We had a fatal overdose tonight. Crystal meth, same kind of stuff as these boys, I imagine, only her people didn't get help in time to save her."

Gabe blanched. "Who was it?"

"One of the Weddell girls, Amanda. Fourteen years old. Knocked Marc for a loop, I'm afraid."

"And not you?"

"Oh, yeah. Me too. But nothing I haven't seen before."

Shaking his head, Gabe scowled. "All too often, lately. The Weddell's own stuff, I expect. Did anybody admit it?"

"To the contrary." Frankie repeated what she'd heard the girl's father—or perhaps grandfather—say. "And he should have some idea, shouldn't he? Seeing it's pretty obvious some of the family are both using and cooking."

"I'll have a talk with him," Gabe said, grimly enough that Frankie didn't envy the person he interviewed. "Tomorrow. But for now, I'll follow you to the hospital. Did Benton alert the department?"

"I think so. Some of the Weddells are part of the Coeur d' Alene tribe, if you didn't know, so it'll coordinate with Rudy." She stopped and chewed the inside of her lip for a second. Normally, she never asked how an investigation was proceeding, but this time, she felt entitled. "Have you discovered how many red Lexus sports cars there are in the area? Or gotten any information on Eric Benedict?"

"We're taking a close look at him," he admitted. "How about we talk later?"

"Right." Frankie was surprised he'd said that much. "We've gotta get these kids to Kootenai Medical anyway."

He gave her a quick salute and a trace of a smile before going off to talk with the boys' parents. Frankie climbed into the ambulance with her patients, leaving Marc to drive and trusting the responsibility would calm him. To her relief, the run to the hospital proved uneventful.

They had one more call out that night, one that turned from a heart attack to a bad case of indigestion, even though the run kept them a couple hours beyond the end of their shift. Frankie felt ready to collapse when at last she parked the Ranger in her slot to the house's back door.

Gabe had backed his Tahoe into its usual spot, showing he'd finished preliminary investigation into the overdoses. That or been taken off the fatality case and had it turned over to tribal jurisdiction. Depended on which mother the girl had, Frankie guessed. She'd had dark hair and brown eyes. But then, so did Frankie, so that meant nothing.

The dogs ripped out the doggie door to greet her, Shine spinning eager circles and Banner crowding her left knee. A blessing of so much love. Smiling, she slipped quietly into the kitchen, wincing as the dogs' toenails clattered on the floor. A note lay on the counter by the sink. Big print, full page, saying tersely, Wake me up. We need to talk.

"Oh no." She whispered, but it must've been as good as a shout as Gabe, scrubbing his hands over his face, emerged from the main floor bedroom clad only in jeans.

"You're late home." He looked at his watch. "You must

be beat."

"Worst night yet. She was so young. The death so unnecessary." She didn't mistake the direction this talk would go. "If only they'd called for us sooner, we might've saved her."

"And kept what'll be ruled a homicide to a simple, comparatively speaking, accidental overdose."

"Homicide?"

"That's what the tribe is going to push for."

Frankie could only shake her head. Not denying, just sadness and dismay. "Against who? Her own family?"

"Who else? Happens all the time. But nothing is sure yet. Franklin Weddell swears nobody in their clan would let that girl, he called her a little girl, get hold of drugs. He's saying somebody else, somebody from outside, poisoned her. His word, by the way. Poisoned." Gabe moved on into the kitchen and sat at the old enamel topped table, tapping the chair across from him as an indication for her to sit.

Taking the hint, she settled herself and lifted Shine onto her lap. Banner moved closer to nestle on her feet. Which she liked. Even though the kitchen was warm, a chill had her in its grasp.

"Who is he accusing?" she asked.

"He didn't name names. Just said there are people out there who have it in for his younguns."

"Younguns?" Frankie smiled at the old southern term. "What did you think? Did you believe him or is he just trying to weasel out of any responsibility?"

Gabe shrugged. "A little of both would be my guess. Do you have an opinion?"

She thought a moment. "Well, I doubt he'd deliberately set out to try to get her, or any other family member, hooked. On the other hand, several of them are, so obviously he hasn't done enough, or maybe anything, to stop them."

"You think he knows what they're mixed up in?"

"Sure. That sort of thing is right up his alley. I remember my grandparents talking about the Weddell family. A hundred years ago, during prohibition, they had a big still up on Hawkesford mountain. Were famous for it, claimed it was part of their Scottish slash southern heritage. And afterward too. Used to keep the high schoolers supplied. Their reputation indicated they made some pretty good stuff. That's how they made their living. Way back when, they'd lost out on the good farmland and made do with a hardscrabble stump ranch. Grew a few cattle, put up other people's hay, cut firewood for winter."

Nodding slowly, Gabe sighed. "Sounds like a hard life."

"I'm sure. Meth is probably making a very good living

for them, comparatively speaking, just like the booze did in earlier years. Not such hard work, either." Resting her chin on Shine's head, Frankie leaned forward. "Probably be better if they didn't have so much competition. And that's one reason Franklin may have real cause to blame others for Amanda's overdose. Except nothing can erase the fact the whole damn bunch of them just ignored her until it was too late. There was nothing we could do."

Her anger rocketed through the kitchen. Banner swung his head to look up at her.

Reaching out, Gabe took her hand. "Easy, Frankie. You did all you could."

"But I couldn't do enough."

They were silent until, Gabe taking a deep breath, said, "So tell me what you saw out there, this evening. Who you saw. Did anyone say anything that might be helpful? The boys, too. Were any names mentioned? I'll be talking to Marc in the morning, asking him the same. It's uncanny how these people can keep their activities buttoned up so tight. We've got people dying left and right around here lately, and I want to know if they're all connected, some of them, or none of them."

Frankie admitted to being surprised. Really, hadn't Gabe figured it out? She was certain they were connected. "Of course they are connected," she blurted.

Face grim, he nodded. "Easy for you to say, Frankie,

and you're probably right, but I have to have proof. Tell me why you think so. That Weddell bunch . . . I don't know. Doesn't seem like their style, somehow."

"Oh, it's their style, all right," she said.

Gabe hadn't been the one threatened, or on the forefront of treating the affected people. It hadn't touched him like it had her. He'd come in afterward, with the worst already in the rear-view mirror. The situation felt a lot more personal to her. But they all were depending on him—or maybe she should say, on the sheriff's department—to clean up the mess now. Him and Rudy. And sooner rather than later.

Setting Shine on the floor, she got up. "I received something in the mail today that you should take a look at. Two somethings, actually."

His eyebrows quirked up. "In the mail?"

"Yes. Probably not too smart, huh?"

Having stuffed the letters in a drawer by the kitchen sink, she got up to retrieve them.

"Oh," Gabe said, all offhand. "Speaking of not too smart, I have some news for you."

"News? Of what?" She rummaged in the drawer. How did the simple act of shutting one allow the contents to jumble into total chaos, anyway?

"About us getting shot at the other night. I had the bullet dug out of the door jamb and had it compared to the one from Blake's gun."

"You did?" He hadn't mentioned it before, and she hadn't even noticed. "And?"

"And they didn't match. Not that gun anyway. He's got several registered to him. Even so, you'll be relieved to know Strohmeyer is resting tonight in the county jail."

"He is? Why?"

Gabe smirked. "Drunk and disorderly."

Oddly enough, Frankie laughed.

Successful in her search, she handed both letters to Gabe and sat again. "Well, these will probably interest you."

He opened the first one. The one with the threat and the misspelled word she believed came from the Weddells. Most likely the Harley-riding brother, Galen. Replacing the letter in the envelope, he sighed. "Should've used gloves. We've screwed up evidence."

"What evidence? It's just a couple hokey sounding sentences that could be a joke."

"But you don't think it is."

"I don't know what to think, except I'm convinced my motorcycle-riding 'friend' is who sent it. Actually, it's the second letter that scares me."

Gabe read. "This? Tell me why. It seems quite straightforward to me."

"Does it? Except from its tone, I think it might be

from the same man who tried to kill Ruby Lyons. And maybe Mister Ginz. And Gerald Green." She paused. "And maybe others."

He read the letter again before placing it on the table and tapping it with his forefinger. "I agree the message is overbearing and takes a lot for granted, but, Frankie, I don't see a threat."

She stared at him. "Don't you? I hope you're right. But do you at least see what could be a connection?"

He shook his head. "Unless we can prove involvement, right now all I'm finding is a competition."

A gigantic yawn almost split her face in half. Exhaustion made her incoherent. "Forget it then. I'm going to bed."

He let her go without argument, saying only, "I promise you, Frankie, I'm not discounting this letter or anything else you've told me. I'm only saying it requires something more substantial. I won't stop looking."

Frankie didn't know if that made her feel any better, or not. Substantial? Like her being shot at, even if Blake had missed, or having her house burned down around her ears?

Her sleep, broken yet again by dreams of blood and death, did little to rest her. Sometime in the morning, heavy pounding on the front door interrupted even that. A glance at her bedside clock said she'd been in bed a mere six hours. Not nearly long enough, guaranteed. And poor Gabe, he must've left the house long ago.

Banner stood at the bedroom door, his mane ruffled and standing on end.

She sat up. "I hear it." An emergency? Or another threat? One premise seemed more likely than the other.

The pounding continued. She pulled on a pair of jeans and, accompanied by two irate dogs and a nice little twenty-gauge Mossberg she'd taken to keeping in her room, went downstairs. A glance through the peephole confirmed her first thought. Most probably not an emergency.

Opening the door no wider than necessary, she made sure the visitor noticed the shotgun before saying, "Hello, Blake. What're you doing out of jail? You're going to rouse the whole neighborhood with your racket, not to mention ruin my door."

His reply as to what the neighbors could do to themselves struck her as more uncouth than necessary. And that he included her in the general disrespect of anyone and everyone did nothing but rouse her temper.

"Oh, be quiet." She cut him off, her impatience clear. "I'm tired. I had a bad night last night and unless you have something to confess, in which case you need to talk to Gabe or Rudy, why don't you just go away and leave me alone. I don't have time for your crap. "

"Yeah?" He pushed forward as though meaning to enter the house with or without an invitation. "But you've got time to make up stories about me and my dad, don't you?"

A motion of her shotgun stopped him. "I don't need to make up stories, Blake. You do pretty well at drawing attention to yourself without my help. Look around."

A pickup crept past the house, the driver's window rolled down, and the driver himself looking their way. With his attention diverted, he barely missed hitting young Pamela Caine out walking her Sheltie. Pamela had raised her phone and apparently taken Blake's picture. Next door, Mr. Furnough's window went up and the old man's tousled head appeared.

Blake's volume of sound lost a decibel or two. "This is your fault, Frankie McGill. I heard you've been spreading word all around that me and Dad are drug kingpins. Well, we're not. Dad's lawyer says we ought to sue you. I say you need to shut your mouth before I shut it for you."

"Like you tried to do the other night when you missed?" A leading question. Her own shot in the dark.

His lip curled. "I missed on purpose, then. Maybe I won't the next time."

"There'd better not be a next time. I can shoot back, you know, and I'm a better shot than you. Ask Galen Weddell. You're friends, aren't you? He'll tell you."

He went still. "Galen Weddell?"

She couldn't help chuckling, even though she saw it fired Blake's temper to even greater heat. "By the way, I don't think you're kingpins, drug or otherwise. I do think you know more about this drug mess than you're letting on. However, it's not my job to prove it. I leave that to law enforcement. If I see anything, I'll tell Gabe. That's it. You don't like it?" She paused for effect. "Tough. There's an old saying that runs something like, 'do the crime, and you'll do the time.' If you don't, you won't. Simple as that. Now shove off and quit trying to intimidate me. It won't work."

Blake's mouth worked, spewing filth as she stepped back inside and slammed the door shut. Shaking, she threw the bolt and looked down at the dogs. They looked back.

"Holy Moly." She drew in a deep breath and let it out slowly. "What a way to start the day. And who let that man out of jail?"

A question with no answer.

Banner's tail wagged once. Shine's stayed tucked between her hind legs and dragged at her hocks. Evidently, they agreed.

Jesselyn called a little later, about the time Frankie calmed down enough to think about stretching out on the couch and napping for an hour or two. Sighing, she answered.

"Are you okay?" Jesselyn asked, sounding worried.

No, Frankie thought, I'm not. I'm tired and sad. And Pissed with a capitol P. Aloud, she said, "Yes. Why wouldn't I be?"

"Oh, I don't know. Maybe because of the way the Weddell clan is saying you let Amanda die. That you just sat there and did nothing when they called the paramedics. One of them, you can probably guess which one, said you laughed about it."

Any trace of sleepiness whisked away on the surge of red-hot emotion that kicked through her veins. "I let Amanda die?"

"That's what they're saying."

Speechless, Frankie couldn't say a word. Pain slashed through her head. Bright lights and black lightning took the place of actual vision. She felt herself swaying as though tossed by waves beneath her feet instead of standing on solid floor.

Banner whined and nudged up against her, his body a brace holding her upright. Seconds passed. The pain eased and she could breathe again.

"Frankie? Frankie, are you there? What's happened? Answer me."

Jesselyn's voice sounded from the speaker, and when Frankie looked down, she saw she'd dropped the phone on the floor.

Slowly, afraid she'd fall if she moved too fast, Frankie picked it up.

"I'm here," she said.

"What happened?"

"I dropped the phone," Frankie said. "It slid under the couch, which took a minute to reach. Sorry." The lie slipped easily from her lips.

"Oh."

Frankie could tell when Jesselyn made up her mind to believe the dropped phone story. Mainly because she didn't mention the Weddells again, asking instead about the boys and trying to find out how the investigation was going.

Aware her answers sounded short and stiff Frankie was relieved when the conversation ended. Talking to Jesselyn had been bad enough, she could only imagine what Maggie and Karl and Lew were going to say. Dread of going on shift tonight pushed the anger aside.

Nothing she said would prevent either Blake Strohmeyer or the Weddell clan from spewing their venom. All she could do is the best job possible and refuse to dignify the accusations.

Easier said than done.

CHAPTER TWENTY-TWO

"I heard you laughed when the Weddell girl died." Aaron Baxter looked up at Frankie with what appeared to be pleading in his eyes as he repeated the rumor. Green eyes, she noticed, that looked like diluted lake water. But full of pain, too, no surprise since she was in the process of fixing a splint on his badly broken arm while trying not to disturb the shattered bone sticking through the skin.

Not the best thing to say to the person helping you, she thought. And how should she answer? You bet. A fourteen-year-old girl dying as I watched made my day? I always laugh when people under my care die? I thought it would be interesting to observe the family's reaction?

Best, she knew, to keep her mouth shut and pretend she hadn't heard. Except she just couldn't do it. At best, she managed to keep the sarcasm at bay.

"Who's saying?" Seeing her hands shake, Frankie sucked in a lungful of air and held herself under control. Halfway, anyway. Her anger still raged.

Marc had heard, though, and answered for her, his voice rough with anger. "What a load! Do you think she's laughing at you right now?"

Baxter opened his eyes, which he'd clenched shut after that one plea, and peered up at Frankie. "Sorry. No. Don't seem as if. I didn't believe it anyway. Uh, say, is there anything you can give me for the pain? This hurts like a sumbitch."

She kept her face blank—or thought she did. Right at that point, she did feel like laughing. Oh, not at his pain. Never. Because the whole situation was so ridiculous.

"I'm giving you something right now, Mister Baxter." A small dose of fentanyl went into the I.V. line Marc had set up. Enough to hold him until they reached Kootenai Medical. He'd be whisked right into surgery there and they'd take care of the pain issue. Sometimes Frankie wished she could administer meds sooner, but in this case, not. Best not to leave herself open to censure in case anything happened.

"Anyway," she continued as they loaded him onto the gurney and wheeled him toward the back of the ambulance, "you're not dying."

"I'm not?"

"Absolutely not." She forced a smile. "You don't know how lucky you are to come out of this wreck with only a broken arm." Best, she figured, not to mention the months of therapy ahead of him.

"What about my motorcycle?" His head turned from the sight of his mangled arm toward the crumpled red and chrome metallic mess lying intertwined with the carcass of a deer. Hard to tell which of the blood spills belonged to the animal and which to the man. They'd both bled, the deer copiously. Then there was the oil and gas from the bike.

"Yeah," she said. "I'd say it's as dead as that deer."

Marc snorted. "Cunningham will be here in a few minutes and load your Harley onto his lowboy. And we'll clean away the rest with the pumper truck."

Baxter nodded, or at least made a motion with his head, constricted though it was by the cervical collar Frankie had affixed, and with that, passed out. A quick check showed his vitals strong. He'd simply fainted, the only surprise being that he hadn't done so earlier.

Apparently, Frankie thought with some amusement, the sight of his ruined bike affected him worse than his arm had. Even so, using due caution, she went through a series of checks anyway.

He never did wake up enough during the run to give Frankie her answer on who, exactly, had spread the rumor.

Except for Baxter's accident and a simple run in the middle of the night concerning a pregnant woman with ill-timed and ill-named acute morning sickness, their shift proved uneventful. They treated the pregnant lady for dehydration and provided anti-nausea medications. Otherwise, no threats, no humiliating confrontations, not even ribbing from the others on shift.

At home, Frankie fell into bed after giving her dogs a love and a treat and slept undisturbed for eight solid hours. The phone awakened her. Not so many people knew her number so, still half-asleep, she answered without checking caller ID.

"Miss McGill?" The question struck sharp and loud to her mumbled "hello."

Beside the bed, Banner stirred and raised onto his haunches, his head cocked.

"This is Eric Benedict of Benedict Properties." A man's harshly pitched, super loud voice rose from the speaker. "We need to meet and discuss the sale of your property. Time is of the essence on this offer."

Blinking, Frankie shook her head to clear the cobwebs. Too much sleep? Banner growled. Her attention caught she eyed the dog as he stared at the phone in her hand.

"What?" Her question could have been aimed at either Banner or at the caller. The caller took it to mean him, as he was the one who verbally answered.

Answered impatiently, Frankie duly noted. Sitting up, she pressed a button on her phone.

"What is known as the old Buchanan place. I warn you this is the only offer you'll get. Meet me out there in an hour and we'll get the paperwork signed."

"Who is this?" Oh, she'd heard him clearly enough. Eric Benedict of Benedict Properties. The same outfit that had been hassling Ruby Lyons, according to Victoria Pettigrew. She swung her legs over the side of the bed, her back stiff, her heart racing.

"I think you heard me," he replied.

"Yes. I believe I did. Eric Benedict of Benedict Properties, correct?" She waited for his assent before continuing. Gratified to get it on the recording, she said, "Now you hear me because I'm only going to say this once. The Buchanan homestead is not for sale. Isn't now, never has been, and never will be. There is nothing more to discuss. Any further communication will be construed as a threat and harassment. Are we clear?"

The phone went dead.

She had no doubt she'd made an enemy. A deadly enemy? Shrugging, she punched a speed dial number on the phone.

Gabe picked up on only the second ring, somewhat of a record, especially since she could hear people talking in the background.

"Is this a bad time?" Frankie knew she sounded worried. Sounded? She was worried.

"Kind of busy," Gabe said, his standard sentence after saying hello. Sometimes even before saying hello. "What's up?"

"I just had a phone call I want you to listen to. I didn't get all of the beginning of the conversation since I didn't know what he'd say, but I can send you the rest."

"You recorded it?"

"Yes."

"Send it. I'll see what I think and call you back."

As usual, he hung up with saying goodbye. Two minutes later, before she could even get her prothesis attached, her phone rang.

"Promise me, Frankie, that you'll stay away from the homestead. Under no circumstances are you to go out there alone. I'd prefer you never meet this guy, but especially, you won't meet him anywhere unless plenty of people are around. Me, if possible, Rudy, if not."

"Believe me, I have no intention of meeting him at all. I thought I made that clear."

Gabe chuckled. "I'd say so too. But I don't know about this guy."

The knot that had been forming in Frankie's belly since Benedict's first imperious, "Miss McGill," began to ravel apart. She hadn't been imagining things. Gabe had heard the threat this time as well. As had Banner, she realized.

"There's something else," she said. "I'm almost positive now that he's the guy who tried to kill Ruby."

A pause indicated Gabe's surprise—and maybe doubt? "What makes you think so?"

"Because—" Frankie hesitated. What would any level-headed cop say about this? With a mental shrug, she continued. "Because of Banner. In his own way, I believe he just told me so."

"I'm not even going to ask." Gabe went silent for a moment, then his voice came again. "I'll look this Benedict guy up, Frankie, but we need something more solid than a dog's . . . word. In the meantime, watch your back."

"I intend to." Something else she intended to do involved posting no trespassing signs around the Buchanan property. But not alone. She wouldn't go back on her promise to Gabe regarding that. She'd ask Marc to accompany her. Maybe he'd even wield the hammer if she bought him a six-pack of his favorite brew.

Sure enough, a few hours later as she and Marc—he being the agreeable sort, especially when bribed with expensive micro-brewery beer—finished nailing a series of signs around the property, Frankie saw a car stop down at the main road. Evidently, whoever was driving hadn't spotted Frankie's Ranger parked just around the bend. Anyway, she had an eye on it when someone got out of the car and started walking toward the house.

It was the blonde. She wore the same blue sundress Frankie had seen at Roland Ginz's house. The car, an old blue beater, also struck her as familiar. The woman stopped when Marc, previously hidden, appeared around the corner of the house.

"Watch my back?" Frankie said to him. She'd had to explain to him the reasons she needed his help. He'd agreed, even though she knew the whole idea made him nervous.

"You know I will," he said. He waved his hammer as though it were a mace.

"Thanks."

Frankie, assured of backup, started toward the blonde. "Hi," she called. "You're just the person I wanted to see. I need to talk to you."

There were too far apart for her to make out the woman's expression, but her body language verbalized as clearly as words. The woman dithered, took a step forward, then held her ground. But only for a few seconds. As Frankie moved closer, she suddenly threw up her hands, spun, and ran.

"Wait," Frankie called, running after her. "Please wait."

"I'm sorry." The woman flung herself into the car. "I can't talk to you. I'm sorry." With that, the door slammed, and she drove away, a dust cloud rising under the car's wheels.

"What the heck?" Marc, taking the job of watching over his partner seriously, had followed. He spoke from behind her. "Who is that woman, Frankie? What did she want?"

Frankie, hurrying before she forgot, picked up a stick and wrote the car's license plate number in the dust of the road. Finished, she looked at Marc. "I think that's the woman who helped save Gerald Green's life."

Marc's gaze narrowed on the car's dust trail. "And the one you saw at Ginz's."

"Yes." Frankie had seen her one other time, too, when the woman had been looking for the non-existent Frank McGill. She'd run that time, too, just as she had now.

* * *

"The car belongs to an Emily Walker. Do either of you know her?" Gabe had stopped in at the station to give Frankie the news. She and Marc had been cleaning the ambulance and double- checking the drugs Lew had re-stocked after an accident just before shift change. Frankie finished locking the drug box and put away the key.

"Never heard of her," Marc said, slamming the ambulance's rear doors shut.

Frankie almost added her ditto, but then her eyes narrowed. "Not exactly."

"Not exactly? What do you mean?" Gabe seemed a little impatient.

"Not to put the face with the name. But I think I can tell you who employs her."

"If you're thinking Eric Benedict, you're right."

She hesitated. Damn her memory, but this next part he needed to know, and she felt a fool for neglecting to tell him. "There's something else, though, and I don't know how it all ties in. Or if it ties at all, for that matter."

The way Gabe tapped the side of his holster indicated she should get on with it. "Let's hear it."

"Well, Jesselyn and I were looking through some old high school yearbooks the other day. And there was a photo of a girl I didn't remember. Jesselyn told me it was because I was in Boise for three months at a medical training course during my senior year. The girl came and went during the time I was gone."

"Yeah?" Gabe's mutter seemed meant to encourage.

"Yeah. Seems the girl lived with the Weddells for a while, while her mother was shacked up with Bob Weddell. Then they split and that was the last anybody saw of either of them. Until now."

"Don't tell me, Emily Walker?" Gabe didn't even seem surprised.

Marc snapped his fingers. "I thought I recognized that beater Honda she was driving. Galen Weddell sold it when he bought his Harley."

"So, does this clarify anything or just make it all more complicated?" A rhetorical question, as Frankie hoped Gabe knew. "Who do you suppose she's really working for? The Weddells or this obnoxious Eric Benedict?"

Marc had an answer. "Both? Playing them off against the middle?"

"Possible." Gabe wore a thoughtful expression as he straightened from where he rested one foot on the ambulance bumper. "My job is to find out. And I guess I'd better get at it."

Brow puckering, Frankie felt a headache coming on. Another of her doozies. "And maybe hurry. Either way, Emily Walker could be in danger."

Gabe nodded even as Marc leapt on the premise. "Why? Why should she be in danger?"

Frankie ticked items off on her fingers. "One, she's tried to prevent people from dying. Late, but maybe she wasn't in any position to do any better. Two, she knows I'm on to her. Three, her boss probably knows I'm on to her."

Gravely, Gabe nodded. "And four, because of her,

Gerald Green survived and can likely put a name to his shooter when he wakes up. If he wakes up. And if he can't, the Walker woman can. I'll put a BOLO out on her right away."

Marc frowned. "If the old boy doesn't wake up, there's only her, Emily, isn't there. Because I heard that Missus Lyons is still in a coma and may never come out of it."

Frankie nodded. They'd heard that at the hospital on their last run.

Every muscle in Gabe's face tightened. "So that leaves Green, Frankie, and Emily Walker who can."

He tipped his hat to Maggie on the way out but didn't stop. Which no doubt is why the dispatcher pounced on Frankie as soon as his Tahoe left the parking lot.

"What was that all about?" She tossed the question to land evenly between Frankie and Marc but the way she eyed Marc meant she knew him to be the weaker vessel. "Is there a problem?"

"No problem." A slight shake of Frankie's head warned Marc not to answer. She said the first thing that came into her head. "One of the officers mentioned he'd like Mick Boyd's phone number and Gabe said he'd get it for him. No big deal."

Marc gave a start, although if she hadn't been watching for it, Frankie probably wouldn't have noticed. Apparently, thank God, Maggie didn't.

"Oh," she said. "It's just . . ." She looked out the window as though to catch sight of Gabe's vehicle. Too late. "He seemed in a hurry."

Frankie shrugged. "You know Gabe." She tried for airy and unconcerned. "Isn't he always in a hurry?"

Their shift dragged after a single run around the dinner hour that involved an emergency from the café down the street where a woman had choked on a grape from her fruit bowl. Frankie grabbed her bag and, with Marc, simply ran the two blocks. Marc's longer legs and whole feet made that faster than getting out the rig. When Frankie reached the café, Marc had already performed a Heimlich maneuver to expel the grape and was collecting backslaps and accolades, not to mention the slightly inebriated woman's gushing thanks.

At quitting time, Marc declared himself dog-tired and, speaking of dogs, wanted to get home to Elmer who was overdue for some meds. It turned out the first thing he'd done when he took responsibility for the old mutt was to take him to Violet Kelly, the same veterinarian who cared for Banner and Shine. The old fellow had an infection and Marc was meticulous about his antibiotic schedule.

"See ya tomorrow," he said, saluting as they parted ways in the parking lot. "Just watch your back."

Frankie only hoped tomorrow would be better.

CHAPTER TWENTY-THREE

At 2:45 AM on the dot, Frankie's phone awakened her. The name Emily Walker lit up on the caller ID screen.

Hesitating, thoughts awhirl, Frankie sat up. Shine, lying on the other pillow, raised her head and, from the rug beside the bed, Banner got to his feet and stretched front to back.

The phone rang twice more. "Rats," Frankie said, "should I, or shouldn't I?" She didn't need to be psychic to know the call portended nothing good. Dangerous, even. But to whom? And what sort of danger?

Sighing, she answered. After all, no one could actually shoot her through a cell phone.

"Frankie McGill?" a woman asked.

"Yes. Who is this?"

"You don't know me, but my name is Emily. I . . ." As the voice died away, Frankie thought she heard someone else in the background.

"I know who you are," Frankie said, then went quiet to let the other woman speak.

After a moment, Emily resumed. "I'm in trouble. You're a paramedic. I need your help."

"I'm off shift. You should call emergency services. Dial 911." And I should hang up and go back to sleep. But she didn't.

"I can't. If I . . . I just can't. Please."

Frankie sat straighter. "What kind of trouble?"

Another of those pauses left her hanging.

"Are you hurt?" Banner jumped onto the bed and crouched across Frankie's legs as she waited.

"Yes. I think so. I'm . . .I'm bleeding." Emily said, too quickly to be believable. "But I. . . I had a little too much to drink and wrecked my car and I can't afford to have a DUI on my insurance. Please, can you help me?"

Listening hard, Frankie's certainty grew that someone in the background stood by coaching the woman on what to say. Eric Benedict. She knew it in her bones.

"Call 911," she said, and poked the red button on her phone. To her relief, Emily didn't call back.

Undecided on whether she should wake Gabe and tell him about the call, sleep eluded her the rest of the night. No real surprise. Which meant when she heard him stirring about in the kitchen, she got up to speak to him. Downstairs, she stood in the kitchen doorway where sunlight blazed through a window open to the morning air. Both dogs dashed past her legs and zoomed out the doggie door.

"I had a call during the night," she announced, stepping into the old-fashioned room.

A sleepy-eyed Gabe, in the act of pouring milk over a mound of brown flakes topped with banana and cinnamon, turned to look at her. "Yeah? Anyone I know?"

"I don't believe know, but someone I'm certain you'll be interested in."

The coffee maker burbled a few final sputters and beeped. Frankie lost no time in fetching cups and filling them, setting one at Gabe's place at the table, and another at her own.

Gabe nodded his thanks and sat. "Who was it?"

"Emily Walker."

Gabe's spoon, laden with cereal and banana and dripping milk, stopped half-way to his mouth. "Emily Walker?" The spoon moved, then stopped again. "Does she know we're looking for her?"

"Didn't seem too."

"Did you tell her?"

"Nope."

"Why do you suppose she called you?" Now, at last, the food made its way into his mouth.

"I'm not exactly sure." Frowning, Frankie couldn't hold back her real anxiety. "I think someone was with her directing the conversation."

"What do you mean, directing?"

"I mean, as we talked, she kept hesitating, as though someone was telling her what to say."

Gabe went back into his bowl for another spoonful, the crunch as he chewed loud in the quiet room. "So, what did she want?"

Taking a sip of coffee, Frankie savored the rich liquid. Gabe always made a darn good pot, as long as you drank it while fresh. Otherwise, it grew too bitter for her taste. "She asked for my help."

"Help at what? Was she in an accident?" His eyes narrowed.

"She implied that. Said she wrecked her car anyhow."

"Did she say where?"

"No. She mentioned bleeding but no specific injuries. I don't believe that's true. She also said she's in trouble, which I do believe."

"But not what sort of trouble?"

"No."

Gabe waited.

"I told her to call 911."

"Good thinking. And what did she say then?"

"She said she'd had too much to drink and wanted me

to help her out."

"Which meant what, exactly?"

"I don't know. To draw me out, I suppose. Do these people think I'm so stupid I'd do something like that for someone I don't even know? I'm not a total fool, Gabe. Of course I wouldn't go haring off into the night. That's when I told her to call 911 and then I hung up. The thing is, she may have been in trouble, all right, but not from wrecking her car. The longer I think about it, the more sure I am someone was telling her what to do. I think she's in danger."

Gabe's spoon clattered into the bowl. "Frankie, if you had said you'd meet her, I swear I'd disown you."

"Disown me?" Her eyebrow arched.

Face reddening, as though realizing how ridiculous that sounded, he grinned a little, while still firm in his intent. "You know what I mean."

She let him off the hook. "Um, I guess." Even so, unable to let the matter drop, she said, "But, Gabe, I've been thinking—"

Eyeing her levelly, Gabe shook his head. "Best you don't, Frankie. No second guessing. It's apt to get you in trouble."

Something she couldn't deny.

Even so, after Gabe left, she tried the number Emily had called from last night, hoping to find out more. The phone rang and rang, but no one answered.

Frankie spent the morning putting sealer on the new porch, a soothing activity that gave a satisfying sense of accomplishment. Of course, Mr. Furnough, spotting her at work, came over to supervise and drink the lemonade, his spiked with just a tad of gin, she offered him.

"You doing all right, young lady?" he asked, easing down onto one of her new rockers and sipping his drink. He pointed at a spot she'd missed.

Dipping her brush into the can of sealer, she slapped some where he indicated.

"I'm fine," she said. The kind old man didn't need to know any different. She was just relieved he didn't own one of the original homestead properties, or she'd have to fear for his life, too.

By the time she left for work, she felt almost normal.

Until, with barely time to lock away her purse, Chief Mager called her into his office.

"Take a pew, Frankie." He pointed at the chair opposite him.

Frankie sat. What now? she wondered. Karl's round, rather florid face wore a serious look. Had she done something wrong? Had there been complaints about her work other than the hassle crap from the Weddells?

"What's up?" She perched self-consciously on the old oak kitchen chair that served for Karl's 'guests'. Most of the volunteers referred to it as the 'ass chewing' seat.

Leaning back in his leather office chair, he shrugged. "Oh, nothing much, unless you count the manure those rattle-brained Weddells are spreading. I suppose you've heard they've been accusing you of dereliction of duty or some dang thing over the way their girl died."

"So I've been informed." Frankie knew she was scowling and didn't quite know how to remove the expression. "What do you want me to do about it?"

He blew a gust of air from his nose forcefully enough to stir the papers on his desk. "Nothing," he said. "Nada, zilch. Folks around here know you better than that and know there isn't anything to the rumors. That's what I wanted to tell you. But, if by chance one of them, or anyone else for that matter, jumps you and starts in with any rat-brained accusations, I want you to zip your lips and refuse to answer. I expect that might be tough, everybody oughta be able to defend their own self, but it'll be best if you refuse the provocation."

Slowly, Frankie nodded. "Do my best not to bring shame down on the fire department, sir."

"Atta girl, that's the spirit." He nodded.

She started to rise, but he waved her back down.

"There's one other thing," he said, picking up a pen and rolling it between his fingers.

Uh-oh. She'd been in the department long enough to

know when he had bad news to deliver. It always made him fidgety. "What else?"

"Some ladies from the Hawkesford Women's Club came to me asking for a favor." The pen clicked rhythmically as he worked the nib in and out.

"Did they?"

"They did."

Apparently, he wanted her to ask what that favor might be.

Frankie resisted. She'd learned to keep her mouth shut in the military, especially during the weeks she'd spent in the VA hospital. She waited Karl out.

"Yeah." His impatience got the best of him. "They asked for a paramedic to make a presentation to their group about stroke signs and what to do in case of a heart attack. You probably remember Jane Lansdale, one of their members, had a minor heart attack a while back and followed it up with a massive stroke. Scared the ladies pretty bad."

"As well it should." Frankie certainly remembered the heart attack, which she and Marc had treated not long before he got shot. Lew and Chris had worked the stroke portion. "Has Jane recovered any of her speech?"

Oh, she knew what he was getting at. He wanted her to volunteer to be that paramedic. She ramped up her resistance. Public speaking scared her spitless. What if she had one of her blackouts? Stress often brought one on, and while so far, she'd managed to hide them from everyone but Gabe, that record could change at any moment. And then what? Not a good result. She knew that much.

Karl brushed her question about Jane aside. "The point is, I've scheduled you to do the presentation. They meet next Monday and want you there about two PM. You'll be paid an hour overtime."

Frankie went cold. "Scheduled me?" she squeaked. "No, no. I can't do it. This should be Lew's job. He's the head paramedic. The ladies will enjoy a man's perspective, especially since he handled Jane's stroke."

Karl settled a hard stare on her. "Whaddya mean you can't do it? Of course you can. You will. Being head paramedic means Lew has perks you don't. For instance, he gets to push this off onto you. Sorry, Frankie. Two PM on Monday at the senior center. It'll take about an hour, what with answering their questions. Better start getting your ducks in a row right away."

His dismissal seemed extra abrupt.

At the door, she turned around and glared. "I'm the one who's apt to have the stroke," she spat at him. "Then what?"

He laughed.

CHAPTER TWENTY-FOUR

"You can do a presentation on heart attack and stroke in your sleep," Marc assured Frankie as they drove toward Alex Henderson's place north of town. At ten o'clock, they hoped it would be the final run of the night. "You know this stuff frontwards and backwards. Better than Lew, sometimes. Quit worrying. You'll do great."

Frankie had, sometimes to the detriment of her driving, spent the last ten minutes pouring her vexation into her partner's sympathetic ear.

Flattered at Marc's praise even though she questioned the veracity—how would he know, after all—Frankie still had her doubts. "I know I'm a decent paramedic. That doesn't mean I'm a good teacher. I'm definitely not a good speaker."

Marc rolled down his window, filling the cab with the pungent odor of smoke from wildfires burning as much as two hundred miles away. The summer had been super dry. Global warming at its finest. "Just pick one of the women—Missus Gagne is a member and would be a good choice—and pretend you're having a conversation with her."

"Why Missus Gagne?"

"Because she is a teacher and likes to learn new stuff. I think she wanted to be a nurse at one time. She'll be fascinated."

Frankie looked over at him, a little surprised at the wisdom of his advice.

He grinned. "Besides, that's what our debate teacher in high school taught us."

"Does it work?"

"Dunno. I think so. Never tried it myself but I had a girlfriend who said it did."

She had to laugh.

The ambulance's headlights flashed on the Henderson's mailbox, then caught the glow of some animal's eyes as they turned onto the long drive. A deer or a coyote, maybe. She hoped the critter wouldn't run out in front of them.

Alex had been a year ahead of Frankie in school, she remembered. He'd married his college sweetheart, and now that his dad had retired, Alex worked the family farm. He was also the father of a two-year-old with asthma. The child suffered attacks triggered by the forest fire smoke that swept in and clogged the air at this time of year. This was not EMS' first trip to the farm to treat the little boy. They knew the way well.

Jolie Henderson awaited them at the door, her whole body wired and tense. "Thanks for coming, guys," she said, leading the way down a meticulously clean hall to Alex Jr's room. They could hear the child, whom they called Lex, gasping for breath before they saw him.

Alex the elder sat in a rocking chair with the boy on his lap. The table beside them held a litter of medication. An inhaler, and both a standard oxygen concentrator and a portable were nearby. A mask meant to deliver medication covered most the boy's small, pinched face. Lex's distress showed it didn't seem to be helping.

As Frankie knelt beside them, Alex shook his head. "This is a bad attack, Frankie. The worst yet. Do you have something you can give him?"

Marc stood back as she got out the oxygen meter, her stethoscope and a tiny blood pressure cuff. "What've you treated him with?"

Smiling reassuringly at the toddler, she noted his dull eyes and general miserable appearance. Quick sympathy stirred in her. Poor little boy.

While Frankie took vitals, Jolie, blinking back tears, reeled off Lex's latest meds. They all knew the drill by now, leaving EMS with few treatments.

"I'll give him albuterol," Frankie said. "He responded well to it last time. Just be sure to get him to the doctor tomorrow. I think the pediatrician needs to check his treatment plan." Her mouth compressed. She knew the doctor by reputation. "Don't let him put you off."

Grim-faced, Alex nodded.

"And be sure to keep the house buttoned up. We don't want smoke coming in," she added.

"Always," Jolie said.

An hour later, as she and Marc hit the highway on their way back to town, headlights in her rearview mirror flashed across her eyes. The glare almost blinded her. Some idiot without the sense, or courtesy, to use his dimmer switch when following another vehicle. Frankie slowed. The road ahead ran straight and clear of traffic.

"Wish he'd hurry up and pass," she grumbled.

But the other driver didn't. It struck Frankie that he deliberately had set out to destroy her night vision. Settling into a distance behind her likely to cause the most potential harm, he weaved from side to side, lights catching not only in the rearview, but in the ambulance's big side mirrors as well.

Marc, watching the bright light play over Frankie face, tightened his seat belt. After a minute or so, apprehension dawned. "He's doing this on purpose, isn't he?"

"Looks as if." Her fingers tightened on the steering wheel.

"Who in the . . ." Mark began, but she cut him off.

"Hold on. We're coming up on the turn off to Pearson's place. I'm going to steer the bus onto their road, but I'm not going to hit the brakes or slow down first. Don't watch what I'm doing. If this works out right, the car will have to go on past us. Either that or rear-end us. I'm hoping the first choice. Your job is to see who is at the wheel. At least, try to get what kind of car he's driving and the plate number if you can. Got it?"

Eyes bugging, Marc said, "Got it."

"Get ready."

Far from slowing, she pressed the accelerator down. The ambulance gained speed. Ahead, a reflector showed on a post, their marker for the turn off. Choosing her moment, Frankie spun the steering wheel, causing the heavy rig to go into a skid. Gravel slid beneath the wheels, splattering on the undercarriage. They came to a stop in a swirl of dust on the unpaved side road. To her relief, the following car swept past, swerving madly from one side of the yellow line to the other, the red glow of its taillights showing brightly.

Frankie leaned into her seatbelt. Sweat ran down the sides of her face. Warning flashes of an eye migraine bounced in her vision. Not now. Oh, dear God, not now.

"A man," Marc yelled, so loud the noise startled her. "In a red sports car. Maybe a Corvette, but definitely a red sports car."

"You're sure?"

"You bet I'm sure."

She let out a breath. "Good job."

His face, in the dashboard light seemed a little pale, but his teeth flashed in a grin. "You too. Where'd you learn to drive like that? This old bus hardly even swayed."

"Military." Wryly, the thought flashed through her head that Marc may have been delusional. Hardly swayed? Fighting the wheel in the turn, she'd thought they were going to roll.

To her relief, the flashes were rapidly fading. Maybe having someone besides the dogs to talk to helped.

Marc loosened his seatbelt, which had tightened around him as the bus juddered in the turn. "Figures. One thing for sure, Frankie McGill, every trip with you is an adventure. A downright scary adventure." He passed a hand over his face and took a shaky breath. "Never a dull moment. That guy, he did that on purpose, didn't he? He's out to get us, isn't he?"

She had to be honest. "Afraid so. Me, at least."

"Why?"

"If I had to guess, it's because he's afraid I saw him when he set Ruby's house on fire."

"Holy crap, Frankie, that was him? Emily Walker's boss? The cops need to get this guy!"

An involuntary chuckle gurgled to the surface. "You're telling me?"

But even Marc, although excited by their encounter with the tailgating car, chose to take a softer approach when it came to reporting the event.

"Uh, maybe you can wait to talk to Gabe," he said as Frankie backed the ambulance into the station garage. "It's almost quitting time. I don't want to stay half the night answering questions, do you?"

No, she decided. She didn't, especially those she had no answer to. And if, by chance, Gabe had actually gotten to bed on time, maybe he'd wouldn't be so growly when he heard about this in the morning. She'd write him a note.

The growly assumption turned out to be only partially correct.

Instead of him ringing her phone, Frankie woke up to find Gabe sitting on the edge of her bed giving Shine an ear rub while Banner waited his turn.

"Got your note," he said when he saw her eyes open.

He'd been in her room before, but only a couple times. For instance, when she'd been having bad dreams, complete with cries and calling out.

Oh, Lord. I wasn't doing that, was I? No. Not possible.

Her heart rate and stress level seemed normal. All was well.

"I thought you might be able to go back to sleep if you didn't get up," he went on, switching his attentions to Banner. "What's so important it can't wait?"

She stuffed a pillow behind her back and sat. When the rented duplex where she lived got blown to smithereens a while back, all her clothes and other possessions had gone up with it. Consequently, she had on a pretty black nighty with pink trim that Jesselyn had selected as a replacement. Quite a change from Frankie's normal night gear of oversized T-shirts. Right now, she was kind of glad.

On the other hand, she felt certain her hair stuck out in rat tails, no doubt detracting from the desired effect.

Sighing, she said, "We had an incident last night. Marc and I."

Unblinking, Gabe stared at her until Banner bumped his arm as a reminder it was his turn for attention. "An incident? What kind of incident?"

"We'd gone out to Henderson's on a run and were almost run off the road on our way back."

"Where?"

She told him, going through the particulars.

He resumed petting, although his mind didn't seem on it. "Could it've been an accident?"

Frankie shook her head. "No accident. Definitely on purpose." She smiled a little. "It's a good thing that old ambulance is so much like my deuce-and-a-half, though. I learned some trick evasive maneuvers driving in Afghanistan."

"You're all right? You and Marc?"

"We're fine. Do you think I'd be sleeping now if we weren't?"

He stared at her, his eyes as dark as shadowed lake water. "No." His mouth twisted. "I don't suppose you caught sight of the driver. Or the rig."

"I didn't really, too busy keeping the bus on all four wheels." She skipped some of that part, finishing swiftly when his expression turned stormy. Or, she corrected internally, growly. "But Marc did. I'm not going to tell you what he told me, though. I want you to speak with him yourself."

"I will." Giving Banner a final pat, he stood up. "From which I understand you have an opinion you're keeping to yourself."

She nodded. "For now."

"Then I'll get back with you." He took a step toward the door but stopped and spun back to face her. "Dammit, Frankie, be careful. I wish to God you could hole up someplace for a few days, until we get this guy put away."

"I have to work."

"I know you do. We'll talk later when I hope to update you on what's going on. I can't do that just yet. Just know that the whole department is working day and night. I promise. It'll be over soon."

She snorted. "Even Armbuster and Rimmel?"

"Even them."

He closed the door softly as he left, a snick of the latch that resounded as loudly as a slam.

Although, she thought, he might as well have slammed it. Wouldn't have made any difference since she was done sleeping anyway.

She heard nothing during the day, not even from Marc. Surprised when he didn't call to let her know what Gabe had said, it came as a relief to head over to the station.

Maggie, taking her turn in the evening shift dispatcher's chair, surprised her by not uttering a word or asking one question about last night's close call. Frankie could only assume Gabe had gotten to Marc soon enough to keep him from announcing their incident to the whole department. Which suited her. She had no desire to go over the story again.

Of course, that didn't mean Maggie hadn't kept her ear close to the ground, as Grandpa used to describe the quick spread of gossip. But the dispatcher's usual sparkle was missing.

"I see your shift got called to Henderson's again last night," she said. "Little Lex, he's in bad shape, isn't he?"

Frankie felt a flash of anger that quickly dissolved into sadness. "His mom and dad do everything they can, Maggie. And so do we when they call us."

"Well, sure. That goes without saying. But personally, I think they need to change doctors."

Frankie, heading for the lockers to put her purse away, acted as though she didn't hear. She remembered saying something of the sort to the Hendersons, last night. Oh, not in so many words, but an indication. It would probably be worth her license if she came right out and said as much. Maggie had surprised her by doing so.

In the end, Marc didn't make it to work on time. Lew, to his aggravation, had to stay a half-hour late to cover when a call for service came in right at shift change. Marc's excuse, Lew told her, involved something he'd seen and had to report to the police.

"I don't know what," he said as if it were a personal affront. If one thought Gabe got growly, well, he could take lessons from Lew. "He wouldn't tell me."

Frankie asked just enough questions to direct suspicion from herself. Or at least, she thought she did.

Between dodging Maggie and some of the other night crew members, Marc, when he finally arrived, and Frankie had no chance to talk until a dinner time run called them out.

"I remembered something else to tell that detective. Armbuster. Weird name, huh?" Marc took the wheel for the run, and Frankie had a hunch he hoped something would happen so he could try her driving technique.

She, as fervently, hoped just the opposite.

"A very weird name. So, what else did you remember?"

"I remembered the license plate is from Idaho, but it's a special plate, not just a plain old state one."

"Good going." She smiled across at him. "Did you catch the design?"

"Yeah. They had me look at all the available plates until I found it. And then Gabe came in, and he had the idea I should look at some pictures of red sports cars. So, I did."

"And?"

He made a wry face. "So, I found out the car wasn't a Corvette after all."

A pulse starting a heavy throb in Frankie's temple. "Not a Corvette?" She paused, thinking she knew what he'd say. "So what was it?"

Marc let out a breath. "A Lexus LC500." He grinned. "Nice car, by the way."

CHAPTER TWENTY-FIVE

Roland Ginz's heirs gathered after a week-long delay caused by one of his grandsons having flown in from Hong Kong. At the memorial service held at the homestead, the old house was overrun with relatives and neighbors. The Women's Club ladies had pitched in to tidy the house and prepare foods and practically the whole of the Hawkesford community turned out to show their regard. Given the horror of Ginz's death, that aspect held a certain sway over the proceedings.

Frankie, wearing her best black slacks and dress boots, picked up Jesselyn and drove out to the farm in her Ranger. Various rigs were packed headlight to tail-light along the gravel drive, while the relatives' vehicles occupied the yard. A cluster of tables had been set up under a couple huge red leaf maple trees.

"I wonder what the heirs are going to do with the

place," Jesselyn said, glancing about as she tripped along on high-heeled sandals.

"The heirs?" Frankie, keeping pace, had an easier time in her boots. "None of them are farmers, are they? Aren't they all college professors or businessmen or something?" She'd never known the Ginz clan well, all of them being many years older than she. She thought Jesselyn might have a connection through her older brother Russ. Or maybe even Victoria.

"VIPs?" Jesselyn snorted a little. "Yes. All but one, I think, and he runs an alpaca ranch in central Washington. I doubt he could buy the others out even if he wanted to—or if they wanted to sell."

Frankie thought they'd sell all right, especially if the offer proved . . . um . . . persuasive.

"Has Victoria contacted them? Or have they contacted her?" If anyone would have the lowdown, Frankie suspected it would be Victoria.

"Not that I know of." Jesselyn stopped to catch her breath as they neared the central gathering spot where the Protestant minister had set up a portable sound system for his eulogy. "In fact, I think she said . . ." she frowned suddenly, as though at a bad memory.

Frankie's attention sharpened. "She said what?"

Frown deepening, Jesselyn stared at her. "She mentioned a letter she received. Hands off being the implication. She's pissed, big time."

"Did she say who sent it?"

"Unsigned." Jesselyn's inflection showed exactly what she and her sister thought about this. "She figured at first it from one of heirs. Now she's not so sure."

"Why? Why change her mind, I mean? Did she tell you what the letter said?"

"Not exactly. Maybe the attitude just struck her as wrong. You know, someone telling her to butt out always ruffles her fur."

Frankie thought Victoria had better be careful. It sounded remarkably like the letters she'd received. "My advice? Do as they say."

"Hah. You know Victoria."

To Frankie's surprise, a couple of the older Weddells were present, even as the family were preparing a funeral of their own. And once Frankie caught sight of a woman she thought was Emily Walker, but when she tried to cut a way through the crowd to speak to her, the woman had disappeared.

Two incidents stood out in Frankie's mind. One, after the service ended and she'd entered the house to use the bathroom, she spotted a man rifling through a desk in what appeared to be Roland Ginz's bedroom. A slim, nattily dressed man, with sandy hair and furtive attitude. He reminded her of someone, but she couldn't think who. Later, she discovered he wasn't one of the heirs. Nor a local. Questions rose in her mind. Or maybe those were suspicions. The second incident was when the minister made an announcement that Ruby Lyons, in a strong sign of recovery, had awakened from her coma.

Needless to say this brought forth a roar of approval from the crowd, and several pats on Frankie's back when someone recounted Ruby's rescue at her hands. Frankie just wished for one of those proverbial holes to crawl into.

"Hooray." Jesselyn grinned at her. "Now maybe the police can get the name as to who tried to kill her."

"Yes. I wouldn't mind knowing that myself. In fact, I think I'll see if I can speak to her. Maybe tonight, after work. Check in on her anyhow."

"Will they let you in to see her?" Jesselyn knew about the guard posted outside Ruby's room.

Frankie smiled. "One advantage of being with EMS. I can walk around the hospital and nobody stops me."

Except they did. Although she'd been the first to advocate posting a guard on Ruby's room, she hadn't anticipated being the one prevented entry. To her amazement, the ICU staff was in an uproar at being checked themselves. Not one, but two guards were stationed outside the doors.

She snagged Elaine Durkson, an RN she'd come to

know quite well in the last few weeks, as the woman rushed past pushing a depleted crash cart. "What's happened," she asked. "Is Ruby all right?"

"She is now. Five minutes ago, it was touch and go." Elaine looked grim. "One of the interns decided to check on her before he went off for a nap—she'd been restless this evening—and he found a guy holding a pillow over her face."

Frankie's eyes opened wide. "What? Did they catch the guy?" Unconsciously, her fingers crossed, only to be disappointed when Elaine shook her head in disgust.

"No. The would-be murderer knocked the intern down and while everyone's attention was on Doc Macy and Ruby, he slipped past the guard. Nobody knows how he got in the room. Doctor Macy didn't even get a good look at him, unfortunately. Said he had a hoodie pulled around his face and that the guy was sweating like a horse. Oh, and he smelled strongly of some expensive cologne."

Frankie pulled a face. "Dunno how much that'll help. Has Ruby been able to talk yet?"

Somber expression in place, Elaine shook her head.

"Who's the detective in charge?"

"Armbuster." Lip curling, Elaine continued, "And Rimmel. Dumb as posts, both of them, if you ask me."

Frankie blew a raspberry. "Dang."

"Yes. The deputies are still searching the facility, for all the good it'll do. I'm surprised you made it this far."

"I imagine whoever attacked Ruby and the doctor is long gone." Looking around, Frankie didn't see anyone moving with any sense of urgency. She suspected the cops knew a search now was a waste of time.

"No doubt," Elaine agreed. "Well, I'd better get this cart replenished, and you better get out of here before somebody, meaning Rimmel, tries to throw you out. He's such an ass."

As she followed Elaine's advice, Frankie had to agree. She never had understood how Rimmel got promoted to detective unless it was because nobody else could tolerate him. They probably just wanted him out of their ranks.

* * *

He knew right where to ambush her. At one a.m. Frankie had nothing on her mind except getting to bed. But then, after turning off the highway onto the road home, a figure moved from the side of a stopped car. Arms waving, the woman walked out in front of the Ranger and Frankie had no choice but to stop.

She stomped hard on the brakes in a purely reflexive reaction.

Illuminated by the headlights' beam, the figure

resolved into that of a woman. A female wearing a familiar blue sundress, although at this time of night Emily Walker must've been a tad chilly with her bare shoulders exposed. The decidedly cool air coming in through Frankie's rolled down window indicated a note of autumn on the way.

At the same time that Frankie recognized Emily, she realized she'd made a mistake. She'd have been better served to do her stomping on the gas pedal and go around. Emily would've gotten out of the way. It wasn't as if she were tied to the middle of the road.

Although, in eyeing the scene from her pickup, Frankie had an idea the man who stepped from behind Dave Pendleton's overgrown lilac bushes may have been holding a gun on Emily. Before he pointed it at her, that is.

"Get out of the truck," the guy said, his voice a high-pitched tenor.

He ignored Emily now, although the Ranger's headlights held her pinioned. She looked dejected. And, according to the dark shadow on her cheek in an otherwise pale face, like she'd been beaten.

Frankie turned to look at the guy. She'd seen him at the memorial, messing around in Roland Ginz's desk.

Smirking, he waved the automatic at her and said, "So, at last we meet."

What did he expect her to do? Celebrate and say, "So

happy to make your acquaintance?"

"Get out of the truck, now," he said, and when she still didn't move, pointed the gun at Emily. "I'm not beyond shooting her if you don't do as I say."

She believed him.

Furious, she opened the Ranger's door. Too bad he stepped back when he did. She'd intended to slam it into him and knock him ass over teakettle.

"Who are you?" she demanded. "What do you want?"

"You know who I am." His smirk didn't falter. "And you know what I want, too. Make me a deal and all this will be over."

"All what will be over?" Keep him talking, Frankie thought. Any minute now, maybe Gabe would come along. Or if he'd already made it home, maybe the dogs had gotten restless waiting for her and awakened him. They'd been known to do so, once or twice. She always found them waiting for her at the door and suspected they were able to recognize the sound of her truck from quite a distance. Although from here she needed to drive around the block to get home, she was only a couple backyards away as the crow flies.

But nobody came. And Eric Benedict didn't intend to hang around and wait.

"Emily," he said, a snap in his voice. "Get over here. Search her."

Emily, her shoulders slumped, moved to obey. Eyes downcast, she ran quick hands over Frankie, her touch light. Shoulders, particular attention to the waist where people often carried guns, down her legs.

Frankie stood frozen. The woman would find her revolver.

But oddly enough, although the search touched the ankle holster, Emily stopped short. "Nothing," she said, and now her eyes met Frankie's for the briefest of moments before she stood up and moved aside.

"All right." Benedict gestured with the automatic. "Get back in the truck. You and I are going to follow Emily." He stared hard at the woman. "You know where to go."

Lips trembling, Emily nodded, dejection in the way she turned and walked to the car parked at the side of the road.

Not a Lexus, Frankie noted, and not the beater Civic, either, but Emily got in. The car started with a roar. Even Eric Benedict winced at the racket of the untuned engine.

"Stupid blonde bimbo," he muttered. "She'll wake everyone in the neighborhood." Then, "There she goes. Follow her."

Frankie took her time climbing into the truck, shifting the Ranger into drive and pressing lightly on the gas.

Benedict poked her in the ribs with the gun barrel.

"Step on it. I want her aware that we're right behind her."

Flinching as she pulled out of an inadvertent swerve, Frankie thought of several things she might have said. That she wanted to say. Like, Why should I make this easy for you, asshat? Like, It ain't over 'til the last drink is drunk, buddy. Like, I'm in no hurry to let you kill me.

She said none of them. Glancing over at him, she said, "This is an old pickup. A '93. It's prone to breakdowns if I push it too hard."

A rattle coming from the center console seemed to punctuate her words. Her phone, she remembered. Best if Benedict didn't find the phone.

"What's that?" he demanded, reaching to open the console.

Good thing it had a trick catch, she thought as he struggled with it. One her grandfather had rigged when the original went TU. Easy enough to use when you knew how. "A wrench rattling is all," she hastened to say. "Although I wish it was a fully auto AR15."

Chuckling as if she'd pulled a good one, he gave up.

Movement caught at the edge of Frankie's vision as from habit, she glanced in the rearview mirror. Whatever it'd been, she didn't see it now.

After a few miles, when they turned off the highway onto an almost hidden road, she realized their destination. She almost had to admire Eric Benedict's thinking.

A body could lie out there for a long time before anyone chanced upon it. Gerald Green lived only because someone, and Frankie knew now it'd been Emily Walker, had called in the alarm. The old man would have to go in a home now, and there'd be no cause to check on the place. Maybe for years.

Brush and weeds scraped along the sides of the pickup, their acrid stench rising through her window. She had to wonder how the car Emily drove made it through without being shaken to pieces, but at last both vehicles stopped outside Green's ramshackle old house. Emily remained in the car, the motor still running, so Frankie left the Ranger running too. It helped cover some of the noise from a band of noisy crickets and an owl in the tree.

Benedict opened his door allowing the dome light to come on. He took a sheaf of papers from his pocket. Frankie saw the title on one. A quit claim deed. She had no doubt he'd made it out with all the t's crossed and all the i's dotted and that all it lacked was her signature.

"Let's get this over with." Benedict pulled an expensive-looking pen from his pocket and held it out to her. "Sign this."

"What is it?"

"A bill of sale, for starters. One that states that for a reasonable sum, you've sold that old homestead property to me."

"Reasonable? How much?"

He pointed at a figure on the paper. How he kept his face straight, Frankie didn't know.

Her laugh, so dry it almost burned a hole in her throat, mocked him. "Really? I thought that was the down payment. Why would I even consider such a ridiculous deal?"

He smiled. "So I don't kill you?"

"Oh, I expect you plan doing that anyway. So why would I make it easy for you?"

His dry laugh echoed hers. "Not so dumb, are you? But look at it this way, easy on me, easier on yourself. And maybe you'd even save Emily's life. I've begun to suspect the old man who owns this place owes his life to a phone call she made. As long as our transaction turns out well, I'll keep her around. She's handy in some cases. Just needs taught a lesson."

Frankie drew in a shaky breath. "Is this what happened to Ruby Lyons? Wouldn't she cooperate? Is that why you left her to burn? But that seems to be your MO, doesn't it? Setting things afire. Those two murders on the Berthold place? And Roland Ginz? Burning from the inside out is far from an easy death. Punishment for thwarting you, I expect."

"Like I said, you're smart as a whip. Smarter than the cops, for sure. They'll never figure this out. Now, sign this paper." His already high voice rose.

She snorted. "Don't be silly. They already have. You shouldn't have used your Lexus, Eric. It's a bit too obvious. People noticed."

His mouth set in a thin line. "Get out of the truck."

Desperate now, Frankie had to keep him talking. "But what I haven't figured out is why you want all these old places so badly. There's other farmland for sale. What's so important about these?"

Although she didn't expect him to, he answered. "Aside from out-of-the-way sites for my drug operations? The Weddells will soon be out of business, you know, and my people will be in place. I'll see to that. The final straw was them moving in on your land. Luckily for them, you've taken care of that. Saves me from having to do it."

She could only imagine his plans for them. "So, you're the one who overdosed Amanda Weddell?"

"Was that her name?" He shrugged. "Not much of a loss. Besides, she was more than willing. Although those two boys were an unexpected complication. If it hadn't been for you, they would've been dead too. "

Did Gabe know about that? Why hadn't he told her?

But now Benedict wanted to brag. "I plan on owning most of this part of the reservation before long. The old parts, in particular. Those are the very places the tribe wants to buy back." His laugh came again. "When I close down my drug business, I'll still be able to get double what I'm paying for the properties."

Frankie, unable to stand the sight of him any longer, glanced in her side mirror and saw a pale shape cross the road behind them. A deer? Brave of it to come so close to running vehicles. Brave and uncharacteristic. Unless it wasn't a deer at all. Knowing it might not be wise, still she said, "And yet, if I'm not mistaken, you've not yet managed to acquire any of the homesteads. Not even Berthold's, although I imagine the Strohmeyers are cooperating with you. Blake anyway."

"Not he. He's dumb as a box of rocks. No. Harvey makes a much better player than his son. He's ripe for retirement and knows that son of his can't run a big farm on his own. Why, I had to take care of that pair of out-of-town squatters the Weddells had parked there myself. But the Ginz place is in the bag. I managed to place a notarized sales document in his office while at the memorial today. It's a done deal. Your land will be the second. The other two will follow." He poked the pen at her again and rattled the paper. "Enough talk. There's nothing you can do about it anyway. Sign this and be done."

This time she took the pen. And promptly dropped it.

"Pick it up," Benedict said, voice rough. "No more delay."

But it wasn't the pen Frankie came up with. It was her pocket Sig Sauer and she shot Benedict in the shoulder. The wrong shoulder, although he howled as he pulled the automatic's trigger. The bullet gouged past her knee tearing the cloth as it banged through the pickup door.

He only got the one shot.

Already on the move, she leaned toward him, slamming his head with the pistol barrel. He managed to grip the door handle and open it. Falling out sideways, he yelled for Emily.

Not that his shouts did any good when like a white ghost, Banner appeared out of the darkness and leapt, teeth gnashing, on him.

It was probably a very good thing when Gabe, only a few yards behind the dog, got there. Even so Frankie took her time about calling Banner off. And Gabe didn't interfere. She thought he kind of enjoyed the sight.

* * *

"How did you know I needed help?" Frankie, tired to her bones, leaned against Gabe as her own strength seemed to have disappeared. Funny how having an avowed killer hold you prisoner could wipe you out.

His arms were wrapped around her as they waited for EMS' arrival to treat Eric Benedict's gunshot wound. It would be another long night for Gabe as he followed the ambulance to the hospital and got Benedict booked.

Frankie couldn't remember the members of the EMS back-up shift. Maybe the heavy-handed volunteer that everyone hated to work with, and patients complained about? She hoped so.

She looked up at Gabe and repeated her question. "How did you?"

He bent to speak in her ear so Benedict, on the ground on the other side of the pickup with Banner growling at him, didn't hear. "Emily. She called it in before you ever left 1st Avenue. But I already knew something was wrong. The dogs came barreling into my room and woke me up. And Banner jumped in the Tahoe with me before I could stop him."

Frankie smiled into his shirt front. There! She'd known the dogs had her back. And Gabe, too.

"I think he's having fun being a police dog," she said.

Gabe's chest moved as he stifled a laugh.

"But Emily," she whispered, "she took an awful chance. He said he might keep her around, but I'm sure he meant to kill her when he got done with me. He'd figured out she saved Gerald Green. Oh, and you'll have to contact the Ginz heirs to be on the watch for an official looking document in Roland's desk. Benedict sneaked into the house at the memorial and put a forged sale paper in

Ginz's file. As chance would have it, I saw him do it. I just didn't know who he was at the time."

Gabe gave a start. "That's good. We have a witness."

"You sure do." Frankie couldn't wait to testify against Benedict. All these murders, he'd surely get life. It wouldn't hurt her feelings if he got the death penalty.

"Emily will have to testify too, won't she?"

"Absolutely. She'll be a good part of our case. And she's agreed."

Gabe had let the blonde woman leave. Frankie didn't know what all he'd said to her, but she'd goosed the car into spinning its wheels on the grass filled driveway as she beat it out of there. She'd still looked frightened, but not as browbeaten and scared as she had an hour ago.

There'd be troubled times ahead with this case, Frankie knew. The Weddells, the Strohmeyers, Ruby and Mr. Green. So many people, from criminals to victims. All in her own little town of Hawkesford, Idaho. Disgusting to be out of the formal war, but still required to tote a gun.

"Dang!" She reared back, jerking from Gabe's embrace as a new thought occurred to her.

"What?"

"You'll have to take my Sig. This will be the second gun the cops have confiscated from me. Will I ever get either of them back?"

"Think you'll need them?"

Arms akimbo, Frankie balanced on her good foot. "Do you?"

Gabe sent her a look. "I'll buy you another 9 mm, myself."

She guessed that was answer enough.

For now. But what next?

A LOOK AT LOST GIRL LAKE
BY C.K. CRIGGER

The day Truth Diamond and her dog, Razz, find a woman's charred hand at one the Golden West Resort's campsites, is the day her busy life spins out of control. A search for a body turns up nothing. Truth believes her resort on Lost Girl Lake is in the clear, but when the rest of the body comes to light, the situation goes from bad to worse. She receives one of those "offers you can't refuse" for the resort, her flirty young employee, Becca Keene, vanishes, and a camper is murdered. Why? That's what Truth wants to know.

Finding whoever is doing the killing should be quick and simple. Plenty of law enforcement is around. There's Pratt, the quiet and appealing undercover FBI agent; Hunter, the dishy Fish and Wildlife officer; the Sheriff's department detective and his hardworking deputy. Can't anyone find Becca before she ends up gone forever? It's beginning to look like Truth has to do everything herself, unless she becomes the next victim

.

AVAILABLE NOW ON AMAZON

ABOUT THE AUTHOR

C.K. Crigger was born and raised in North Idaho on the Coeur d'Alene Indian Reservation, and currently lives with her husband, three feisty little dogs and an uppity Persian cat in Spokane Valley, Washington.

Imbued with an abiding love of western traditions and wide-open spaces, Crigger writes of free-spirited people who break from their standard roles.

Her short story, Aldy Neal's Ghost, was a 2007 Spur finalist. Black Crossing, won the 2008 EPIC Award in the historical/western category. Letter of the Law was a 2009 Spur finalist in the audio category. The Woman Who Built a Bridge was the 2019 Spur Award winner for best western romance.